The Great Holdup Mystery

And

The Mystery of
Wilfrid Usher

ISBN eBook:
ISBN-13:978-0914303-25-1

DEDICATION

To mystery lovers everywhere, and to those who love the behind the scenes mystery of those who wrote the stories in the first place. Wilfrid Usher is nearly unknown today and was so in his own time. He only wrote 3 or 4 mysteries and then disappeared like the next heir in line. Finding out about this writer is a mystery for us all...

CONTENTS

ACKNOWLEDGMENTS

To the great mystery writers who everyone knows like Loren Estelman and Dutch Leonard , who gave so many of us so much fun and to the writers like Wilfrid Usher that no one knows and who deserve better.

THE GREAT HOLD-UP MYSTERY

CHAPTER I

THE MAN WITH HAY-FEVER

At the moment when the three shots rang out, Peter Brown was sitting alone on the stone wall that runs by the quay at Tregenneth, the little Cornish fishing-village, smoking a final pipe before turning in as he watched the play of moonlight on the river. The sound at such an hour—for it was after eleven—was so unexpected that for a few moments he continued to sit in a kind of dazed astonishment. Then the patter of running feet made him turn his head sharply, and he beheld a man a hundred yards away, racing towards the quay as if for his life. And a little distance behind

him ran several others.
He was a fat man, the foremost runner, with a bare bald head that gleamed white under the moon, but despite his bulk he covered the ground well, and by the time he reached that part of the quay near where Peter was sitting he was fully fifteen yards ahead, apparently making for some steps which led down to the water. Before he could reach them, however, disaster overtook him in a singular fashion; for suddenly, as he ran, he gave a tremendous sneeze. Whether this circumstance was in itself responsible, or whether his foot caught in something on the surface of the quay, it is impossible to say; at any rate he tripped and fell;
and before he could recover, his pursuers—Peter

1

counted four of them—were upon him.

It was at this juncture that Peter decided to take
a hand in the game. Normally an amiable individual
who disliked rows, he disliked still more the
spectacle of a middle-aged man of stout aspect being
set upon by four others. He hesitated only long
enough to take off his spectacles and slip them in
his pocket; then he darted forward with that agility
which had once made him one of the most famous
rugby three-quarters in England. And since he was
wearing rubbers on his feet, his approach possessed
in large measure that element of surprise which
constitutes in all warfare the surest prelude to
success.

There was no doubt about the surprise. Indeed, if
a tornado had burst above the heads of those four
men they could hardly have been more astonished.
One of the ruffians was kneeling on the prostrate
man's chest, apparently trying to tear open his
waist-coat, when an iron hand seized him by the
neck from behind, another grip fastened on the seat
of his trousers, and he was flung full into the bosom
of one of his friends who unwisely chose that instant
to slink up; with the result that he, in his turn,
cannoned into yet a third. All fell in a mix-up on the
ground; while Peter was in time to meet the rush of
the fourth man, a huge mulatto. One rapid glance
was sufficient to convince Peter that he was no
match for the coloured man at close quarters, so he
dived like lightning for his legs. The mulatto's head
met the ground with a crack, and for a time, at least,
his interest in the proceedings was negligible, while
Peter had a moment's leisure to see how the
situation was developing elsewhere.

The fat man, profiting by the respite, had regained
his feet. Peter had a glimpse of him in the act of
charging his assailants like an enraged bull, but it
was no more than a glimpse, for he suddenly became
aware of a new peril. Creeping towards him with a

peculiar sinuous movement was a slight man, some
kind of foreigner, who held in his hand a weapon
that looked like a razor without the handle. His lips
rolled back in a malevolent grin as he saw his
approach was discovered, but he did not cease his
stealthy advance, planting one foot in front of
another with the soft tread of a marauding cat.
With a queer constricted feeling in the region of the
breast-bone Peter waited for him, leaning a little forward on the balls of his feet, his arms hanging
loosely
at his sides. Of the methods of attack practiced by
razor-slashers he was in entire ignorance, but he
remembered how years ago, during the War, a
Canadia gunner, by way of passing the time in a
convalescent home, had taught him the trick of
defeating an aggressor armed with a knife. The ruse
depended largely for its success upon watching one's
adversary's eyes, and he breathed a little prayer of
thankfulness that he had the moon behind him.
To this fact he undoubtedly owed his safety, for, just
before his assailant sprang, there leapt into his
eyes an unmistakable warning of his intention. And
in that instant, with a frantic movement, Peter
hurled himself to the right. The razor swept
harmlessly, and then, before the man could recover
himself, Peter's hands were upon him. There was a
quick twist—no violent effort—followed by a yelp of
pain and a sound like a stick being broken under
water.
The weapon fell to the ground, and Peter, stepping
back a pace, let the other have his left on the point
of the chin. And number two of the attacking party
flopped over like a dead thing.
So far as Peter was concerned, that ended the fight.
The remaining two ruffians, who had been having an
uncomfortable time at the formidable hands of the
fat man, now, on Peter's approach, immediately took
to their heels; and hardly had they disappeared,

when the big mulatto, recovering consciousness, staggered to his feet. He gave one wild look round, and finding himself deserted, promptly followed the example of his companions and bolted.

"Cleared out, by George, the whole bunch!" declared the fat man breathlessly. "Laddie, I don't know who you are, but—"

He broke off, staring over Peter's shoulders, and turning, Peter saw why. Crawling along the ground in the evident hope of escaping observation, was the man whom he had hit on the jaw.

Suddenly Peter perceived his objective—the razor which lay near the edge of the quay, where he had carelessly kicked it after knocking out his man. He sprang forward, and immediately the man, abandoning all efforts at concealment, leapt to his feet. It was Peter who reached the weapon first, however, and he covered it with one foot.

"I think not," he said quietly.

The next moment the fat man, coming up behind, had seized the enemy by the coat collar.

"Now, you scum!" he cried. "Try to murder me, would you! Why, you damned little squirt, for two pins I'd tear you in half. Did he hurt you just now?" he demanded of Peter.

"He had a jolly good try to. I rather think I broke his arm, though."

"Broke his arm?—pity it wasn't his head!" growled the fat man. "Got anything to say, you?"—this to his prisoner, whose sullen eyes were fixed on Peter.

The man slowly felt his dangling arm, and Peter noticed that his face was disfigured by a huge scar that ran across cheek and nose.

"I not forget you," he said deliberately. "One dese days—I kill you!"

The fat man laughed in a soft and particularly unpleasant fashion.

"Indeed," he said, in a silky voice, "and pray what

4

makes you think you're going to live so long? Kill, by George!"—and here his voice began to gain in volume.

"I reckon the boot's on the other leg! Listen here, little man. I'm not going to kill you here and now, because you'd be a nuisance, and I've no time to waste on coroner's courts and things. But by the living God, if ever I lay hands on you again after this I'll break every bone in your body and dance on the remains afterwards. D'ye hear? Now go before I change my mind, and thank your lucky stars I'm a humane, kind man. Understand? And if I catch you monkeying round here again to-night, sure as my name's Jim Bridgewater I'll smash your ugly face in, broken arm or no broken arm! Now run away back to Horstman. Impshi! Futsack! Or by the Lord, I'll"

Here he suddenly gave his prisoner a mighty shove that sent him ten paces, and then, taking a run. launched a tremendous kick at the flying man which, had it taken full effect, would assuredly have given him cause to remember the moment for long afterwards. Mr. Bridgewater returned, wheezing audibly, but with his face agleam with laughter.

"Filthy little swine, ain't they!" he said cheerfully.

"I must apologize for my language, but it's the only kind that sort of blackguard understands." He sneezed twice, then added: "We'll collect the spoils of war."

Picking up the razor, he glanced at it and pitched it into the river. "Hurt?" he inquired.

"Not at all, thanks. How about you?" said Peter. "That was a nasty purler you went just now."

Mr. Bridgewater gave a contemptuous snort. "Pooh, that was nothing. My dear fellow, it takes more than that to hurt me. What I'm sorry about is having to let 'em get away so easy, but there's no alternative, unfortunately. I don't suppose this place has a policeman, let alone a lock-up. The dirty cowards—

they came on me suddenly, five of them—and one
started getting busy with a gun, damn him."
"I heard him," said Peter.

"That was Horstman—you didn't see him," went
on Mr. Bridgewater, who seemed to find relief in
talking. "He's too lame to go running races in the
dark.
Well, I'm not a tenderfoot cowboy that I should go
about with a six-shooter in my hip, so not carrying a
gun I ran for it, remembering a wise tag about a
lame dog. I'd have got clean away, too, if my cursed
hay fever hadn't come along and made me trip and
embrace Mother Earth with rather more affection
than I usually bestow on that hard-bosomed lady.
But it was worth my trouble to see the way you set
about them—upon my soul, I couldn't have done it
better myself. Quite sure you're not hurt?" he
insisted, casting an anxious eye over his rescuer.
Peter laughed. He rather liked this large
garrulous man who could show such solicitude for
another when he had only just escaped what had
every appearance of being a violent attempt on
his life.
"Not a scratch," he assured him. "I suppose, by
the way, your friends are not indulging in what the
newspapers used to call a strategic retirement,
and intend coming back with reinforcements?

"Come back? Not they!" cried Mr. Bridgewater
with a confident laugh. "They won't trouble us again
if I know anything of the breed. They've had their
bellyful for one night, I fancy. But look here, laddie,
I haven't properly thanked you"

"Please don't," said Peter hastily. "In any case I
suggest we move away from here, in case your friend
with the pistol decides on a forlorn hope. I don't
know whether you live here or not, but I'm staying
at a cottage about half a mile away, if you'd care to
come and have a cleanup."

Mr. Bridgewater consulted his watch. "Thanks,
I will. It's too late now to find the man I'm looking
for. Excuse me one moment."

Whereupon this strange man produced a small
glass instrument with a bulb attachment like a scent
spray, and proceeded to apply it to his nostrils.
The treatment was evidently effectual, for he drew
several deep breaths with every appearance of
satisfaction.

Peter began to put on his spectacles, when he
noticed that his new acquaintance had paused, and
was regarding him with an amused smile.

"Do you usually have time to take your glasses off
when you come to the rescue of middle-aged men in
distress?" he inquired with a chuckle.

Peter smiled. "Well, as a matter of fact, I see much
better without them," he confessed. "They aren't
really necessary, but I happened to have a slight
accident to one eye during the War—" he broke
off, for Mr. Bridgewater's large face had changed
like a conjuring trick, and he was staring open-
mouthed.

"Well, if this ain't providence I don't know what is,"
he said in a new voice. "Are you by any blessed
chance P. J. Brown, the rugger-man?"

"Yes. Why?" asked Peter mildly.

"It's a sign from Heaven," Mr. Bridgewater declared

solemnly. "You're the very man I've come to these parts to see."

CHAPTER II
DOINGS IN THE SMALL HOURS

It was ten minutes past two when Peter, having seen
his visitor comfortably accommodated on the parlor
sofa, at length retired to his room. Slipping off his
clothes and donning pajamas, he did not get into
bed, but sat on the edge of it with an unlighted
cigarette in his mouth, gazing thoughtfully at the
candle. His mind was troubled and confused, and he
wanted to sort it into some condition of order before
he went to bed.

His refusal to accept Bridgewater's proposal had
been bluff, pure and simple. Partly from a certain
obstinate disinclination to be forced along a course
he disliked, and partly in order to see to what length
the other would go in efforts to cajole him, he had
affected complete disbelief in the urgency of the
suggested expedient. But in his heart of hearts he
knew he stood committed. Fantastic and unusual as
the story was, it had the ring of truth. Dick
Cartwright was not the kind of man to appeal to him
for help without just cause. Yet Peter could not help
a slight feeling of resentment against him for
dropping the bombshell into his tiny garden of
contentment. He had been so happy in his work, and
his friends, and his games. Looking at it in
retrospection he realized what it meant to him. And
now he must give all these things up to embark on
an adventure which he knew he would loathe.

He turned the question over in his mind: was he
in duty bound to accept? Many men, he knew, would

9

jump at the chance for the sake of the adventure
itself. That reason held little appeal for him, but he
certainly thought there must be men, trained in the
ferreting out of secrets, more competent to under-
take the job than himself The mechanical part of the
role—the driving and looking after the car and so
forth—presented no difficulties; but what about the
other and more important part? Hangerson, a
professional, had failed in this; What were the
chances of a mere amateur? Yet Dick Cartwright, no
mean Judge of men and their capabilities, had
thought him not unworthy. It was all very puzzling.
He rose from the bed, and lighting the cigarette,
moved to the open window, where he stood with his
arms on the sill, looking out over the moonlit
landscape.

The sight of the river below him brought to his mind
the violent attack made on Mr. Bridgewater earlier
in the evening, and he wondered what had become of
the gang. Probably they were miles away by now.
Having failed so completely in their purpose with all
the advantages of surprise, it was hardly likely they
would linger on in the hope of achieving it now that
their intended victim knew of their presence in
Tregenneth, and was sure to be on his guard.

The window at which he stood overlooked the road,
a thoroughfare bounded on the far side by a low
stone wall, beyond which the ground fell steeply to
the river.

Peter had finished his cigarette and was still
ruminating on the strangeness of his proposed
mission when his eye chanced to fall on a green light
moving slowly up-stream. As it drew nearer he could
see the dark outline of a small boat and hear the

faint throb of its engine. Idly wondering who it could be at such an hour, he was watching it when suddenly the light went out, reappeared for a space, and vanished again, only to appear once more for a similar period before it again ceased. Almost immediately it was there again, a mere flicker this time, and Peter suddenly realized it had spelt the letter "G" in the Morse code. As the light continued to wink away he read the message mechanically. It said: "Going to Creek."

Peter's heart was beating a shade faster as the green light, shining steadily now, continued up the river. The flashing of a message implied the presence of a recipient—and who, other than himself, was there awake and alert in Tregenneth at that time? Peter had little doubt as to the right answer. And even as the light, having passed the village, began to draw in to the Tregenneth side of the river, he made up his mind as to his course of action. Half a mile above the village was a small inlet, called Benton's Creek, for which the motor-boat was obviously making. Here was an opportunity not to be missed. Since there was no way of avoiding the part Dick Cartwright had cast for him, he might as well start at once—and what better beginning could be imagined than scrutinizing at close quarters the members of the gang with whom he had to deal, while remaining invisible himself:

During the fight on the quay he had been unable to gather more than an impression of their appearance, and he had not even caught a glimpse of Horstman—"the lame one" of Mr. Bridgewater's narrative. Benton's Creek, surrounded as it was by trees, was an ideal spot for such an espionage.

11

There was no need to rouse Mr. Bridgewater. Hurriedly slipping on some clothes he stole downstairs, and cautiously opened and closed the front door; then he ran swiftly and silently in the direction of the village.

Two minutes after he had gone, a man emerged from the shelter of the wall opposite the cottage, and putting his hands to his mouth, uttered a strange cry, which floated down through the quiet night like the plaintive call of a night-bird. Peter, hurrying through the silent village on noiseless rubbered feet, heard the cry, but being occupied with keeping a wary look-out for lurking members of the gang, he gave no heed to it. He had no reason to suppose that they were familiar with his personal appearance, but he was taking no chances.

Once clear of the village he felt more at ease, for he took a short cut of which he knew his enemies would be ignorant. It led along a deep-rutted lane between high banks which presently became a path that crossed a field to the foot of a little hill with a ruined stone tower on top, like the spike on a policeman's helmet. He reached the top of this hill a little breathless, for he had made good time, and he eagerly scanned the several miles of river up-stream which its height commanded. But there was no sign of any boat. Below him, its shores thickly fringed with trees, lay Benton's Creek. Here, he decided, the motorboat must be hidden.

He had some anxious moments descending the hill. It was as bare as a new railway embankment, and he was afraid of being seen. Half-way down, as luck would have it, he put his foot in a hole, and ended the descent at a run that nearly brought disaster,

12

his impetus sending him into a tree-trunk with a painful force. In an agony of apprehension he listened, holding his breath. If there was anyone in the creek they certainly heard him.

Came a man's startled voice, low and sibilant.

"What's that, Dan?" it demanded.

A peevish voice replied:

"Oh, for cry-sake shut it, can't yer! You give me the ruddy jumps, you do. Scared of a blinkin' 'orse movin' now!"

"That weren't no horse, I know," returned the first. "Shove 'er in a bit, Dan. I'll just 'ave a look"

"Not in this boat, you won't!" interrupted the other with sudden heat. "I don't shove no boat up to the stage till 'Orstman comes, not for you" nor no one. I've 'ad enough trouble with this ruddy engine this trip without startin' 'er up every time you 'ear a ghost. 'Sides, the tide ain't up yet. Chuck them fags over and siddown."

"Horstman said—" began the first speaker.

"I don't care wot 'Orstman said," snapped the irritable one. "I'm in charge o' this boat, not you. Chuck them fags overl"

The other subsided, muttering, and silence descended on the creek. Peter began to pick his way carefully through the trees. Presently he perceived the sheen of water, and a few more stealthy strides brought him in sight of the small landing-stage. Twenty yards from the shore lay a motor-boat containing two men.

One, little more than a lad, sat forward in an alert attitude; the other, presumably the surly Dan, lolled in the stern, cigarette in mouth, and Peter saw a villainous face with a shield over one eye. There

was a stretch of mud between the boat and the
stage; it would be the best part of an hour, he
decided, before there was sufficient depth of water to
float the boat alongside. Peter settled himself to wait.
Slowly the night wore on. The men in the boat
hardly stirred. Once the younger of the two essayed
conversation, only to be immediately snubbed by his
morose companion. The moon sank perceptibly lower
in the heavens. Silently the tide crept up to the
landing-stage, but still the men made no move. At
length, when his vigil seemed to have lasted for
hours, Peter heard the melancholy call of a night-
bird in the distance. The occupants of the boat at
once bestirred themselves, the younger busying
himself with the anchor-rope, while the peevish Dan,
to the accompaniment of much profanity, bent over
the engine.
"About time, too," he grumbled, as the engine
started with a splutter. "We'll be lucky if we get out
o' this before daylight, I tell you. 'Orstman can say
what he likes—'ullo," he broke off, staring up the
creek. "Wot's all this?"
At the far end of the creek, where the road came
down to the shore, a party of men came into sight,
and commenced to advance along the path to the
stage.
Among them strode a huge man with a conspicuous
limp, a monstrous bulk of a man who towered above
the others like a damaged battleship amidst a swarm
of destroyers. Fascinated by the spectacle Peter did
not at once observe the rest; but when at length he
took his gaze away from the giant his heart missed a
beat with sudden horror, for the others were carrying
the limp body of a large man.

14

"It's Joseyl" declared the young man in the boat excitedly.

"Josey be Mowed," rejoined Dan, standing up as the boat glided to the stage, "it's Big Pedro. Say, boys, wot's happened?" he called out. "Is he dead?"

"Dead?" answered one of the bearers as they laid down their burden. "Ah, I should think 'e was dead. As mutton."

Stray beams of moonlight filtered through the trees, weirdly freckling the face of the dead man; and Peter saw with inexpressible relief that it was the giant mulatto with whom he had tried conclusions earlier in the evening. For several ghastly moments he had thought it was Mr. Bridgewater.

"Aye, but he gave as good as he got," piped the huge man in a shrill voice that contrasted unpleasantly with his enormous size; "trust Pedro for that. Pity he didn't get the other swine as well, blast his bones. Get him in, boys; we don't want to stop here no longer'n we can help. I suppose you ain't seen no man round 'ere, Dan?" he asked.

"There I" cried the young man in the boat.

"You 'old yer ruddy tongue—'e didn't ask you, did 'e?" answered Dan angrily.

"I only said—" commenced the other.

"Stow it!—who wants to 'ear your opinion." retorted Dan. "There wasn't nothing, Mr. 'Orstman. There's been no man 'ere, I'll take my oath."

"Dan couldn't 'ear—'e was half-asleep," said the lad with spirit. "About a hower ago, it was, Mr. 'Orstman . . . ."

"Look 'ere—" began Dan in menacing tones, but the big man interrupted him.

"Well, it don't signify if he ain't here now," he

squeaked. "If I got my hands on him I'd tear his
eyes out, curse him. Josey here 'ud like to have a
word with the swine, too—broke his arm, he did—eh,
Josey?"

The miscreant addressed—it was the dago who had
tried to slash Peter with a razor—replied with a
threat so dreadful that all except the angry Dan
laughed loudly.

"Any'ow, we got no time to waste on him now,"
said Horstman with finality. "We done enough for
one night I reckon—leastways, Pedro has. Got those
stones, George? Well, chuck 'em in—we'll tie 'em
on outside. Get a hustle on, boys."

With a strange sinking of the heart Peter watched
them haul the dead body of their fellow-conspirator
on board. What was the meaning of these sinister
allusions to the dead Pedro?—to whom had he given
"as good as he got"? If anything had happened to
Mr. Bridgewater while he was away—he clenched his
fists at the thought. By Heaven! if there had they
should pay for it. If he had to spend a year searching
for every member of the gang they should pay.

A wave of anger swept over Peter. He wanted to
hurt these men physically, make them suffer, shake
them out of their vile complacency. And he was
helpless—absolutely impotent. He had no more
chance of injuring those six desperadoes, unarmed
as he was, than a fox had of killing a pack of
hounds.

And then suddenly Peter grinned faintly as an idea
came to him. The men were all aboard now; all
except the monstrous Horstman, who had stopped to
light a cigar. Peter considered the relative sizes of
the boat and its last passenger—and his grin grew

wider. It was madness, of course—but how inexpressibly gorgeous if it came off. And assuredly there was no reason why it should not. After all, it was dark under the trees; the boat was a small one for so many passengers; and he was wearing rubbers. And it was only a matter of a thirty-foot sprint to the boat.

The man Horstman probably never knew quite how it happened. He stood on the edge of the wooden stage, tentatively feeling with one foot for the gunwale of the boat. A hand was stretched forth to help him, and he took it. All at once he heard a sound behind him, while simultaneously a hoarse cry of warning came from the boat. Caught in two minds he hesitated, and then tried to step back, tugging furiously at his hip-pocket. But he never had time to draw. Peter's outstretched hands caught him full in the back. There was a crash as twenty stone odd of human flesh fell sprawling athwart the gunwale; and then a mighty splash as the over-loaded boat, tilting up suddenly to an acute angle, flung the whole of its human freight overboard.

Dawn was beginning to lighten the eastern sky as Peter, reaching the village on his return journey, dropped into a walk. He had run from Benton's Creek, not for fear of pursuit from the dripping gang, but urged on by the dread in his heart. The elation of the glorious moment when he had seen his victims struggling in the shallow water had gone, leaving the fear of what he would find at the cottage.

When he came in sight of it he was partly reassured by a light in the sitting-room window, which was wide open. Now, to reach the front door he had to pass this window, and he naturally looked in. What he saw struck him stiff with horror.

In the room stood three people. One was his landlady, her head and shoulders enveloped in a shawl;
she had evidently been weeping, and she was looking
pathetically at a short man whom Peter recognized
as the local doctor, who lived nearby. By the couch,
in helmet and unfastened tunic, stood the familiar
figure of Police-Constable Trethewy, examining some
object like a walking-stick in his hand. A figure lay
stretched at his feet—a bulky motionless figure with
its boots towards the window. Peter gave it one long
fearful look; then he again fixed his gaze on the
object held by the constable. This time he recognized
it. It was a heavy niblick which usually reposed in
his golf-bag in the corner; and on the head and part
of the shaft was a dark stain.

Even in the frightful moment of his discovery Peter
realized that he must not enter that room. The con-
sequences of such -a step were only too apparent. In
the first place he could do nothing to help: Bridgewater was obviously dead and the vital documents
stolen; in the second he clearly foresaw the equivocal
nature of his position. What kind of story had
he to tell? The truth, to the stolid village constable
and the hard-headed country practitioner it would
sound like the ravings of a lunatic; the deduction
they would draw, with the damning evidence of that
golf-stick in front of them, obvious. Nor would they
hesitate to act on their conclusions. He was
practically a stranger in Tregenneth. Apart from a
few fishermen, his landlady, and some members of
the golf-club at Polhaven, ten miles away, he knew
not a soul in Cornwall. It would be nothing less than
the duty of the constable to detain him, if only upon

suspicion.

That his detention would only be of short duration
he knew; he had not the slightest fear of being
unable to prove his innocence, given time. But until
his innocence was established in the eyes of the law,
even if he were not put to the ignominy of arrest, a
watchful eye would indubitably be kept upon his
movements, and his liberty of action be curtailed.
And at all costs he must keep his freedom if he were
to get into touch with Dick Cartwright. He realized
that must be his first aim.

While these thoughts flashed through his mind the
doctor had been bending over the prostrate figure on
the floor; and now he straightened his back and said
something in an undertone that resulted in the constable turning to the window. Peter drew away just
in time. The voice of Constable Trethewy came from
the window:

"Likely he be twenty mile away by now," he
remarked.

A woman's voice, his landlady's, said tearfully,
"He didn't do it sir—that I do know. There wasn't
a kinder nor simpler gentleman you'd ever meet than
Mr. Brown. You know that well, Mr. Trethewy. Don't
'e take away a man's character behind's back!"

"I got my duty to do, Mrs. King," returned the
constable. "Never spoke tu' chap t'arl meself. He
looked a decent well-set-up sort o' chap—I will say
that for'm."

"Give me a hand here, Trethewy," said the doctor's
voice.

A pause followed, and then the constable's voice
again: "It do put me in mind of the War, doctor."

Peter waited to hear no more. It distressed him to

19

leave his landlady to face the music alone, and she standing by him so loyally; but there was no help for it. Some day later he would put things right with her; at any rate, apart from the inevitable trouble and publicity, she would come to no harm.

He started off down the road to the shed where he kept his car—and then he pulled up, swearing under his breath. His keys and all his money were in his bedroom; there was nothing for it but to retrace his steps. Ducking under the open window he found the front door ajar and silently slipped inside. As he tip-toed up the stairs he caught a glimpse of Trethewy busy with a note-book, and he wondered irrelevantly why it was that policemen invariably used such stubby pencils.

Once in his own room he lost no time in slipping into his pocket such articles as were necessary for his flight; and then, going to the window, he speculated on his chances of jumping down without making too much noise. Better to risk the stairs, he decided; but he regretted his decision a few moments later when, on reaching the bottom step, the burly figure of the constable emerged from the sitting-room.

"'Ullo, 'ullo!" exclaimed that worthy, pressing the back of his neck importantly against the collar of his tunic. "An' where have yu' been arl this time, might I ask?"

Peter thought quickly. Should he affect ignorance of the whole business or tell them the truth—or as much of the truth as was necessary to clear himself? There was no reason why he should encourage them to think him a murderer. At the same time he was certainly not going to allow himself to be detained. On that point he was determined.

"Why, what's the matter—and what are you doing
here?" he gasped in what he hoped was a voice of
suitable astonishment.

"You'll know soon enough! Going to sneak out,
wasn't yu', now?"

Peter's nerves, though he did not know it, were
all to pieces, and the man's tone irritated him.

"And what the devil has it got to do with you if I
am?" he said angrily. "Do you propose to try and
prevent me?"

"Yais!' said Trethewy with a grim nod, and put
his broad back against the front door.

It was the constable's complacent assumption of
his guilt that made Peter lose his temper. Afterwards
he realized that his action, besides definitely putting
him on the wrong side of the law, was stupid and
unnecessary; he could so easily have temporized and
sought a later opportunity to slip away. Had he
taken the wiser course the subsequent trend of this
narrative would have been entirely different. But
reason is apt to melt in the heat of anger, and Peter's
course was the unwise one. He feinted for the
constable's jaw, and as Trethewy's arm flew up he
smote him on the unguarded mark; the man doubled
up involuntarily, and before he could recover Peter
was through the door.

He ran down the road as hard as he could go. Daylight was rapidly gaining, and looking back, he saw
the heavy figure of the constable lumbering after
him.

Of the doctor there was no sign. Well, he had not the
slightest desire to hurt Trethewy, but he would
persist in getting in the way ... it would be a harder
blow next time, he thought grimly.

Wilfrid Usher

Reaching the shed he thrust in the key and flung
back the doors; then he jumped into the car,
switched on, and pressed the self-starter. The engine
fired at once, and shoving in first gear, and
regardless of the unwisdom of speeding up a cold
engine, he trod on the accelerator and let in the
clutch. The car lurched forward just as Trethewy
appeared at the entrance.

Peter steered straight for him: it was the only thing
to do, and he knew the constable wouldn't wait to be
run over. Trethewy leapt aside with a yell, but as
Peter turned into the road he jumped on the
running- board—and then, in a ghastly moment for
Peter, the engine made a peculiar hissing noise,
coughed, and was silent. Well Peter knew that
sound—no petrol!

In the excitement of starting he had forgotten to turn
the petrol-tap; the amount left in the float-chamber
of the carburetor had been sufficient to take him a
few yards, but no further.

Whether the constable had his truncheon with him
Peter never knew; at any rate he did not use it.
Instead, he threw himself on Peter like a tiger and
endeavored to drag him from the driving seat. He
was a big strong man, full of righteous anger at the
way he had been treated; but then so was Peter.
Moreover, Peter was in the finer condition. Out of
the car they rolled, twisting and turning, speaking
no word, the breath whistling through their lungs as
they struggled. There was no question of finesse; it
was the old elemental game, man to man, with
victory to the strong arm and the quick brain.
Trethewy fought desperately; but he was by twenty
years the older man, and he began to weaken. Peter

felt the lessening resistance and put forth all his
strength. And when presently he arose, shaken and
panting, it was a sense-less figure that lay at his
feet.

Stooping, he lifted the inert body of the plucky
constable, and with some difficulty carried him to
the side of the road. It would take Trethewy about
ten minutes, he reckoned, to recover consciousness,
and by that time he would be well started on his
journey. But how far would he travel before the hand
of the law overtook him? Only too well he realized
the seriousness of his position. He was no longer an
innocent man fleeing from justice; to the crime for
which everyone would hold him guilty he had now
added that of a murderous assault on the police. No
amount of explanations would palliate that offence.
Truly, he reflected bitterly, as he re-started the car,
violence always recoils on the head of the violent.

But with the freshness of the morning, as he
bumped along the narrow lanes, his spirits rose.
After all, granting the original folly of having
assaulted the constable, he did not see how he could
have acted differently. He began to think of the
future. Obviously he must make some sort of plan.
In good open country his car was capable of doing
sixty miles an hour; on the Cornish and Devonshire
roads he could, he thought, average from thirty-five
to forty at that early hour, though it would be bumpy
going. In four hours, then, given luck, he would be
well into Somerset or Dorset where the roads were
better, but where, with the coming of the working
day, he would need to be on the alert for those three
flies in the speed-merchant's ointment—corners,

cross-roads, and cattle.

Provided he was not stopped he calculated he would reach London, two hundred and sixty miles away, in the early afternoon. But in the meantime the ether and the telegraph-wires of Great Britain would be humming to the description of a certain yellow two-seater car, driven by one Peter Brown, motor-engineer, aged thirty, in height 6 ft., etc., etc. . . "The devil!" thought Peter. "It will take some doing!"

Exeter—that bottle-neck to the south of England—it was there he might first meet trouble. Impossible to avoid that long High Street, with it numerous white-coated policemen, without making a tiresome detour. Better, perhaps, to get rid of the car and go on by train. The risk of detection would be immeasurably less. He would be able to get a much-needed sleep in the train, too, for he was beginning to feel the effects of having stayed up all night. For the present, however, he would have to be content with the car; there would be no train running yet for several hours.

It was a steam-roller, snorting merrily out of a deep-sunk Devonshire side-lane some two or three hours later, that solved the problem of the disposal of the car. The thing happened with that swiftness which characterizes most motor accidents. One moment the speedometer needle was quivering near the fifty-five mark; the next the brakes were squealing a frenzied protest as Peter jammed on everything hard, klaxoning furiously. But the steam-roller kept on its course, completely blocking the highway. Peter had a vision of the scared driver, spinning his steering-wheel like one possessed; then seeing a

smash was inevitable he turned the car into the side
of the road.

It hit the bank at twenty miles an hour, slithered
round, and fell over on its side, pitching its occupant
out onto the grass. Rising unhurt his first thought
was for the car. It was out of action—he saw that at
a glance. The near-side front wing was crumpled up
like paper, the wheel beneath being bent at an angle
of forty-five degrees.

The steam-roller had stopped, and the driver
climbed down from his cabin with an indignant
face. He was a little man, and the reaction from the
alarm of the averted collision rendered him abusive.

"Now don't get angry," Peter told him. "It won't
do you any good and you are entirely in the wrong.
What do you mean by coming out of a side-road like
that without knowing the coast was clear?"

"You 'adn't no business to go ser fast. Think you
own the ruddy 'ighway, you motorists—'airin' along
at that rate!"

Peter looked at his weak, angry face, and realized
the uselessness of argument.

"Where's the nearest garage?" he asked, with what
patience he could summon.

"You was a-doin' seventy if you was a-doin' ten,"
declared the man doggedly. "I know! I gotter motor-
bike meself. Racin' you was! 'Ow was I to know . . ."
And so on, and so forth.

The dispute might have gone on indefinitely had
not a commercial traveller in a Ford Sedan driven
up, and learning the facts of the case, offered to give
Peter a lift to Exeter, whither he was bound. Peter
accepted gratefully, and after exchanging names and
addresses with the still-simmering driver of the

steam- roller, mounted up beside the traveler and ensconced himself between two cardboard boxes and a suitcase.

Shortly after they had started they met two police-men on bicycles, who subjected them to a keen scrutiny, without, however, stopping them. As Peter's companion thoughtfully observed, they seemed to be "on the look-out for somebody". Peter consulted his watch. It was a quarter to eight. Constable Trethewy had apparently not been long in spreading the glad tidings

CHAPTER III
THE GIRL AND THE MOTOR-SCOOTER

In Exeter, having parted from the obliging
commercial-traveler, Peter took a tram to St. David's
station. It marked the terminus of the route, and he
was about to descend when the sight of two
uniformed constables, lounging outside the station
entrance, made him resume his seat somewhat
hastily.

There was no reason to suppose that they were
there on account of him, but he was hatless and still
dressed in the flannel trousers and shabby sports-
coat which he had worn at Tregenneth; his damaged
eye, in the absence of his glasses, was a fairly
conspicuous object; all of which rendered him easily
recognizable should his description have already
been circulated. The risk, it was true, was only a
slight one, but he wished to take no chances. As the
tram journeyed back to the centre of the town he
told himself he was giving way to panic: that it was
absurd to suppose that the machinery of the law
could have been set in motion in so short a time. But
he changed his mind when, alighting at Queen St.,
the other of the two main stations in Exeter, the
familiar uniform once again met his eye in the
booking-hall. The double circumstance was too
strange to be a coincidence, it looked as if the task of
leaving Exeter was going to prove more difficult than
he imagined.

27

He left the station in a thoughtful mood. The
police, he supposed, must have come across the
abandoned car, the information of the driver of the
steam-roller having done the rest. Probably by now
the whole police force of Exeter was in possession of
a description of his appearance. It became
increasingly evident that if he was going to leave the
town by any of the recognized exits—and short of
adding to the list of his crimes by stealing a motor-
cycle or car he saw no other way—he must adopt
some sort of disguise.

Towards this end, the hour being now after nine
and the shops open, he paid a visit to a ready-made
clothing store, and purchased a suit of reach-me-
downs of cheap dark serge, into which he presently
changed in a public lavatory. A call at an
unpretentious barber's shop in a side-street resulted
in the loss of his mustache; then he purchased a
road map of Devon, and a quarter of an hour later,
equipped with a pair of green-tinted spectacles,
shiny black shoes and a bowler hat with a straight
brim, he entered the Commercial Room of an hotel
and ordered breakfast.

No one took any notice of him. With his flowing tie
and imitation pearl pin, his well-oiled hair and
general appearance of commercial smartness, he
might have passed for one of the cheaper kind of
travelers in that diversified trade known on the road
as "The Rag".

As soon as the meal was over he obtained a time-
table. It appeared that there was a train leaving
St. David's station at 12.30, which would land him
at Paddington at 6 o'clock, and he determined to go

28

by it. In the meantime, as he had nearly two hours to wait, he decided to try and snatch a little sleep, of which he was beginning to feel strongly in need. Espying a smoking-room which appeared at the moment to be empty, he told the Boots what he proposed to do, and asked him to rouse him half an hour before the train was due to start; then, making his way to a couch, he stretched his tired limbs on it with a feeling of infinite weariness. His body had begun to ache all over, and there was a dull pain in his left shoulder which was the result of his tussle with Constable Trethewy; nevertheless, it was the first peaceful moment he had enjoyed since the episode on the quay at Tregenneth eleven hours before, and he sighed for the sheer delight of it. Five minutes later he was asleep.

Out of the formless land of shadows, that impalpable world of half-impressions that lies between sleep and waking, in which he had yet been dimly aware of some sinister happening that menaced his safety, Peter was jerked, with a suddenness that set all his pulses racing, into complete, panic-stricken wakefulness, with every nerve taut, his whole being alive to the proximity of some imminent danger. Indeed, so real and unmistakable was the warning that, without being conscious of actual volition, he slid his legs from the couch and stood up, gazing fear-fully round the empty smoking-room. And then, just as the memory of a dream, clear enough at the moment of waking, quickly fades under the rush of new perceptions, so the feeling of apprehension began sensibly to diminish. He laughed uneasily. Nerves—that was what was the matter with him: his cursed imagination was playing him tricks again. It was as well no one else was in the room—a pretty fool he would have looked, starting up like that at nothing. He glanced at the clock on the mantelpiece. It was half-past eleven— there was still time for another forty winks. Determined not to let his nerves get the better of him, he resolutely lay down once more. And as he did so he noticed a curious thing.

In the opposite corner of the room two doors stood close together at right-angles—the one through which he had entered, and another marked "Writing-Room".

His eye had chanced to fall on the handle of the former door, and been arrested by the fact that it was being slowly turned from without.

Lying with eyelids almost closed Peter watched the sinister movement: saw the handle become still, and the door begin to open. Then a head was thrust cautiously through the gap. It was that of the commercial-traveler who had given him a lift in his Ford.

And his eyes went straight to the couch and stayed there.

There was something unnatural about that scrutiny. It was not as if the intruder had looked in search of a friend, but rather as if he had come solely to examine the figure on the couch—to identify it, perhaps. The train of thought suggested was disquieting. It looked as though Peter's efforts to evade capture had failed, and his tracks been followed. He continued to lie quite still, while his brain took in this new development.

The Great Holdup Mystery

At length the head was withdrawn and the door
softly closed, but not latched; whereupon Peter
once more rose, and tiptoeing to the door, peeped
through the crack. What he saw confirmed his
suspicions, for in the hall of the hotel were two
police-men, one evidently a sergeant, talking
earnestly to the manager, while the commercial-
traveler, a few yards distant from Peter, was
beckoning excitedly.

The sight galvanized Peter into violent activity.
With a couple of bounds he reached the windows,
only to perceive that they looked out upon a busy
street, with a white coated policeman directing traffic
not a dozen yards away. Obviously there was no
escape in that direction, and he promptly flew to the
door of the writing-room. Two men were sitting at
desks with their backs turned towards him as he
entered. They did not look up, and he strolled
carelessly to the door, and whipping off his now all
too betraying spectacles, walked out into the
corridor.

He was banking on the hope that the watchers, if he
attracted their notice, would be so firmly convinced
that he was still asleep in the smoking-room as to
mistake him for an ordinary hotel guest.

This was apparently what happened. Peter treated
himself to a swift glance up the corridor, to be
rewarded with a sight which, in less trying
circumstances, would have filled him with laughter.
Creeping along on tiptoe towards the smoke-room
door with every appearance of stealth, looking
ridiculously like stage conspirators, were the
sergeant and the constable, followed by the manager
and the commercial-traveler.

Undoubtedly they saw him emerge from the writing-room, but Peter was half-way down the corridor, walking as slowly as he dared, before they realized who he was. A sudden shout warned him of recognition; and the next moment, casting aside all pretence, he was sprinting down the corridor, praying that the closed door which faced him at the end did not lead into another room or cul-de-sac. Reaching it amidst a growing uproar of shouts, he flung it open, and slamming it to again, found himself in the courtyard of the hotel, empty save for a man in brown overalls busy washing down a car near the entrance gates. To pass the man without being seen was impossible, yet there seemed no other way of escape, and Peter was on the point of making the attempt when his eye fell on a wicker skip or case, such as travelers carry samples in, standing open against the wall by the side-door—and it was empty!

In an instant Peter was inside with the lid down, just before the hotel-door burst open, and the chase cascaded noisily into the courtyard.

Peter would have enjoyed the scene which followed if he had not been so desperately anxious as to its outcome. For a few minutes there was nothing but the sound of men running about and voices raised in excited comment and inquiry, dominated by the parade-ground bark of the sergeant. He seemed to be a man of explosive temper. Peter imagined him as being thick of jaw, with choleric, protruding eyes— as, indeed, he was.

"Where in Hades is he!" he cried. "Talk about thick heads—God bless my soul, you've got eyes in your head, man haven't you?—you must have seen him come out!"—this, presumably, to the man in brown overalls.

"I didn't see no one," the unfortunate man returned surlily. "How could I, with me back turned and all?"

"I don't want none of your sauce," retorted the sergeant. "A little more lip from you, cocky, and you'll find yourself in trouble! Any other exits bar them gates, sir?" he demanded of the manager.

"Not unless he climbed the wall," was the reply. "It's me belief he's hiding somewhere in those old stables yonder."

"We'll soon find out. Edwards, you stop by them gates. Now, sir, if you please."

The next half-hour was one that was long remembered by the hotel management and staff. The day had become uncomfortably hot, as the result of which tempers were already in a sensitive condition and the sergeant's energy, as he raged about like an angry lion, did nothing to soothe them. In his zeal he peered under motor-cars; he climbed into disused lofts; he insisted on having two lock-up garages unlocked; he entered the stock-room of a traveler in lady's lingerie and outraged the indignant salesman by feeling into a large case of his daintiest wares with hands soiled by a previous visit to the coal-hole. Yet it never occurred to him, or to anyone else, to look into that much more obvious case by the side-door. Finally, he invaded the servants' quarters, which were on the ground floor at the back of the hotel.

And it was while he was there, engaged in a passionate altercation with an irate elderly female cook who resented his declared intention of searching her bedroom as a slur on her good character, and whose name and address were duly taken by the furious sergeant as the result, that Peter for the first time dared to raise the lid of his hiding-place.

"Holy Moses!" he gasped. "Talk about the Black Hole of Calcutta!"

He looked round the yard. The man in the brown overalls was lying half-under the car; the other men had gone to their dinner; the manager and the obliging traveler were nowhere to be seen. Only one policeman stood between him and freedom. It was a case of now or never.

Leaping from the skip he rushed to the gateway. The constable saw him coming, and made a gallant attempt to grapple him; but with the experience born of many runs on the rugby field Peter handed him off, and raced down the street like a hare, with the policeman, vigorously blowing his whistle, after him.

Fortunate it was for Peter that it was the dinner-hour and there were few people about, or his period of freedom would have been short. As it was, the only person to attempt to stop him was an old lady with an umbrella, which she valiantly brandished in front of him as if he were a runaway sheep. Dodging her, he slipped down a side-road; and running as fast as he could lay foot to ground, he reached the end of it just as the pursuing constable hove in sight. It was a comparatively easy matter to avoid the chase then; and presently he dropped into a walk. And soon afterwards, coming upon a field with a gate which bore the legend "The Chavverton Croquet Club", and seeing no one about, he slipped through, and finding a large tree in one corner, lay down in its grateful shade to take stock of his position. The problem of reaching London was going to prove less easy than he had thought. It looked as if he would have to wait until darkness before he attempted to leave Exeter.

The Rev. Charles Barkleigh-Claughan was winning his game. As he strode about the croquet-lawn, bare-headed and in his shirtsleeves, his face glowed with pleasure and perspiration. It always afforded him keen delight to beat Rear-Admiral Bodmin, the best player in the club, for the old sailor's dislike of coming off second-best was notorious. Whenever the clergy-man made a particularly long break the Admiral's frown, always formidable, would have been terrifying to anyone but his opponent, who was not easily intimidated. Finally, when Mr. Barkleigh-Claughan had ended the game by pegging out both his own balls, the Admiral gave tongue.

"It's outrageous!" he declared explosively, "'it's positively a disgrace!"

"What is that, Admiral?" asked the young clergy-man innocently.

"The state of this lawn, sir! If I had my way the grounds man should be strung up at the end of a yard-arm. The ground isn't fit to play polo on, let alone croquet. It's like the present condition of this country, sir—a damned disgrace to those who are supposed to look after it."

"Oh, come, Admiral," said the clergyman. "I thought you were playing rather well. You had most atrocious bad luck, you know. That last shot of yours, for instance. Dead on all the way it was, until the last moment."

But instead of appeasing him, as Mr. Barkleigh-

Claughan hoped, this commiseration served only to
raise the Admiral's ire.
"Exactly, sir! Precisely what happened!" he
barked. "It was entirely the fault of the ground.
One might as well play croquet on a ploughed field.
I shall make it my duty to lodge a complaint with the
Committee."
Saying which Admiral Bodmin bit furiously into a
new cigar and stumped off to the pavilion. The
clergy- man sighed, and knocking about a ball or
two, mopped his glistening brow.
"Wouldn't care for your revenge, I suppose?"
he said casually to the indignant sailor, who was
changing his shoes on a small chair in front of the
pavilion.
The Admiral, struggling hard to get a hot foot into
an obstinate shoe, breathed heavily without replying,
whereupon Mr. Barkleigh-Claughan repeated his
request.
"Sure you wouldn't care for another game?" he
said insinuatingly.
For answer the Admiral gave a savage tug at the
shoe, but his hand slipped, and with the sudden
movement he lost his balance and rolled completely
off the chair. Mr. Barkleigh-Claughan hastily turned
his shaking shoulders to the pavilion.
But he again sighed regretfully when the Admiral
had left. These elderly men with livers were very
trying. He had hoped to play croquet for another
hour at least, and there was no other member on
the ground.
And then his eyes fell with some surprise on the
figure of a man walking past the end of the lawn—
a complete stranger, dressed in blue serge and

wearing tinted spectacles. It occurred to the clergyman to ask him what he was doing there, but being a companionable soul he nodded instead, and remarked: "Hot, isn't it?"

"It is," agreed the stranger. "Nice, though."

"Oh, rather; I'm not complaining," returned the clergyman. "New member?" he asked.

"As a matter of fact I came here to find a man," was the reply. "A man named Smith; but he doesn't seem to be here."

"Smith, the accountant, do you mean? He only comes here on Saturdays."

"No, my Smith is—a doctor."

"No doctor of that name here," the curate informed him. "You must have made a mistake."

"I'm afraid I must have," confessed the stranger. "What a jolly little club you have here."

"Yes, isn't it! By the way, I suppose you—er—you don't happen to be a croquet-player?" asked the clergyman tentatively.

"Well, I used to play a bit some years ago. You fond of it?"

"I love it," said the Rev. Charles Barkleigh-Claughan. "Greatest game out—for the summer. You don't spend half your time in the pavilion like you do at crick when you reach the green in two and take four more to hole out. Trouble is it's so dashed unpopular. In novels and things. The only writer I know who really appreciates it is Chesterton. Ever read that little thing of his on croquet? 'The game which is no game' or some such title. How he played in the dark and kept hitting balls he couldn't see . . . jolly true, too. I suppose you wouldn't care for a game yourself?"he suggested.

Wilfrid Usher

The stranger's gaze rested thoughtfully on the
distant figure of a policeman walking slowly and
majestically past the railing that separated the field
from the road. "I should like one very much," he
said.

"Only I'm afraid I shouldn't be able to give you much
of a game."

"Splendid!" cried the clergyman. "As a member I
enjoy the privilege of inviting a friend to play. You
can borrow the Admiral's shoes and mallet—he won't
know, and if he did it couldn't make him madder
than he was five minutes ago. Come in."

"I like your pavilion," observed the stranger,
glancing over the box-like structure. "Nice and
compact."

"Yes, isn't it? It was once a kiosk at some open-
air exhibition or other, and we picked it up for an old
song. It hasn't got a window—still, it suffices, and
the door is strong enough."

"It locks, I suppose?" the stranger asked carelessly.

"Oh, yes, rather. We couldn't leave all these things
lying about without. I'll get the book and put your
name down."

The clergyman disappeared inside. The stranger
said," I like this game and it's nothing like so
maddening as golf," glanced back at the policeman,
now safely past the gate; then his eye came back to
the clergyman's hat and coat, which were lying on a
chair, and from there travelled to a bicycle leaning
against the pavilion, presumably belonging to the
clergyman also. Then, feeling an utter cad, he
stepped to the door and turned the key.

"Hello, what's up?" came the clergyman's voice
from the pavilion, and the stranger heard him trying

the door. "Here, I say!" he protested.

"I'm really awfully sorry!" said the stranger apologetically. "I assure you I wouldn't do this if it was not absolutely necessary. I hope you don't mind if I borrow your clothes."

"Borrow my clothes—what do you mean? Unlock this door."

"I haven't the time to explain, but when you know the circumstances—"

"What the deuce do you mean?" the clergyman interrupted angrily. "Let me out at once, do you hear?"

The stranger had already removed his collar and put it on back to fore, and he now slipped on the clergyman's hat and coat, and seized hold of his bicycle.

"I'll get someone to let you out," he called. "I'm leaving you my coat; it's a nice new one, I only bought it this morning. Good-bye. I'm so sorry to be so rude, but you'll understand some day. I'll send the bike back if I can."

To the accompaniment of a thunderous banging on the door the stranger wheeled the bicycle into the road. On the footpath was a small boy with a dirty face, and the stranger felt in his trouser pocket and produced a coin.

"Like to earn sixpence, sonny?" he said pleasantly. "You see that pavilion over there—well, there is a friend of mine, a very angry gentleman, locked inside. You can hear him talking to himself if you listen, but he's quite harmless really. Run and let him out and the sixpence is yours. Or better still," added the stranger with a sudden grin. "Run to that policeman and ask him to let him out. It'll make him happy for days to think he's been so near to me with-out knowing it."

So saying he mounted the bicycle, and overtaking the policeman, graciously saluted him, to receive a dignified salute in return.

"Nice fellers, them curates," was the mental comment of the constable as he watched the cyclist disappear; but whether this attitude of mind survived the next half-hour, when he discovered that the curate who had given him such an affable salutation was none other than the man for whom half the county was looking, history does not relate.

Picture now the spectacle of our Mr. Brown, strangely clad in clerical coat and collar and blue serge trousers, toiling along the Taunton road through that hot after-noon on a bicycle several sizes too small for him, tired in body, the calves of his legs already beginning to ache from the unaccustomed exercise, but in great spirits on account of his lucky escape from Exeter.

Since leaving the town cars had passed him in plenty travelling in both directions, but as none had show the least interest in him he was full of hope that he had eluded the police for good.

It would take them the best part of an hour, he calculated, to identify the miscreant in the hotel with the stealer of the clergyman's bicycle, and by that time he reckoned to have put many miles between himself and Exeter. To remain long on the main-road, however, was asking for trouble: and when, shortly, he came to the summit of a hill which com-manded a wide prospect of the vale through which the road travelled, he dismounted and brought out his map. He had a plan in mind. The hill on which he stood was, roughly, the center of a circle twelve miles in radius in which there were about a dozen railway-stations, from one of which he was convinced he would be, able to catch a local train and make his way to one of the larger towns, and thence to London.

There was obviously a limit to the number of police who could be spared to join in the search, and the risk of being discovered at a wayside station seemed less than that of trying to get a lift in a passing car, the driver of which might easily have been warned to be on the look-out for him. Accordingly, therefore, he mounted his machine, and a few minutes later, coming upon a side-road with a finger-post bearing the name of one of the villages with a station, he turned down it. As he did so the thought occurred to him that he could not be far from Okewood Hall, the residence of Sir Mortimer Drude. Mr. Bridgewater had omitted to name its exact locality, for the necessity had not arisen; but Peter had gathered that it lay in a region to the north-east of Dartmoor. He made a mental note to inquire if it was anywhere near, should the opportunity arise.

It struck him that thunder was about. As he followed the winding course of the lane, now plunging through a tunnel of green foliage to cross a tiny bridge over a stream that tinkled pleasantly in the oppressive heat, now topping the rise of a hill that opened up extensive views of the rich Devon landscape, it seemed to him that over everything there hung that ominous stillness which generally precedes a storm. He rather hoped the weather was breaking up, and that it would rain hard—anything to damp the ardor of the police.

And then, on a bend in the lane, he came upon the motor-scooter.

It stood temptingly by the side of the road in front of a cottage, a squat, ugly-looking machine with small wheels; and there was no one in charge of it. Here was a Heaven-sent gift. The rights and wrongs of stealing something which did not belong to him failed to trouble him at the moment. Larger issues than the loss of a motor-scooter depended on his movements within the next few hours; indeed, he would have stolen a motor-car if one had been handy. So, with a quick glance about him, he dismounted, and leaning his bicycle against the wall in front of the cottage, he laid hands on the scooter and kicked up its tiny stand.

And as he was about to push it off a girl came out of the cottage—a tall girl, straight of limb and body, who said "Oh, but—excuse me, please, that's mine," she protested, and came quickly through the garden-gate with a resolute face. Then, confronted by a clergyman, she stopped in some perplexity.

Peter raised his hat and smiled. "Madam, I am aware of it, and I apologize. I admit I was about to steal it without a by-your-leave, and I therefore humbly ask you—may I borrow it?"

Her expression of perplexity deepened. "Yes, of course," she said hesitatingly. "Take it by all means," and she ran her dark brown eyes over his attire. "Someone is ill, I suppose?" she asked.

"I'm afraid I can't even plead that," said Peter with a twisted smile. "I am not even a clergyman. On the contrary, I am a criminal fleeing from justice." She looked at his ingenuous face, sun burnt and comely except for the disfiguring scar over one eye,

and she felt a sudden desire to laugh. Anyone less
like a criminal in appearance she had seldom seen.
"It sounds interesting," she said composedly. "All
the same I don't see why you should steal my
scooter."
He made a grimace of resignation. "I see I shall
have to explain. I am supposed to have murdered a
man in Cornwall last night, and early this morning
I committed a foul and unprovoked assault on a constable. Since then I have assaulted another
constable in Exeter, and had the misfortune to steal
a suit of clothes and this bicycle from a parson. Even
at this moment stout and perspiring policemen are
climbing into Ford cars in order to get on my tracks.
And yet I assure you I am entirely innocent. Do you
believe me?" moved with the supple grace of an
athletic boy.

During this recital her face had gradually softened,
and at its conclusion she laughed outright.
"You poor man," she cried. "Of course I believe
you. But why do you run away if you are innocent?"
she asked seriously.
"Why?" He gave a gesture of mock despair.
"Because, my dear lady, I have a deep-rooted
objection to spending the night in Exeter gaol, or
wherever it is they put wicked malefactors
nowadays. I want to enjoy the country while I can—
Devon—England'
"Her sights and sounds; dreams happy as her day;
And laughter, learnt of friends; and, gentleness
In hearts at peace, under an English heaven.
"I beg your pardon," he ended lamely. "I'm afraid
the sun must be getting to my head. Only the very
best criminals quote poetry, and I'm only a bungling

43

amateur. I can imagine my friend Horstman spouting Keats by the hour."

He had spoken lightly, and she had listened with a half-smile on her lips; but at the word "Horstman" her face changed as though she had been struck, and the colour slowly drained from her cheeks.

"Horstman," she said in a low voice. "You know him?"

"Intimately enough to have been the means of giving him a good ducking," returned Peter dryly. "He's not a friend of yours, I hope? A nasty fellow with a carcass like a bull and a squeaky voice."

She had regained her self-possession and some of her colour.

"Tell me exactly what happened," she demanded.

He looked at her curiously. "You don't happen to know the fellow really, do you?" he asked. Probably, he reflected, she had met the brute somewhere in the neighborhood, for if all Mr. Bridgewater had told him were true, nothing was more likely than that he had been in the habit of visiting Okewood Hall. He was conscious of a certain thrill of indignation at the thought that a girl like this should ever have been brought into contact with a blackguard of Horst-man's character.

In reply to his question she nodded. "Tell me what happened," she repeated.

"There isn't very much to tell," he said carelessly. "Mr. Horstman and some friends of his happened to annoy me in a certain way, and the opportunity presenting itself for me to annoy him, I took advantage of it. To be exact, I pushed him into the river."

"You didn't!" she cried, beating her hands together

44

in a sudden ecstasy. "Oh, how lovely." Then, her eyes narrowing, she added viciously, "I hope you hurt him."

"I'm afraid it was only his dignity that suffered," said Peter sorrowfully. "I rather gather that you don't like him," he went on. "Will you think me curious if I ask you where you met the charming gentleman?"

She laughed evasively. "I met him at a friend's house."

"It must have been a jolly party. The sight of Horstman in the drawing-room, balancing a teacup on one knee and a plate on the other, must have been worth seeing. By the way," Peter added carelessly, "Do you happen to know where Okewood Hall is, where Sir Mortimer Drude, the scientist, lives?"

"Oh, yes," she answered composedly. "It was at his house that I met Mr. Horstman. It's about four miles from here."

At that moment a motor-horn of a peculiar penetrating note sounded some distance away, and the girl started as if she had been stung. She looked round wildly, all her colour gone again in a trice.

"Quick!" she cried. "Take this—oh, don't stop to ask why, but take it! Get right away from here—at once."

He looked at her in amazement. "But why—" he began, when she interrupted him fiercely, stamping her foot.

"Do as I say! Oh, hurry, you fool—hurry!"

A great suspicion, born of something Mr. Bridgewater had told him, took possession of Peter. The horn sounded again, nearer this time. After a moment of hesitation he caught hold of the scooter

45

by the handlebars. Then he turned once more to the girl.

"Before I go," he said, meeting fully the anxious gaze of her dark eyes. "Won't you tell me your name?"

A faint flush crept into her cheeks. "Jane," she said, "Jane Smith."

"Thank you," said Peter. "Mine is Brown—Peter Brown."

And with that he lifted the valve release lever and ran the machine along the ground; the engine fired with a loud explosion; and the next instant, with a noise like a small quick-firing gun, the motor-scooter was streaking up the lane with Peter on its running-board, while from somewhere behind, clearly audible above the roar came the ominous note of the motor-horn.

In the lane, or rather in that part of it where the following scene was enacted, the predominating feature was dust. It lay on the ground in miniature mountain-ranges where cart-wheels had pressed it aside; it tinted the green of the tall hedges and the long grass at the side with grey. A haze that was visible only at a distance had arisen and partially veiled the sun, whose white glare had given place to a blazing disc; and strangely enough the veiling process seemed to intensify rather than diminish the heat. So oppressive was the atmosphere that one might have imagined there was an actual physical presence, infinitely great, brooding over the scene. And the quiet was such that when at long intervals there came the low growl of distant thunder the sound was like a menace.

Presently another sound emerged from the stillness;

a far-away but insistent throbbing that grew
steadily louder until, with a roar, a squat, ugly
machine, with a man standing on it, came rapidly
into view round a bend of the road, followed by a
dense cloud of dust.

Down the lane it came at great pace, filling the air
with its hideous noise. And then—something
happened.

The roar suddenly ceased; simultaneously the front
wheel of the machine seemed to stop still for an
infinitesimal moment, tipping up at the back and
shooting the rider forward over the handlebars as if
he had been discharged from a catapult, so that he
fell all of a heap, rolled over and lay still, his limbs
sprawled out like a starfish. The dust slowly settled.

A few minutes later a motor-horn sounded, and a
limousine swept round the bend at speed, only to
pull up suddenly with squealing brakes. Two men
got out, one tall and spare, with white hair and pale,
ascetic features, the other enormously bulky and
walking with a limp, and they approached the
prostrate figure in the roadway. But before they
could reach him a girl had sprung from the car and,
overtaking them, had stooped down and raised his
head, gazing fearfully at the closed eyes and blood-
stained cheek.

The white-haired man looked down at her with an
expressionless face.

"I must confess, Una, that your conduct sometimes
causes me a little surprise," he said dryly. "It would
almost appear as if my wishes went for nothing.
Since this unfortunate young man seems to have
stolen your machine, may I ask why you did not at
once inform me?"

His eyes, pale as marble, fixed themselves coldly on her troubled face, as without waiting for her reply, he went on: "I understand now why you suggested that we should go home by another route. I presume he imposed on your good-nature by some credulous tale or other. As it happens no great harm is done, but if through your connivance I had missed him, I rather think, Una, we might have had a slight disagreement. I suppose this is the fellow, Horstman?" he added, turning to his huge companion. "I never set eyes on him meself," piped the giant in his queer falsetto voice. "If it is him I'll have a word to say to him on me own account, curse him! And so would some of the boys—he broke Josey Gomez's arm. Is the young swine dead?"

"Permit me, my dear Una," said the other, gently moving the girl aside, and he proceeded to make a swift examination of the unconscious man. At length he stood up. "I am afraid you will be disappointed, Horstman," he observed. "He is not only alive, but very little damaged. I have no doubt that he will come to his senses before long."

"What are you going to do with him?" demanded the girl.

"We will offer him the hospitality of Okewood Hall," the white-haired man returned with a singular smile on his thin lips. "Such a resourceful young man deserves the greatest care and attention. Bring him into the car, Horstman."

The girl watched the huge man with an angry glint in her dark eyes as he stooped, and, picking up the limp body, bore it to the car. Twice she seemed on the point of uttering a vehement protest, but each time she refrained as if conscious of the fact that it

48

would not be of the slightest use.

"Perhaps, Una," remarked the white-haired man, when the car started again, with Horstman beside the chauffeur and the still unconscious victim of the accident stretched on the seat in front of him and the girl, "perhaps it might amuse you to read this." He handed her an early edition of an evening news-paper, folded back at the following:

CORNISH OUTRAGE

MAN BRUTALLY ATTACKED IN COTTAGE

FAMOUS RUGBY INTERNATIONAL DISAPPEARS

THRILLING CHASE OVER TWO COUNTIES

A shocking discovery, involving a well-known rugby-footballer, was made in the early hours of this morning at a cottage in Tregenneth, Cornwall. Mr. P. J. Brown, the footballer in question, had, it appears, been holidaying at Tregenneth, lodging with a Mrs. King, who was awakened about four o'clock this morning by hearing a noise in her front parlour. Descending to investigate she was horrified to find a man lying in a pool of blood with terrible injuries about the head. Mr. Brown was nowhere to be seen, nor, when she visited his room, had the bed been slept in.

Mrs. King states that the injured man, whose life is despaired of, is an entire stranger to her.

P. C. Trethewy and Dr. Armitage were at once summoned to the spot, which showed signs of having been the scene of a severe struggle. While making their examination they were suddenly surprised by Brown, who, it is supposed, had been concealed on the premises and violently assaulted. Brown, a man of powerful physique, is reported to have first attacked Dr. Armitage, knocking him down, and although P. C. Trethewy made a gallant attempt to arrest him, he was unable to prevent his escape.

Brown then, it seems, made for a shed where he kept his motor-car, and was on the point of leaving when P. C. Trethewy, who had followed him, again made a plucky attempt to detain his man, only to receive several violent blows in the face, which had the result of partially stunning him. Brown was thus enabled to effect a complete get-away. When last seen he was heading in the direction of Bodmin. The ex-international was next heard of near Okehampton, in Devon, where, between seven and eight o'clock, he had a narrow escape of colliding with a Steam-roller. In an Endeavour to avoid the steam- roller Brown, who from all accounts must have been travelling at a terrific speed, ran into the bank, severely damaging his car, but without, apparently, receiving any injuries himself. He was given a lift into Exeter by Mr. James Nolan, a commercial-traveler, who, of course, had no knowledge as to the identity of his passenger, who has not been seen since. P. J. Brown is, of course, the well-known rugby wing three-quarter whose famous try against Wales at Swanport in 19.., the only try scored in the match, will long be remembered by followers of the handling code. He received a D.S.O. and M.C. for services during the War, since when he has been engaged, we understand, in the motor industry. He stands 6 feet high, is well-built with a bronzed complexion, wears glasses, and has an artificial eye, the result of a war-time injury. When last seen he was wearing a tweed coat and grey flannel trousers.

LATER

It is reported that Brown has been seen in George
Street, Plymouth, wearing the uniform of a petty-
officer in the Navy. The police are making inquiries.
The girl handed back the newspaper with a weary
smile.

"I suppose it's all true," she sighed unhappily.
"But he never did it—I'm sure he never did it."
"I wonder," said her companion with an enigmatic
smile. "I wonder."
"You won't'—give him up to the police?"
"No," was the thoughtful reply. "I don't think,
my dear Una, you may have any apprehension on
that score."
And his cold eyes rested meditatively on the
unconscious figure in front of him.

CHAPTER IV
SOME ADVANTAGES OF A
THUNDERSTORM

A bump on the head is an unpleasant business.
When Peter first opened his eyes following his
mishap on the motor-scooter, he was forced to close
them again hurriedly, while great waves of pain
surged through his head. For a while he lay still,
trying to think, his whole being concentrated on the
intolerable torment in his head, inside which a great
wheel was rotating with nauseous and maddening
deliberation. Gradually the pain became more
bearable, and he opened his eyes again, to realize
that he was lying fully dressed on a bed in a room.
He tried hard to think where he was.

This was never the bedroom in which he had gone to
sleep at Tregenneth the night before. Indeterminate
memories rose in his mind, of a fight in the dark and
a big fat man, mingling with others, of a girl with
dark eyes, who seemed to be riding along a lane,
unaccountably mounted on a croquet-mallet. He
groped feebly for the thread which would lead him
through this dark mental labyrinth to light and
recollection, until his brain ached again with the
effort, but there was nothing now but two dark eyes,
brown and enormous, that stared at him
unwinkingly. . . .

And suddenly, like a blurred picture on a screen
which is moved into focus, the incidents which had
led up to his present position leaped into his

52

memory.

The escape from the hotel, the appropriation of the curate's bicycle, the meeting with the girl of the motor-scooter and the subsequent driving of the abominable thing along the bumpy lane—he remembered them all, even to a fleeting reminiscence of the fatal moment when the machine went wrong. The wretched engine must have seized, he supposed, tipping him over the handlebars onto his head. He wondered how long he had lain there, and glanced at the watch on his wrist, only to find it broken, the hands having stopped at a quarter to five. The sky, visible through the window, however, presented much the same appearance as before the accident, and he was convinced it was still the same day. Twisting his head he looked around the room, and was surprised to find he was alone. He lay for some time puzzling over this fact. Presumably he had been brought to the house or hospital or whatever it was, after having been picked up unconscious, and it was surely usual under such circumstances for someone to remain beside him. He also had the idea that ordinarily he would have been put inside the bed instead of on it.

There was something strange in his being left alone like this fully dressed—or was it perhaps that he wasn't so seriously hurt as he imagined?

With an effort he sat up and slid his legs over the side of the bed. The movement made the room swim round, but he persevered, and by holding on to the foot of the bed he raised himself unsteadily to his feet.

Then, with the gait of a drunken man, he went to the door and tried to open it. It was locked.

That settled it, thought Peter. They were keeping him prisoner until the police arrived. With a feeling of resignation he lay down once more on the bed. He had tried his utmost, but circumstances had been too strong for him. There was nothing more to be done.

He felt as if there was no fight left in him. His head was still sore; the wheel went on turning in his brain.

He closed his eyes in utter weariness and dejection of spirit; and presently sleep came.

He was awakened by a hand shaking his arm and started up to find a man bending over him, a burly fellow with "pug" written all over him. He carried some clothes over one arm.

"The Guv'nor says you're to put these on," he ordered shortly.

Peter stared at him in surprise, and then at two other men standing nearer the door. Night had fallen, and the electric light was switched on, plainly revealing all three; and not one bore the least resemblance to a policeman.

"Who are you?" he asked.

"Never you mind," said the bruiser. "You got to put them togs on."

"What for?"

"Do what he tells you and don't talk," put in one of the men sharply.

"I'll do anything you like in reason if you'll tell me who you are and where I am," said Peter. "You're the police, I suppose?"

"Police!" The bruiser gave a contemptuous grunt. "You jest nip into them togs and don't ask no questions."

"And get a move on," added the man who had
spoken before. "We're not going to wait here all
night."

"Your consideration overwhelms me," murmured
Peter. "I begin to think you aren't the police at all."

"What you think and don't think doesn't matter"
retorted the man. "Please yourself whether you
undress yourself or force us to make you. The point
is Sir Mortimer has given his orders that you're to
wear these clothes, so if you're wise you won't give
any trouble."

Sir Mortimer! It needed every atom of self-control
of which Peter was capable to refrain from showing-
how deeply the mention of this name affected him.
He was a prisoner in the house of Sir Mortimer
Drude, the very man whose secret he was pledged to
try and discover! How this extraordinary practical
joke on the part of providence had been brought
about he had no conception, but the possibilities
which it at once suggested were so vast that he
found difficulty in collecting his thoughts. The one
obvious course, whether Sir Mortimer regarded him
as an enemy or whether he was merely keeping him
until the police arrived, was to provoke as little
trouble as possible.

"Anything you jolly well like," he said resignedly.
As soon as the change had been effected the bruiser
gathered the clergyman's clothes in his arms and left
the room. The two others produced pistols.

"Follow me," directed the one who had spoken
before, "and kindly remember that my friend will
be immediately behind you. So if you have any
hankerings after eternity all you have to do is try to
escape.

Going to come quietly?"

Peter laughed and stood upright. Already he was feeling better, and he was full of intense curiosity to know what was going to happen next.

"My dear old friend, I wouldn't attempt anything for worlds while you're pointing those nasty things at me," he replied pleasantly. "They won't go off, will they?"

"They will if you don't behave yourself," returned the other grimly, as he opened the door.

Peter followed him along a carpeted corridor, and up a flight of stairs, the other man all the time remaining close at his heels. Yet another flight of stairs was negotiated before his guide spoke again; and then, at the end of a narrow passage, he unlocked a door and threw it open.

"In there, please," he ordered.

There was no light in the room, and Peter hesitated, fearing some trick.

"My dear chap," he protested, "I never did like the dark"

"No words—get in," interrupted the man.

Peter eyed him. He was a wiry man, with long arms; his companion, too, looked quite capable of holding his own in a rough-and-tumble; moreover, both were armed. The odds were absurd. With the merest shrug of resignation Peter passed through the door.

"I might add," came the unpleasant voice of his guide, "that I shall remain outside your door all night. So no tricks."

And the door was shut on impenetrable darkness and the key turned.

A young man dressed in clerical garb, in whom the

casual observer might have traced a general
resemblance to Peter, was bidding a grateful farewell
to Sir Mortimer Drude in the hall.
"I can assure you, sir, I shall never forget your
kindness," he said, as he wrung his host's hand—
and even his voice was not unlike Peter's. "You've
been most generous, and without your help I don't
know what I should have done."
Sir Mortimer gravely inclined his white head.

"My young friend, why thank me? Believe me, I
am doing no more than indulge my whim. Circumstances have contrived to place you in a peculiarly
false position, and I see no reason why I should
supply the deficiencies of the law by handing you
over to the police, especially as I am assured you are
entirely innocent. Miles will take you in the car and
drop you anywhere you may choose, and I can only
hope and trust that our rather stupid but well-
meaning police will cease to trouble you any further.
Good-bye and good luck to you, my boy."
"Good-bye, sir, and again—thank you!"
Sir Mortimer waited until the door closed behind
the young man, and was turning thoughtfully away
when a girl came out of a room and seized him
impulsively by the arm.
"You dear old thing—thanks so much," she said,
with a happy smile. "I knew you wouldn't ever
give him up to the police. Was his head all
right?"
His cold face softened a little as he looked down at
her and gently stroked her hair.
"Of course it was, dearest," he answered. "Do
you imagine I would let him go away otherwise?"
"I think it's splendid of you. I only hope the police

won't find out. It might be rather awkward if they
did, mightn't it?"
He laughed quietly and shook his head. "The police
will not find out," he assured her. "You must
remember, too, dear, that in sending him away I am
acting partly in my own interests. You forget our
friends arrive to-night."

"You mean Kreller and Pagleiro?" she nodded.
"What time?"
He glanced at his watch. "About twelve. And—
er—Una—I may have to show them one or two
experiments"
"What—to-night?" she interrupted.
"Quite possibly," he nodded. "It would be unwise
for them to stay here too long and they may be gone
by morning. So if you hear any strange noises in the
night—you won't be alarmed, dear?"
She shivered a little. "I shan't hear any. I hate
them both, and Mr. Horstman, too. Uncle, don't you
think—" she hesitated, a curious look in her eyes.
"Can't we go away, just you and me, and forget all
about these people for a little while? I don't mean
Sark—we seem to meet more people there than we
do here—but can't we have a long holiday together,
Just ourselves, away from all this—" She made a
little grimace of distaste. "Oh, everything here!"
He appeared to be examining the nails of his long
white fingers.
"We may have to leave Okewood Hall sooner than
either of us imagine," he said reflectively. "Come,
let us go into the library. You shall read to me from
that new book of Walter de la Mare which arrived
to-day."

Meanwhile, seated on the bare floor with his back
to a wall in complete darkness, our Mr. Brown was
going through the process of trying to keep up his
spirits in face of the gloomy outlook which the future
seemed to hold. For the prospect, it could not be
denied, was anything but cheerful. Not only was he
a prisoner in Sir Mortimer Drude's hands, but it also
looked as if the scientist was aware of the part he
had played in preventing Mr. Bridgewater from
falling into the clutches of Horstman and his gang.
The uncompromising behavior of the men from
whom he had just parted left no doubt in Peter's
mind that it was not in order that he might be
handed over to the police that he had been brought
to this garret of a room. He had a shrewd suspicion
that Sir Mortimer had ordered him to be taken there
for purposes of his own; and if all Mr. Bridgewater
had told him about the owner of Okewood Hall were
true, those purposes were likely to prove interesting.
Whether Sir Mortimer had any knowledge of the
mission which Mr. Bridgewater had projected he did
not of course know, but the circumstances of his
present position rendered any further consideration
of that plan futile. Even if he was able to escape from
the awkward situation in which he now found
himself, he would never now be able to take a
position as chauffeur in Sir Mortimer's household.
On the other hand he had most miraculously been
permitted to enter Okewood Hall, which was
undoubtedly a definite step in the right direction;
though whether he would ever have the opportunity
to take advantage of it was uncertain. Sir Mortimer
might, even now, hand him over to the police in the
morning; in which case Dick Cartwright would have

to look for a new agent.

Yet if he was to be handed over to the mercies of the law, why had not the police been informed already?

There had been ample opportunity to 'phone Exeter, and Peter knew enough of police methods to guess that little time would have been wasted in coming to fetch him had they been informed he was at Okewood Hall. And why, too, had he been made to change his clothes and forced to spend the night in this poky little room at the top of the house, when the bedroom would have sufficed?

By feeling round the walls he had already discovered the small dimensions of his prison, which was devoid of all furniture and had a small –window overlooking the grounds. The moon, whisk had served him so kindly on the previous night, was hidden behind a sullen pall of cloud stretching from horizon to horizon, and he could make out no detail. His explorations over, he had resigned himself to the discomfort of a night on the bare boards, but though he felt unutterably tired, his head was throbbing painfully and he had been unable to sleep. Once or twice it struck him that he was in for a bout of illness. He was clear-headed enough and felt quite capable of making any call on his physical resources, but his pulse was rapid. He had succeeded in opening the window before he lay down, for the atmosphere was stifling, but it was still uncomfortably hot, and he idly wondered if it was worth while asking his gaoler for a drink. He knew the man was there, because when he had forced open the window the fellow had angrily demanded to know what he was doing.

Suddenly a light flickered on the wall opposite and

vanished, to be followed after an interval by the
distant mutter of thunder. Presently the lightning
danced again, the ensuing growl being louder than
before, and Peter roused himself. The elemental fury
of a thunder-storm had always appealed to him, and
since sleep seemed impossible, he got up and went
to the window.

Towards the horizon the sky was continuously
lightening up, and it was obvious that a considerable
storm was brewing.

He had been standing there for perhaps ten minutes,
leaning his arms on the window-sill as he watched
the quickening display, when he became aware of a
light of another kind drawing near, and the
headlights of a powerful car swept up to the house
and stopped.

Craning his neck out of the window he saw several
men descend from the car, and two other figures
that left the house to greet them. Faintly he could
hear their conversation, and then, in a lucky
moment, one of the group passed in front of the
headlights, and he could have cried out with
amazement, for it was none other than Horstman.
He would have known that bulk and that limp
anywhere. They all went into the house, the car
drove away, and Peter was left to speculate as to
what this visit portended.

Of course he had known that Sir Mortimer and
Horstman were associated, and if he had felt any
doubts as to the truth of Mr. Bridgewater's story the
fact of the girl whom he had encountered in the lane
having met Horstman at Okewood Hall was sufficient
corroboration. But he had not expected to see Horstman again so soon. He supposed he had come by the

car which had just arrived, and he found himself longing to know what was going on downstairs. Yet with a locked door and an armed man between him and the rest of the house he might as well long for the moon. And just then the sky opened with a flood of yellow light, and he saw something that made his heart miss a beat with the sudden idea to which it gave birth.

The window at which he stood was a dormer one, and what the lightning had revealed was a similar window jutting out of the roof, about a dozen yards away. The mad notion had come into his head to try and reach it. Such a feat, even in broad daylight and performed by a man in normal health, was one not to be undertaken lightly, for a slip meant certain death: for anyone in his condition it was stark lunacy. Nevertheless, no sooner had the idea entered his head than he resolved to try it. If he failed—well, it was a quick ending; whereas if he succeeded he might have an opportunity of roaming about the house which would never occur again. The risk, he considered, was justified, and having once made his decision he resolutely shut out all thoughts of failure—a psychological trick which had more than once served him in good stead in the past.

As soon as the next flash came he marked the edge of the rain-spouting, and then, climbing through the window and holding tightly to the sill, he slowly lowered his body until he was lying full length on the tiles, his feet feeling for the spouting. He could not get a satisfactory grip at first, and almost unconsciously he twisted his neck and looked down. And in that moment a blinding figure of light divided the heavens, illuminating the ground far beneath his

feet as if it had been brightest day, so that he
suddenly felt giddy and was filled with terror. And
while the thunder crashed and rolled, for all the
world as if the sky was a huge wooden flooring upon
which giants were trundling cannon-balls, he lay on
the steep roof with his eyes shut, his whole body
trembling beyond his control, while the thought of
that awful drop gripped him like a nightmare.
How long he remained in that position he never
knew, but gradually the giddiness passed and
confidence came back, bringing with it a new
determination to carry out the feat he had set
himself. It was a bad moment when he let go his
hold on the window sill, for although he knew the
spouting in such houses was usually reliable, he
could not be certain that it had not rotted in places.
With the utmost caution, leaning all the weight he
could on the roof, he slowly worked his way along.
And presently, breathing a little prayer of
thankfulness that his nerve had held,
he found himself with his hands on the sill of the
further window. It was shut, but this was a small
matter, and pulling down his sleeve so as to cover
his hand, he smashed the window, taking the
opportunity to do it during a particularly loud clap of
thunder lest the noise of breaking glass should reach
the ears of his gaoler. There was no difficulty in
opening the casement once he had raised the catch,
and he pulled him-self over the sill just as a hissing
noise announced the approach of the rain.
The room in which he found himself was as bare as
the one he had left, and he prayed the door was not
locked on the outside. Investigation revealed the
pleasing fact that the key was inside, and he lingered

a few moments to collect himself, waiting for the
next rumble of thunder ere opening the door. No
sooner had it boomed out than he turned the handle
and cautiously peeped through.

A dozen yards away sat his gaoler with .his back
turned, a candle on a small table beside him, by the
light of which he seemed to be trying to read a book.
Peter lost no time. As before, he waited only for the
friendly thunder; then with half a dozen rapid strides
he reached the man and caught him by the throat.
He was in no mood for dalliance. The man struggled
fiercely, but he had little chance in Peter's powerful
grip; moreover, his revolver was on the table by the
candle. In less than a minute he was lying
motionless on the floor and Peter was unlocking the
door of his old prison, wondering what he should do
to prevent the man raising an alarm if he regained
consciousness.

He decided that it would be sufficient to lock him in;
if he chose to escape the same way he had gone—
well, he was welcome to it. Dragging the man inside,
he locked the door, and after examining the revolver,
which was loaded in all six chambers, he
appropriated the matches and blew out the candle.
Then he stole along the passage to the head of the
stairs and stood listening.

All was still, and he descended to the next landing.
He was in his stockinged feet and made no sound.
He could see that the light was switched on in the
hall below, and treading at the extreme end of each
stair he went cautiously down, and then stopped
near the 'bottom as the sound of voices reached him
from one of the downstairs rooms. Holding the
revolver ready for instant use, he crept from the

shelter of the stairs into the hall. No one was there.
A grandfather clock ticked sedately against one wall,
pointing to twenty minutes to one. There was no
other sound except the drone of conversation from
the one room. Going to the door he laid his head
against it, but it was substantially built of oak and
he could not distinguish the words.

Now that he had reached this stage, however, he was
determined to overhear what was going on, and he
made a rapid examination of the front door. At any
time a servant might appear, and it was imperative
that he should make no noise. Luckily the bolts,
which were shot, slipped back noiselessly, and he
found himself outside in the now torrential rain,
which drenched him to the skin as he slipped round
to the front of the house. There was no mistaking the
room, for it was the only one lit up. He knew there
was a risk in appearing against the lighted window,
but this chance had to be taken; and to his joy the
window was open a couple of inches at the bottom.
With a fast-beating heart he crouched down on to
the flower-bed and listened. A voice was speaking, a
cold professional voice with a very distinct
enunciation, so that he could hear every word clearly
above the fierce hiss of the rain.

"I do—I make the statement with the utmost
confidence," the voice was saying. "It would, in my
opinion, revolutionize the whole theory of radiation."
With the tip of his finger Peter carefully parted the
curtains so that he could see part of the room.
Facing him, smoking a cigarette in a long amber

holder, sat an ascetic-looking man with white hair
and singularly pale eyes, and although Peter had

never seen him before he set him down at once as Sir Mortimer Drude. Opposite a small table on which drinks were laid out sat two other men smoking cigars, one a little fat man with a swarthy skin and spectacles, the other lean and bearded, looking rather like a fierce and hungry goat. And with his back to the window was yet another, in whom Peter had no difficulty in recognizing the gross and bulky Horstman.

"A bold claim, Sir Mortimer," the little fat man replied with the slightest foreign accent. "And you are prepared to prove it?"

The scientist nodded his head gravely. "To-night if necessary," he said.

"High time, too," growled the man who looked like a fierce goat.

"I may as well admit that it was not my original intention to do anything of the sort," Sir Mortimer confessed after a pause. "My work is not yet entirely complete, and it is manifestly impossible for me to give you the results of it piecemeal. Circumstances, however, have conspired to-night to offer me exceptional opportunities for a certain little experiment which I have for some time been contemplating, and I feel sure my apparatus is sufficiently far advanced to enable me to conduct this experiment with enough success to convince you of its extraordinary efficiency.

It will of course be only on a small scale, but it should suffice."

"One hopes so," murmured the little man, placidly contemplating the end of his cigarette.

"First of all, however, I will endeavor to give you some idea of how far my discoveries have

progressed," went on the scientist. "If you will give
me your attention for ten minutes I will tell you the
gist of my discoveries up to the present."
Outside in the soaking rain the watcher thrilled
with excitement. This was the work of fate and
nothing else.
"For many years," the scientist began, "I have been
attracted, like many of my professional brethren, by
the possibility of interplanetary communication. As
you know, there was, some twenty years ago,
considerable excitement in the world because it was
claimed that certain signals had been received from
Mars.
Lowell, if you remember, had already asserted that
there was sufficient evidence to prove the existence
of human activity on the planet, though his theory
was not generally credited; and when it was reported
that definite signals had been seen, the hypothesis
received new life, various ways being suggested as to
how we should reply. The one obvious difficulty in
the way was, of course, the lack of a common basis
of language. Even if we succeeded in transmitting
signals which were actually received, they would be
useless without a suitable interplanetary vocabulary.
"Different means of overcoming this difficulty were
suggested. A French astronomer was in favor of
constructing gigantic figures on the sand of the
Sahara desert, illustrating simple mathematical
truths.
Another astronomer recommended signaling
mathematical truths by means of reflecting the sun
in a huge mirror."

"Mathematical truths—how do you mean?"
growled the man like a goat.

"I mean this. Suppose I were to signal one flash
and then two and then four, it follows that if I get
eight in reply there is clear evidence of the existence
of a functioning intelligence. The process may be
elaborated in a way which it is hardly necessary for
me to go into now, but you may rest assured that
such a method is entirely feasible. It was suggested
also that signals should be sent by the creation of a
gigantic artificial star by electricity, directed by
parabolic mirrors which it was thought would give
light equivalent to a star of the eighth magnitude.
This was, of course, before wireless transmission
had attained to anything like its present stage of
development, and nothing was attempted, for the
simple reason that few influential people could be
persuaded that signals had really been received.
With the arrival of the means of sending powerful
waves through the ether the problem became
simplified, and a definite method was devised by
which messages could actually be sent out
so that they could be read by a sufficiently intelligent
being.
"With that method I am not going to weary you,
since it would take some time to explain and would
necessitate the use of a diagram. Suffice it to say
that the bare outline of it is this. The transmitter
sends out, we will say, ten short signals, then one
long one, and then ten more short, after which he
pauses. Next he sends nine short signals, one long,
one short, one long again, and again nine short
signals, after which he pauses once more. Two lines
of dots and dashes have now been transmitted. An
intelligent being, receiving them on another planet,
might at first put them in one long row. On the other

hand he might not; it is just possible that he might place the second row directly underneath the first, in which case he would have the top angle of the letter 'A' composed of dashes, in the centre of the two rows of dots. You follow me?"

"Admirably," said the little fat man. "Pray proceed."

"A third row would be made up of eight dots, one dash, and so on, until after twenty rows were complete the recipient, supposing him to be taking the signals down, would have the complete letter 'A' composed of dashes in the midst of an oblong of dots. The transmitter would then send, in his last line, the Morse for 'A'. Once the whole alphabet was complete it would not be difficult to begin to send, in the same way rough outlines of familiar objects, such as the figure of a man, with their names underneath in Morse."

"A somewhat long process?" observed the little man.

"An exceedingly long and laborious process," Sir Mortimer agreed. "I am only relating it to you to convince you that it is possible to establish communication. The signals which I was fortunate enough to trap were nothing like so complicated and much more easily, read. I completed my instrument in 1922, just a year after it was reported that Marconi had received some mysterious signals on a long and continuous wave- length, thought to have emanated at the time from Mars."

"These signals of yours—were they from Mars?" the little man asked.

"They emanate from an intelligence functioning on a planet considerably further advanced along the course

of evolution than our own," was the reply. "For three
years now I have been tapping this immense supply
of knowledge which has been trickling through the
ether—such a stream of knowledge and power as
staggers the intellect, and makes our present-day
research seem like the groping of a child in the dark
beside it."

Sir Mortimer paused, his pale eyes fixed on vacancy.
The lean bearded man broke the silence.

"That's all very well, my friend," he said. "We
don't doubt your theories; what we want is proof
that they can be applied for practical purposes.
Those rays you've just been telling us about—
theoretically they may do what you claim for them,
but what we want is a practical demonstration of
their power."

"You shall have it," rejoined the scientist calmly.
"You shall have it to-night."

For the first time since Peter had been at the window
Horstman spoke.

"Tell 'em about the young cub we've got upstairs,"
he suggested.

Sir Mortimer struck a match before replying.

"It so happens, gentlemen, that a young man who
chose to try and interfere with our plans'—I will not
trouble you with the details—has fallen into my
hands by a rather remarkable chain of
circumstances. The point I want you to note is that
not a soul except our-selves knows of his
whereabouts. My niece, indeed, knew he was here in
the first instance, but as she is of a peculiarly
sensitive disposition it was necessary to adopt a
simple ruse in order to convince her that he
had left the house. What, in your opinion, should I

do with him?"

"How much does he know?" demanded the lean
man.

"Sufficient to make this country a difficult one
for us to live in if he were free," Sir Mortimer
answered.

The little fat man sighed placidly. "My friend, my
motto in life is: 'If there is only one wise course to
take—take it.' Did not your Byron say 'Whom the
gods love die young'? I would make no mistake about
the popularity in Heaven of that young man!"

"Precisely my own opinion," the scientist replied.
"There is, however, an alternative."

"Yes?" The little man looked at him inquiringly
through his spectacles.

"Go on," urged his companion impatiently, for Sir
Mortimer had paused and was smiling again—like
some horrible evil satyr, Peter thought, as he
watched him.

"How if I used him for—a little demonstration?"
he said quietly.

There was a profound silence, to be broken by the
soft chuckling of the little fat man as the other's
meaning dawned on him.

"Excellent, my friend, excellent," he murmured.
"The human guinea-peeg! The sufferer in the noble
cause of science! And it will be—what you say?—
killing two birds with one stone! Oh, a lovely scheme,
my friend—very clever!"

Suddenly there came an interruption. The door
burst open and the man who had taken away Peter's
clothes, the ex-pugilist, dashed into the room, his
coarse face flushed with excitement.

"He's got away—Sefton's knocked out! he gasped.

71

"God in heaven, what do you mean?" cried Sir
Mortimer, rising from his seat. "Get a grip of yourself, Copping—what's happened?—Quick!"
"Sefton—I went up to relieve him . . . but he'd
gone," the bruiser gulped. "So I burst in the door . . .
and found him . . . Sefton . . . lyin' unconscious!"
Sir Mortimer's eyes seemed to be shining like stars
in his livid countenance. Horstman and the man
who looked like a fierce goat had sprung from their
chairs; only the little fat man seemed unperturbed,
as he blandly helped himself to a cigarette from the
box on the table.
Whereupon our Mr. Brown, much as he would have
liked to stay to watch developments, decided that it
was high time to be gone

CHAPTER V
ONE EVENTFUL NIGHT

The rain had ceased some little time ago, and the air had that refreshing coolness that often follows a thunderstorm, as Peter sped away down the drive, hurried on by a very real dread of what would happen to him if he again fell into the hands of Sir Mortimer Drude. Sheer luck had enabled him to overhear some-thing of the plans which that enterprising gentleman held regarding his immediate future, and he prayed luck would stand by him until he had succceded in putting himself beyond the possibility of recapture. How this was to be accomplished he had no idea, since he was in entire ignorance of the locality in which Okewood Hall was situated; the only thing he could do was to push on, trusting to the dark and the fact that it would take Sir Mortimer some little time to organize a search-party. For he had no doubt that every conceivable effort would be made to retake him.

Altogether apart from the unpleasing use to which Sir Mortimer proposed to put his body, his escape meant ruin to the occupants of Okewood Hall. It would take them perhaps ten minutes, he thought, to learn that he had actually left the building; and then . . ..

Peter felt the comforting weight of the revolver in his pocket and made a grim resolution that if matters came to a head there would be at least one way of preventing a distinguished but insane physicist from allowing an important discovery to fall into the hands of unscrupulous adventurers.

There was sufficient light to enable him to see the drive stretching away in front of him for a considerable distance, and it occurred to him that there might be a lodge at the other end with telephonic communication to the Hall. It was obvious that he stood a greater chance of escaping if he left the comparative openness of the drive and struck across country until he reached some road, and he accordingly climbed a railing and made his way across a meadow towards what looked like the edge of a wood. The ground was difficult going, for it was pitted with rabbit-holes, and he took a header more than once. It was after the last of these tumbles that the powerful headlights of a car appeared in the direction of the Hall, and swept at terrific speed down the drive he had just left. Almost immediately afterwards another car came into sight round the Hall and sped along a course at right-angles to the first—evidently along another drive. Peter watched it with a kind of dull despair creeping into his heart. The cordon was already being set.

And then suddenly an idea entered his head—an idea that on the face of it was hopelessly insane, yet which, as he considered it, presented extraordinary possibilities. He wondered why he had not thought of it before. If the hunters had already made a thorough search of the Hall and decided that he had tried to escape—the most natural conclusion they could come to—the one place where they would be unlikely to look a second time was the Hall. And in the Hall was doubtless a telephone from which, with a little more of that luck which had served him so well that night, he might possibly seize the chance to inform someone of his whereabouts. More, he might even find his way into that mysterious laboratory whence all the trouble had originated. One or two members of the strange gang of which Sir Mortimer's household seemed to consist might be left on guard, but the majority were far more probably taking part in the hunt in the grounds. At any rate the chance seemed one well worth taking, and once he had put through a connection on the 'phone, even if he ultimately fell into their hands again, his safety would be to a certain extent ensured. It was hardly likely that Sir Mortimer would run the risk of killing him, if he would have to face a possible visit from the police in the morning demanding an explanation of the whereabouts of the notorious Mr. Brown who had so mysteriously rung them up in the small hours from Okewood Hall.

Without any hesitation Peter doubled back on his tracks, and once more approached the Hall. Every room on the ground boor was now brilliantly illuminated, but he could see no one about. The front door stood open, and he approached it cautiously and looked through, only to draw back his head immediately as he espied a man standing by a table in the middle of the hall—a little man whose face was turned half away from the door, and who held a revolver by his side. It is half the battle to be able to recognize at a glance the temperament of your opponent, and Peter decided that here was a man who could be intimidated.

Leveling his revolver he said in a low distinct voice:

"Both hands up!"

And Peter knew he had judged aright. Up went
the man's hands with every appearance of fear, and
the blood drained from his face.
"Put the pistol on the table," said Peter. The man
obeyed. "Any movement and it will be your last,"
added Peter grimly. "Whereabouts is the telephone?"
The man told him.
"Very well. Go and ring up the exchange. I shall
stand by you while you do it."

"There won't be no one th-there," stammered the
badly scared man, staring in a fascinated manner
at the revolver which was pointing so steadily at his
head. Under his breath Peter cursed himself for a
fool.
Obviously the officials at country exchanges
occasionally required sleep the same as other people,
only he had overlooked the trivial fact.
"Where are all the others?" he demanded quickly.
"Outside," quavered the man.
"How many?"
"About—about a dozen, sir."
"And are you alone here?"
"Yes."
Peter considered him. The man was obviously
a weakling, frightened out of his life, and
Peter made up his mind that he was telling the
truth.
"I'm going to give you the chance of saving your
miserable life, but if you don't tell me what I want
to know I'll shoot you," he said peremptorily. "Under-
stand that, you little worm?"
"Yes," said the man, cringing. Peter hated this
bullying business, but he saw no alternative. The
shortest way would have been to hit him over the

head, but he was a creature of such poor spirit that
Peter had not the heart to do it.

"First of all, then—the name of that fat little man
with spectacles who was with Sir Mortimer a minute
ago?"

"Mr. Pagleiro."

"And the other one—the thin one?"

"Mr. Kreller."

"Good. Now take me to Sir Mortimer's laboratory.
If there's a key, get it."

But at this the fellow drew back, and his face took
on an even whiter shade.

"I daren't, sir, really—no one's allowed to go there
at all, and if the guv'nor knew as I'd told you..."

"My little friend," said Peter quietly, "the search
party will be back in a few minutes, and as sure as
there's a God above they'll find a corpse in this hall
if you don't do as I tell you."

The man moistened his ashen lips.

"Very good, sir," he said despairingly. "But if the
guv'nor was to know"

"Please to remember that for the moment I'm your
governor, and you'll obey me. Quick now!"

With many a bodeful glance over his shoulder the
man led the way down a passage to a green baize
door, Peter following with the firm intention of
shooting him down if he made any attempt to
escape.

Beyond the green door was a further covered-in passage with another door at the far end, and here
Peter's guide stopped.

"This is the laboratory, sir," he said.

It was locked, as Peter had expected, and though
he put his shoulder to it, it refused to budge.

"Stand clear," ordered Peter, and taking aim from
a short distance, fired one of his pistols at the lock.
The din in that confined space was alarming, the
smoke almost choking, but he emptied all the
chambers of the revolver before he was satisfied; and
a few moments later the splintered door yawned
behind him.

"Matches," he said to his companion, and when the
man had struck one, only too eager now to ingratiate
himself, Peter switched on the electric light.

He had been in a well-equipped laboratory before,
but never in such a one as this. Of the uses to which
half the instruments were put he had no conception,
but there was no time for indulging idle curiosity,
and after a quick look round he approached a large
cupboard, something about the size of a bathing
van, which he noticed with satisfaction was fastened
with a Yale lock. This was evidently the cupboard of
which Bridgewater had spoken, and without any
hesitation he fired the other revolver at the lock.

"For God's sake, sir," cried his companion in what
seemed like genuine alarm. "Sir Mortimer'll kill you
if he finds this out."

Peter did not answer, for he had opened the cupboard doors and was examining the extraordinary
instrument revealed. From the innumerable valves
and dials and switches his guess that this was the
super wireless set of which he was in search was
confirmed, and he immediately proceeded to wrench
open the huge panel, which swung out sideways on
hinges.

Inside was the most bewildering array of delicate
mechanism he had ever seen—obviously the result of
months of labour. It seemed sacrilege to destroy

work of such ingenuity, but he did not hesitate.
Since he seemed bound eventually to be caught, as
well be killed for a pound as a penny, he reflected,
and at any rate he would die with the satisfaction of
knowing he had temporarily spoilt his enemies'
game. Had not Sir Mortimer said that his work was
not yet complete?

Well, he might not be able to prevent its ultimate
completion, but at least he could defer the date by a
few months—months which would enable Dick Cartwright and his friends to get busy. So with the butt
of his revolver he deliberately set himself to put the
mechanism beyond possibility of repair, until
nothing remained but a mass of twisted rods and
coils and broken wires.

The work of demolition complete, he was running
his eye over the ruined structure in order to see if
any part had been overlooked, his mind already
beginning to work on the old problem of how to
escape, when an exclamation from the man who had
been his guide caused him to turn sharply, and he
found himself looking down a revolver barrel, behind
which gleamed the dark eyes of the girl of the motor-
scooter.

"You—here!" she said in a low voice, as recognition
sprang into her eyes. "But I—I thought . . . what
are you doing?"

It was difficult to know what to say, and he did
not answer. Then, as she realized what he had done,
anger flamed into her face, and she took a step backwards, as if the very proximity of his presence
disgusted her.

"You cur! You unspeakable cad!" she said slowly,

and the contempt in her voice cut him like a lash.
"To come back like a thief . . . and do this . . .
after his kindness to you in hiding you from the
police and setting you free . . ." She could scarcely
speak for the intensity of her emotion. "Oh, haven't
you got anything to say—any explanation to offer?"
she cried, with a sudden trembling of the lip.
Peter was silent. So Sir Mortimer had told her that
he had set him free! Well, if she chose to believe in
her uncle's integrity, it was no business of his to
disillusion her. Yet as he saw how deeply wounded
she was by the thought of his having betrayed her
trust in him, he would have given much to have
spared her this suffering.
She lowered her pistol, and for all the apparent
ignominy of his position Peter nearly smiled. Though
she thought him the vilest cad in creation, the very
action showed that she instinctively trusted to his
sense of honour not to take advantage of the circumstance for he still held his own revolver. It was one
of the biggest unconscious tributes he had ever
received, and he loved her for it.
"And what are you doing here, Davis?" she
demanded, turning with quick suspicion to Peter's
reluctant guide.
Before the man could speak Peter answered for him.
"Please don't imagine he's my accomplice," he
said. "He did all he could to stop me, but—I
happened to be a bit quicker with my revolver,
that's all."
"You needn't think you are going to get round me.
Don't pretending to be chivalrous," the girl said
hotly.
"Is this true, Davis?"

The man gave a malicious side-glance at Peter.
Here was an unexpected chance to get some of his
own back. "Yes, miss, he come up behind me when
I wasn't looking. I never had no chance against
him—hurt me cruel hard he did, too. Shall I take his
pistols away, miss?"

"Yes—and give them to me; I'll keep him covered
while you call the others. You won't be given your
liberty a second time," she added grimly.

The man having relieved Peter of his weapons and
retired, the girl seated herself on a chair and rested
the two revolvers on her knee.

"You can sit down yourself if you like," she said
curtly.

"Thank you," said Peter, and did so. Thus they
waited, while Peter marveled at the queer tricks of
Providence in bringing him to this pass. He felt
strangely indifferent as to his own fate. He could not,
indeed, see a gleam of hope; for Sir Mortimer would
undoubtedly kill him out of hand when he saw his
wrecked instrument. Perhaps he would have enough
humanity actually not to do it in front of his niece,
for whom he evidently cherished some kind of regard
—perhaps not. For her sake Peter hoped it would be
the former. He knew that she had not the faintest
notion of what she was condemning him to; in her
eyes he was simply a common crook badly wanted
by the police, who had not only lied to her about the
crime of which he was thought to be the author, but
had also outrageously abused her sympathy and
help.

Of Sir Mortimer's real intention she obviously had
little idea; nor did he propose to enlighten her. Even

more than the prospect of falling into Sir Mortimer's
hands it hurt him to think that she should deem
him so unworthy; but short of revealing her uncle's
true character there was no other way. And he knew
well that if he so much as attempted to excuse
himself such a course would only serve to increase
her anger and contempt. If she chose to begin a
conversation— well and good; so far as he was
concerned silence was the better counsel.

The girl, for her part, remained on the alert, ready-
to jump to her feet on the instant if he showed fight.
Peter could not, of course, know that behind her air
of grim resolution was a great welling of pity, which
she tried hard to suppress. He was a vile scoundrel,
of course—she knew it and told herself she hated
him for it—but he looked so tired and ill that she
needed all the determination of which she was
capable to keep a severe countenance. And how
humbly he had taken her rough-tonguing! Watching
his face furtively she thought she had never seen
anyone who looked less like a criminal. She looked
away, sternly reminding herself of the well-known
fact that some of the most hardened villains in
history have possessed the faces of angels.

A noise in the passage outside announced the return
of the search-party, and she rose to her feet as Sir
Mortimer rushed in, with half a dozen men at his
heels.

"So you found him, Una? Where ?"

And then he stopped, as if petrified. He had caught
sight of the wrecked instrument board: The next
moment, with a terrible cry, he flung himself at
Peter, and there was immediate uproar. Peter could
have settled his assailant with one hand had he been

so minded, but the presence of the girl made this
impossible; so evading the scientist's frenzied rush
he tried to dodge towards the door, building on the
hope that none would dare to use his firearm for fear
of hitting another. Several men barred his way. One
he hit in the face, knocking him over—it was the
lean bearded man, Kreller—but the odds were
ridiculous, and he presently found himself, bruised
and bleeding, with the gigantic Horstman holding
one arm and the ex-pugilist the other. And for an
instant his self- control gave way.
"You damned lot of filthy cowards!" he cried.
"Let me go, curse you !"
"Shall I finish him off, guv'nor?" Horstman asked
in his high-pitched voice, giving Peter's arm a cruel
twist.
"Stop that, I tell you!"
The voice, young and clear, quelled the uproar
like a miracle, and all eyes turned on the girl as she
stood, like some modern allegorical picture of
vengeance, a revolver in either hand, her eyes
flashing her scorn and defiance.
"Leave the room all of you—at once!" she cried,
stamping her foot. "How dare you behave like this
in front of me! Call yourselves men!—a dozen of you
against one, and him half-dead! As for you, Mr.
Horstman, I've never fired a revolver at a man yet,
but if you don't leave go of his arm at once I'll shoot
you where you stand!"
Whether she would have carried this threat into
execution was never known, for Horstman's great
face turned an unpleasant colour, and he dropped
Peter's, arm as if it had been red-hot. The other men
seemed doubtful whether to obey her orders, but at

a nod from Sir Mortimer, who had recovered his self-possession, although he was still ghastly white, they slowly withdrew until only four were left.

"Vai-ry bravely done, Mees Drude. Permit me to congratulate you on your undoubted courage."

Peter looked round. It was the little fat man with spectacles, placid as ever.

"Thank you, but I don't think I want your congratulations, Mr. Pagleiro," said the girl unsteadily, and Peter noticed that she, too, had changed colour; and suddenly, without further warning, she fainted, and Sir Mortimer caught her as she fell.

"The very best thing that could have happened," the scientist observed with satisfaction. "I was beginning to think she would be a nuisance. Keep your eye on him, Horstman, until I return!"

When Sir Mortimer, with the assistance of the ex-bruiser, had carried the girl from the room, Kreller, the man like a fierce and hungry goat, who was attending to a bleeding nose, stood in front of the prisoner, surveying him with malevolent hatred. He carried a pistol in his left hand.

"This is the young cub, is it?" he said. "I think I have to thank you for hitting me just now—well, I hate being under any obligation, so here's the gift back again with interest," and he struck Peter heavily in the face with his clenched fist.

"I can add one to that," squeaked Horstman, following up and seizing Peter by the throat. "Push me in the river, would you, blast your bones! You'll wish your own mother had strangled you at birth before I've done with you!"

There was twice Peter's strength in those monstrous

arms, and he shook his powerless victim with no more effort than a terrier shakes a rat.

"Peace, my friends, peace," cried the little fat man. "You forget . . . the leetle demonstration . . . Sir Mortimer would not have him killed—yet."

Reluctantly Horstman released his nearly unconscious victim, whose legs promptly sank under him.

There was a great fear in Peter's heart—a fear, not of death, but that, in his physical weakness, he might be tempted to plead for mercy.

As he struggled unsteadily to his feet, Sir Mortimer and the ex-prizefighter returned. The scientist's marble eyes fixed themselves on him with a look of insane satisfaction.

"At last," he said quietly. "We can now continue that little experiment I was speaking of without fear of interruption. What do you think, gentlemen?"

Kreller laughed harshly. "What's the use playing the fool—shoot him and have done with it. No one will ever find out."

"No, no, my friend." Pagleiro put up a fat protesting hand. "The leetle demonstration first. Sir Mortimer promised."

"I agree," said the scientist. "Afterwards, we will consider what to do in the matter of my apparatus—"

For a moment the words seemed to choke in his throat as his eyes lit on the wreck which Peter had made of it; then he recovered himself and went on:

"Horstman, I make you and Copping responsible for him until I am ready. Then, gentlemen, I will endeavor to continue that little talk which was so rudely interrupted a few minutes ago, and try to relieve that attitude of skepticism with which I am afraid you still regard my claims."

During the next ten minutes, while Sir Mortimer busied himself about the laboratory, Peter, who was made to sit on a chair on a small platform, had leisure to think of his position. A kind of indifference had settled upon him. The very thought of escape had receded to the back of his mind. He was without hope, and that state in itself brings its own kind of peace.

If only they didn't torture him he thought he could die with some decency, for after all death was a small thing, and quickly over. But torture—those "experiments", of which Sir Mortimer spoke—that was what filled his soul with dread. From experience he knew the terribly unmanning effect of torn flesh and lacerated nerves, and again he prayed that his courage would hold out till the end.

Chairs had been arranged in a semi-circle in front of the platform on which Peter sat, and on one side Sir Mortimer had placed three instruments not unlike studio cameras. The hum of a dynamo came from the far end of the laboratory. The four men seated themselves, and Sir Mortimer stood by the platform in the manner of an urbane university professor about to lecture his class on some rare and valuable specimen.

"Before we commence operations," he began, "I must say a few words relating to the source of my information. Has it ever struck you, gentlemen, how extraordinarily ignorant we are; how little we have explored of that mysterious continent, infinite in extent, which we call knowledge? I am not referring to the knowledge of one individual man in relation to all that has so far been discovered, but to the knowledge which the world has amassed compared to all that remains to be discovered. We are, indeed, no more than children paddling on the shore of that wonderful continent.

A few of us have struggled up the beach and have peered amazedly through the trees, almost overcome by the dazzling promise revealed, only to be laughed at and derided when we have rejoined our fellows and tried to tell them something of what we have seen. Such was the attitude, gentlemen, of the Roman inquisition towards Galileo. It is to-day the attitude of the world with regard to spiritualism. It-is the attitude which the world would adopt towards me were I to publish the result of my researches into inter-stellar communication, and it is the attitude which you are pleased to adopt towards me to-night. You require proof—the actual proof of your own five senses—before you believe me. Well, you shall have it."

He paused, his marble-like eyes resting thoughtfully on Peter.

"Now let us suppose for a moment that a man on this world does actually succeed in getting in touch with beings on another celestial body. These beings possess intelligence, and it is reasonable to suppose that they exist in some kind of civilization. It by no means follows, however, that this civilization is akin to our own. Evolution, which is more or less at the mercy of temperature and pressure, may have progressed in an entirely different direction. Knowledge will have been brought about in an entirely different way. The chances of their having acquired precisely the same amount of knowledge as ourselves are remote; it therefore follows that they either know more or less—probably more, since they would not otherwise have been in a position to communicate with us. The question which one naturally asks is, how much more do they know? Are they still struggling on the shores of knowledge and scientific discovery, like ourselves, or have they penetrated far inland, and learnt of things which we shall not know, in the natural course of things, for thousands of years?

"Let me put it to you in this way. It is, I suppose, obvious that in, say, a thousand years' time, man will have at his beck and call scientific powers undreamt of by the present generation. Untold sources of energy lie around us unused for the want of the knowledge of how to tap them. Suppose one man were, by a miracle, possessed of the knowledge which will be in possession of the world in a thousand years' time? Or suppose—which would not be a miracle—he obtained the knowledge from another civilization outside the world, which was a thousand years ahead of our own? As I have explained to you before, such knowledge, if he kept it to himself, would simply mean that the world would lie at his mercy, for good or evil. For sheer power Alexander and Napoleon and our modern newspaper millionaires would be babes beside him."

Pagleiro asked a question. "For how long would he be able to keep the knowledge secret?"

"Once his position was established I can see no end to it."

The little man shook his head. "That is not the lesson of history, my friend. Autocracy—dictator-ship (that is the word, yes?) arouses forces which

inevitably bring about"
"You cannot draw a parallel between this and any
other dictatorship," Sir Mortimer interrupted.
"Because absolute omnipotence has never before lain
in the hands of one man. However, you shall see for
yourself. One moment."
With a tense expression the scientist raised his hand
to one of the camera-like objects beside him. And at
that instant every light in the laboratory went out.
There was a moment's silence, everyone being taken
by surprise; then Sir Mortimer's voice rang out,
shrill with anxiety.
"Hold him, Horstman!—Copping!—hold him!"
But Peter, quick to take advantage of this unlooked-
for occurrence, had already slipped from his chair.
Not a gleam of light was visible anywhere, but he
had a clear idea of the position of the door, and he
began to make his way towards it, thankful for the
noise of blows and curses which had broken out,
suggesting that Horstman, and Copping, the ex-
bruiser, had each mistaken the other for him in the
darkness, and were engaged in a praiseworthy effort
to prevent each other's escape. Sir Mortimer was
heard above the din shrieking for matches, but by
the time someone had struck one, Peter, after once
or twice cannoning with painful force into hard
objects that felt like benches, had reached the door,
which, to his surprise, was open.
Into the impenetrable blackness of the passage he
dashed, with one hand on the wall as a guide, just
as a fresh tumult breaking out in the laboratory
warned him that his escape was discovered. He had
no plan, save to try and find a way out of the house,
and he fully realized that, unarmed as he was, his

chance of attaining that desire was microscopic;
nevertheless, he blundered on. It looked as if the
lights all over the house had gone out, for there was
still nothing but darkness ahead. And then, at the
far end of the passage, he bumped into someone,
and with a sudden fury sought for and gripped his
opponent's throat. But the next moment he released
his hold in dismay, for the neck his fingers had
closed round was a woman's.
"Oh!—please!—don't," a girl's voice gasped.
"Quick, there's just a chance," she went on
hurriedly.
"Go through the door on the right, and you'll find a
car—oh, be quick."
From the other end of the passage came the sound
of hurrying feet and furious voices.
"Quick," she cried in an agony of dread.
Then Peter did a thing of which he would never in
his wildest dreams have deemed himself capable.
He seized her hand and pressed it to his lips.
"This is the second time," he said gently. "I shall
remember it always."
The next moment he was gone.

The door which she had mentioned was wide open,
and darting through, he found himself in the drive,
with a car, its headlights full on and its engine
running, standing not a dozen yards away. He saw it
was a make with which he was familiar, and leaping
into the driving-seat he let in the clutch as a revolver
cracked behind him and the windscreen shivered to
atoms.
A regular volley of shots followed, and he felt a
violent blow on his right shoulder, but by this time

he had got up considerable speed and he was soon out of pistol-shot range. Opening the throttle wide he tore down the drive, expecting every instant to see the reflection of pursuing headlights, but none came, and he wondered if the splendid girl who had so opportunely come to his aid had put the other car out of action. From what he had seen of her, he thought it a likely supposition.

Down the drive he swept with the wind cool in his face, nothing between him and freedom now but the gates at the end. There might be a lodge, but after having slipped through Sir Mortimer's fingers he could afford to laugh at the likelihood of a lodge-keeper trying to stop him. The car, however, never reached the gates, for Peter was all at once overcome by a deadly faintness. Feeling himself losing consciousness he thrust hard on clutch and brake, an action which probably saved him from complete disaster; for although the car left the drive, bumping like a live thing over some adjacent grass-land, its reduced speed stopped it from overturning. When consciousness returned he was still in the driving-seat, but he felt desperately ill. And when he tried to start the car again it refused to budge: something had gone wrong with the transmission.

He climbed out of the car and looked back in the direction of Okewood Hall. It was still plunged in darkness, and he could hear no signs of pursuit. Remembering that the car's lights would give away his whereabouts, he hurriedly switched them off; then, hardly conscious of volition on his part, he stumbled towards the drive, along which he walked for some distance with a dazed mind. Every single part of his body clamored for him to lie down and rest, yet difficult though it was to think consistently, he knew he must struggle on. Presently, dimly aware that to continue on the drive spelt danger, he turned aside and began to cross a stretch of turf. There was still no sound of pursuit.

Like a man in a nightmare, he staggered on until he came to an iron fence, which he managed to climb, and found himself in a field of long grass. The longing to let himself fall over and lie down—snug among the thick grass—grew on him as he stumbled across the field. Peace, at any rate, lay there—long abiding peace —and after all, what was the use of struggling? The call of exhaustion was almost overpowering, and there is no doubt that if he had once tripped he would never have risen again; yet somehow he kept his feet and came to the other side. He found he was leaning against a gate—a wooden five-barred gate—and beyond it was a lane. He could see it plainly, and obviously he had somehow got to climb the gate and reach the lane. It took him five minutes of painful concentrated effort to get over this obstacle, and when he had accomplished it he was over- taken with horrible nausea, which made him clutch the gate like a drowning man. Following this came a weak fit of giggling that all but made him collapse but at length he was in the lane, lurching along like some drunken tramp in the gaining dawn, moving almost mechanically. His brain, as apart from his will, had ceased to function.

And so, in due course, as the eastern sky began to be suffused with orange and yellow, he came to a cross-roads where the lane debouched upon a tar-paved highway, and here the last drop of energy oozed out of him, and he flopped on to the grass beneath a signpost.

A motor-car honked, and he looked up wearily.

Sir Mortimer at last, he supposed. Well, he was past resistance—broken, down, and out. It was not Sir Mortimer, however, but two policemen in a Ford car. They peered curiously at the wild figure under the signpost, and the car stopped.

"Is it, d'ye think?" asked the one who was driving.

"It's him, right enough," said the other, and got out. Peter saw him coming, and laughed. "It's me right enough!" he croaked. "Dramatic arrest of famous international footballer in the dawn!" And he went off into a cackle of laughter that told its own tale to the two officers.

"Been in the wars a bit, haven't you?" said the one who had dismounted, in a not unkindly voice. He had been concerned in many arrests, this police-man, and was familiar with the appearance of criminals who had been forced to give themselves up through hunger and other causes after long struggles to evade the law, but he never remembered having seen one so utterly spent as this. Blood was on his face and clothes—what was left of them—and to the trained eye of the officer, he looked not far off the point of complete collapse.

"Just a little," said Peter with his eyes closed, "just a little."

Then he opened them again, and summoning all his remaining strength, spoke in a firmer voice:

"You've got me all right, and I won't make any trouble. But before you take me along I want to make a statement—take it down if you can. There's hell brewing for the old world back yonder, and someone's got to stop it. Sir Mortimer Drude...."

"Yes?" said one of the officers eagerly, for Peter
had paused, tormented by the difficulty of finding a
beginning amidst the tangle of impressions which
confused his mind. And at all costs his story must
be coherent and continuous. He closed his eyes
again hard in the endeavor to concentrate.
"Go to the Foreign Office and find someone who
knows Colonel Richard Cartwright," he said, slowly.
"Tell him to go to Bratislava, Czecho-Slovakia, where
Colonel Cartwright is lying ill, and tell him this.
Bridgewater was right in his suspicions. Sir
Mortimer Drude has got into communication with
another world in a higher state of civilization than
our own, and has in his possession scientific secrets
of enormous power which he is selling to a gang of
inter-national crooks who will probably use them for
their own ends. Got that down? The transaction
has not yet taken place, however, on account
of the gang not being convinced of the efficacy of
Sir Mortimer's discoveries. Through a motor accident
I got taken into Sir Mortimer's house, where I
succeeded in putting out of action the wireless
instrument by which he received the
communications from the other world."
Peter paused once more and put both hands to his
head. Waves of excruciating agony had begun to
surge through his brain, making the effort of
concentrating more difficult. The two officers waited
with open notebooks.
"After I had done this I was caught," he proceeded
at length, "and Sir Mortimer proposed to conduct an
experiment upon me in order to convince some
members of the gang who were present—Pagleiro,
Kreller and Horstiaan—that his assertions were true.

The Great Holdup Mystery

What the nature of this experiment was I don't
know, for thanks to Sir Mortimer's niece I managed
to escape, but I have no doubt in my own mind they
intended to kill me. Sir Mortimer himself is a
madman, and should be put away. The other men
are scoundrels of the worst type—enemies of
society—and if they once get the secret into their
hands God knows where it will end.
The girl—Drude's niece—is, I am convinced,
innocent of the real nature of her uncle's
transactions, and she undoubtedly saved my life.
Tell Colonel Cartwright this—he'll know what to do.
Now that Bridgewater is dead"
"Hold on a minute," interrupted one of the officers.
"You're wrong there. Bridgewater—the man you're
supposed to have tried to murder—isn't dead."
"Not—dead?" said Peter slowly.
"Not a bit of it," was the cheerful reply. "Had a
narrow shave, certainly, but he's a long sight off
being dead. And if it's any pleasure for you to know,
we know it wasn't you who tried to do him in."

"Then—" Peter's mind was spinning like a top—
"there was never any need ... I thought . . ."
He broke off, and gave an odd laugh. "Lord, what a
fool," he murmured.
And then happiness swirled over him like a tide.
Fool he was, no doubt, but in his folly he had not
been entirely unsuccessful, and Bridgewater—
Bridgewater whom he had mourned as dead, and for
whose death he had held himself in part
responsible—was alive, and would carry on the good
work he had begun. Now that the weight was lifted
he realized how heavy it had   been, and his heart
sang with the joy of achievement.

Wilfrid Usher

He rose unsteadily to his feet.
"I'm all right now," he said with the old cheerful
ring in his voice. "Your news is wonderful, and alters
things entirely."
He grinned at the two policemen; the next moment
the world gave a sudden heave and he pitched
forward on to the grass and lay still.

CHAPTER VI
THE HUT ON THE SAND DUNES

For ten long days and nights our Mr. Brown lay in an Exeter nursing-home, battling with the particular species of demon that frequent the bedsides of sick men; at the end of which time, his constitution being sound and his wound not serious, he began to mend rapidly. From the doctors and nurses and various members of the local police-force he learnt many things about which he was intensely curious; but it was not until he had been in the house a fortnight that all doubts and anxieties as to his own position were finally cleared up.

The cause of this relief was a visit from two men. They introduced themselves as Detective-Inspector Claggs of the C.I.D. department of New Scotland Yard and Major Tremayne of the Foreign Office—the first a smart, clean-shaven man with the look of a naval-officer in mufti, the other rugged and kindly, with a broken nose and very bright-blue eyes. Both were pleasant and complimentary. They began by assuring Peter that he need anticipate no further trouble from the police, and invited him to tell his own story. When Peter had done, Major Tremayne spoke: "You seem to have had a most providential escape, and I really don't know whether you deserve commiseration on your bad luck in getting into so many awkward situations, or congratulations on the facility with which you turn them to good account. First of all, however, you would probably like to hear about Mr. Bridgewater. He isn't out of hospital yet, but he's very much better and already itching to be

out and about again. I had a chat with him a few
days ago, and he tells me that on the night he was
attacked the first thing he knew was the noise of
someone getting through the window. He jumped up
and grappled with the fellow at once, and from his
own account they seem to have had a pretty hectic
fight of it, several more of the blackguards joining in.
As you know, he is a powerfully-built fellow, and he
soon settled his first adversary—as a matter of fact
he broke his neck—but what happened after that
isn't so clear. He remembers getting hold of one of
your golf-clubs and laying about with it; then
apparently one of the swine hit him over the head.
The rest you know. Your own story corroborates the
fact that Bridgewater did actually kill his antagonist,
and it's quite clear that after having got the papers
they left him for dead, taking their own dead pal
away with them. The land- lady, hearing the
commotion, had come down, scared out of her life,
and as soon as the attacking party had cleared off
she ran for the police. Then you came back
on the scene and made the same mistake as Horstman's gang—you thought Bridgewater was dead."
"Unfortunately, I did," said Peter. "Looking back
at it now, my running away seems rather absurd,
but given the same circumstances again I don't
think I should do differently. How's the policeman I
had a little difference with?"
Tremayne looked at him with an innocent
expression.
"Policeman?" he said. "I don't know anything
about a policeman—do you, Claggs?"
The detective grinned and shook his head.
"Of course not," said Tremayne. "Neither of us knows

anything about your having a little difference with a
policeman—you must be thinking about someone
else."

Peter caught the merry wink trembling in one of
the Major's blue eyes, and smiled his understanding.
"There was only one officer concerned," went on
Tremayne with much gravity. "His name is Trethewy,
and I am given to understand he—er—had the misfortune to fall and hit his head on the night in
question—an accident from which he happily
recovered with great rapidity. That so, Claggs?"

"As you say, sir," said Claggs solemnly.

"Constable Trethewy, therefore, fades from the
picture," proceeded the Major. "The unfortunate part
is that your friend Sir Mortimer and his household
have elected to do the same thing."

"I heard so," said Peter. "Cleared out, I suppose?"

"Bag and baggage. We raided 'em the same day
we found you. Gone! Vanished! Not a sign of anyone in the whole place. Servants and everyone. The
only things left were a two-seater Climax with its
back-axle broken, the remains of some kind of
wireless set in the laboratory, and one or two locks
that looked as if they'd been opened with a revolver."

Peter nodded thoughtfully. "I certainly made a
good job of that wireless-set. No trace of them, I
suppose?"

"None at all," said Tremayne. "There may be doubts
about Sir Mortimer Drude's mental balance, but
there's precious little doubt about his ability to
disappear into thin air."

"We haven't heard word or sign of him since the
day he vanished," said Claggs, "and the whole
country has been on the look-out for him, I might

tell you."

"What about the Isotta Fraschini?" Peter asked.
"That shouldn't be an easy car to disguise."

"You wouldn't think so," said the detective. "But
ten to one it's locked up in a private garage in the
country. Still, we've got hopes. They can't get out of
the country without leaving from a recognized port.

"Unless they fly," suggested Peter. "I seem to
remember Bridgewater saying something about a
seaplane. And what about that motor-boat Horstman used?" he added.

"They might do that, of course," the detective
admitted.

"The way I look at it is this," said Tremayne.

"Here is this potty genius who thinks he has got into
touch with some civilization on another world which
has advanced in scientific knowledge much farther
than our own. We have yet to receive proof that he
has—it may be all bunkum. On the other hand I see
no reason to deny the possibility of there being
another world inhabited by intelligent beings, nor
would I say it is impossible that someday
communication will be established. Supposing that
Sir Mortimer's assertion is true, and not the mere
ebullition of a deranged mind, I take it that for some
time past he has been receiving a regular flow of this
super-knowledge. Now has he received enough to
satisfy Messrs. Pagleiro and Co., or has your
smashing of his lines of communication
put a stopper on the business until he fits up
another of his patent wireless-outfits? I must confess
I should like to know what it was they proposed to
do to you, Brown."

"Thank you," said Peter with a dry laugh. "I'm

very glad I'm not in a position to be able to gratify your curiosity."

"It therefore boils down to this," continued Tremayne. "If his information isn't complete we have a respite of some months; if, however, it is complete, and is what Pagleiro and Co. want, there'll be squalls blowing up in a very short time. My own impression is that we shall hear of something any day. In the meantime the job is to find Sir Mortimer's where-abouts."

"It rather looks like a case of 'as you were'," Peter remarked. "We're more or less in the same place we were before I started."

"My dear fellow, no, no!" objected Tremayne. "Things are very different. Before your show we were working absolutely in the dark; we knew nothing definite; if we arrested Sir Mortimer we had no case; but now the position is entirely changed. His sudden bolting is a confession of guilt in itself. He dare not show his face anywhere where he is likely to be recognized. There's only one thing I'm really afraid of."

"What's that?" Peter asked.

"Your safety," was the reply. "I'm not going to alarm you unduly, but I should suggest that you walk very warily for the next month or two—very warily indeed. It isn't absolutely necessary that you should go back to your business just yet, I suppose? I mean, you could take another holiday and get thoroughly fit again?"

Peter looked at him steadily. "Do you mean that they will attempt my life?" he asked.

"I think it highly probable," said Tremayne frankly. "Remember, you are the only witness against them.

So long as you are alive they are in danger.
Moreover, apart from expediency, you have spoilt
their game, and I'm afraid they won't love you for it. I
should suggest a crowded seaside resort, where you
are not likely to be alone for long. Why not adopt a
slight change of name?—it might save you a certain
amount of publicity, and you can always explain why
if you happen to meet a friend. I should also
recommend getting hold of one of those compressed-
air revolvers. Your car, by the way, is in a garage at
Okehampton." "I'd almost forgotten all about it, to
tell you the truth," Peter confessed. "Let me see,
there was also the matter of a bicycle I borrowed
from a parson—rather a decent chap—"
"And also, I think, the matter of a motor-scooter,"
put in Major Tremayne, with a roguish twinkle in his
blue eyes. "What is the classical parallel, Claggs?—
I forget—the bold bad baron and the tender-hearted
maiden—what?"
He laughed merrily at Peter's discomfiture; then
his voice grew serious again. "You'll keep a hand in
the game, of course," he added.
Peter did not answer at once. It was the old story,
the same question that had lain between him and
Bridgewater that night at Tregenneth, with all his
inclination tugging the one way, bidding him clear
out of the business while there was yet time. But he
knew in his heart he could never take such a course
now— the issues had been made too plain. Not even
the thought that the bringing to book of Sir Mortimer
must inevitably cause pain and disgrace to fall upon
the girl who had saved his life could alter the
pointing of the finger of duty. But he felt no elation
at the prospect of carrying on the struggle. There

was not even the spur of hatred, for Peter was a man incapable of bearing a grudge. It was the tragic necessity of the thing, the realization that so long as the brilliant but warped brain of Sir Mortimer was at the use of the unscrupulous adventurers under whose influence he had fallen there would be untold misery in store for the world, that made any other way impossible. All of which Major Tremayne doubtless knew; indeed, his last sentence was less of a question than a statement.

Three weeks later found Peter staying alone at the Royal Hotel Seabridge, under the name of Bryan. The choice of Seabridge was not his own. Shortly after the visit of Major Tremayne and Claggs he had received a telegram from Bridgewater which ran as follows:
 'Congratulations suggest another holiday recommend Seabridge golf watch military men's game take care yourself, 'and he had interpreted it as a command.
Seabridge, however, famed for its breezes and notorious for its mud, did not seem to offer much promise of excitement. The population—or at any rate that part which appeared on the front— consisted of bronzed young men in flannels and blazers, and their healthy-looking, free-striding flapper companions; prosaic and perspiring fathers and mothers with brown- limbed children; fierce-looking elderly gentlemen with parchment faces and ramrod backs (ex-governors of a million souls somewhere out East as like as not); mahogany-faced boat-touts ("Trip round the bay, zur"); bathers, balloon-men, bath-chairs and bandsmen, and all the

decent accompaniments that go to make up the
English seaside resort—accompaniments which
Peter absorbed and delighted in for three days, while
awaiting the arrival of his golf-clubs from
Tregenneth—but which were poles apart from the
sinister business which was always in his mind.
During this time he kept mostly to himself; nor
did he meet anyone he knew, a relief for which he
was grateful; for during the few days he had spent at
home he had done nothing but acknowledge the
greetings of friends—in the post as well as the
street—anxious to commiserate with him on his
recent escapade. These friends of course knew
nothing of his adventure at Okewood Hall, all
reference to Sir Mortimer Drude having been kept
out of the papers. All they knew was that Peter had
been wrongly suspected of having attempted to
murder a man in Cornwall, and had been chased
over two counties by the police in consequence. The
month he had spent in hospital, it had been given
out, was due to a motor accident and exposure.
On the fourth day of his visit his golf-bag arrived,
and he made his way to the local golf-club, where,
seeking out the secretary, he inquired if there was
any chance of a game.
"What's your handicap?" demanded the secretary,
an energetic little man with a chubby red face and
spectacles. Peter told him—six
"Six," repeated the secretary. "I've got the very
man for you. Colonel Venning—he's a visitor—been
kicking his heels for over a week without anyone
to play with. Indian army man—you'll like him
immensely."

The Great Holdup Mystery

There was no mistaking either Colonel Venning's profession or the clime in which he had lived. India was written in every line of his tall upright figure, in the deep furrows that ran down cheeks like brown paper, the close-cropped grey moustache and heavily-lidded eyes. He had a quiet manner and his conversation was at all times reserved; the impression altogether being of power and decision. His golf, without being brilliant, was steady, and Peter, who was out of form, lost the match that day. Thus began a very pleasant time. The weather kept fine, and Peter rapidly got into good training. Colonel Venning proved an agreeable companion. After a few rounds Peter found his game, beating his opponent every day, but the Colonel always took his defeat with such excellent grace and good temper that Peter wished the position of affairs could be reversed. He would not, however, allow Peter to give him any strokes beyond those allowed by his handicap, which was nine. "An excellent game—many thanks," the Colonel would observe as they strolled together to the club-house. "I must really have a few lessons from the pro."
But he never did, so far as Peter could observe. That he was keen on improving his game, however, seemed evident by a discovery which Peter made by accident. They played only in the mornings, the Colonel never putting in an appearance after lunch, Peter generally spending the afternoon with a book on the sands, or if it were wet, making up a four at bridge in the club-house. One day, Peter and a member were talking together, and the member happened to ask him if he had ever visited the sands beyond Whale Head, the huge headland, almost an

island, that jutted out into the sea for a couple of miles, and made one horn of the wide bay. Peter replied that he had not.

"You should make the trip," said the member. "It's one of the longest stretches of sand I know in England. Nearly as long as Pendine, I should say. One of the loneliest and most desolate places in these parts, too, I should imagine. There's a muddy river to cross before you get there, and that keeps the folks away. I saw your friend there yesterday practicing golf-shots."

"Colonel Venning?"

"Yes—he seems rather fond of the place; it's the second time I've seen him there. I go there to try out my racing bus—care to come along one day?"

Peter said he should be delighted, and the member, whose name was Atkinson, fixed on the following Tuesday afternoon. The sands, though only about five miles distant from Seabridge as the crow flies, were fully a dozen by road, on account of the detour it was necessary to make to avoid the river, but Atkinson, in his racing Sunbeam, made short work of the distance.

The tide was far out when they arrived, and Peter thought he had seldom seen a more desolate place. For miles the firm sand stretched, a couple of hundred yards wide, straight as a Roman road, flanked on the one side by a waste of mud similar to that at Seabridge, and on the other by cheerless-looking sand-dunes.

"Wonder if the Colonel is here to-day?" Atkinson shouted, as the car roared over the bare sand.

He had barely spoken when in the distance ahead a tiny black figure emerged from the dunes on to the sand. So fast were they travelling that they were level with him almost at once, and sure enough it was Colonel Venning, club in hand. Peter waved to him as they sped past, but he did not appear to observe them, for there was no response. In all the boundless expanse he was the only living thing in sight. Peter thought it was a queer taste to come twelve miles—the Colonel had a small two-seater—to practice shots in that vast solitude.

He was thoughtful on the journey home, and paid little attention to the long diatribes which his companion launched on the subject of his car. Mr. Bridgewater's wire was back in his mind, and he was wondering how much the writer meant by his reference to "military men". From his short acquaintance with Bridgewater he judged him to be one of those men who never do anything without good reason; on the other hand, if he intended the telegram to be regarded as conveying a definite message, why had he not been more explicit?

On the following day, when he and Venning had their usual match, Peter said nothing about having seen him on the sands, deeming it politic for the first reference to come from the other. The Colonel, how-ever, made no mention of it, and Peter concluded that he had not been recognized. The soldier was in an unusually companionable mood that morning, and Peter told himself that he was a fool to suppose for an instant that he was other than what he appeared to be—a typical example of the best type of Indian army officer. He determined to dismiss the absurd suspicion from his mind. If Venning chose to spend every hour of the day practicing golf-shots on the sands it was no business of his. Yet if words had any meaning he had been plainly told to keep his eye on some retired soldier who was in the "game." And the "game" in such a connection could only mean one thing.

The upshot was that next day, after lunch, he hired a bicycle, and with a dozen old golf-balls in his pocket and his bag slung over his back, he pedaled over the same road as he had taken in Atkinson's car.

The sands, when he reached them, were deserted as before. It was truly a scene of loneliness. From a couple of miles away over the mud-flats came the murmur of the sea; except for this, and the occasional croak of a passing gull, the silence was profound. It seemed impossible to believe there was a busy seaside resort less than half a dozen miles away. Laying down his machine, Peter climbed to the top of a nearby sand-dune. Behind him the land stretched for miles as flat as the sea, a dreary waste, intersected by small dykes, and dotted here and there with farm-houses. Far on the one hand he could see the blue haze over Seabridge, and in the same direction, but nearer, the masts and rigging of a small collier marked the whereabouts of the muddy River Yatt. As he contemplated this melancholy picture his eye was caught by an erection of some sort on the dunes half a mile away —a kind of small bungalow—which was evidently invisible from the shore, for he had not seen it on his previous visit. He wondered if it was inhabited—it was an excellent place for anyone wishing to meditate in solitude, he reflected, though hardly the sort of summer abode he would choose himself.

There was no sign of Colonel Venning, and
descending to the sands Peter proceeded to indulge
in driving practice. Some little time later, happening
to slice a ball on to the dunes, he was searching for
it when he realized he was near the bungalow he had
seen in the distance, and prompted by no other
feeling than idle curiosity as to who could build in
such an out-of-the- way place he went nearer to it.
He perceived that it was really a large wooden hut,
without chimney or—on his side at any rate—
window. The purpose for which it was constructed
he could not fathom, until the faint remains of
painted lettering on the wall told him it had been
used for supplying teas for holiday-makers, and had
probably been closed down for lack of support. As he
gazed at it, wondering what manner of person could
be so foolishly optimistic as to put up a tea-shanty
in such a place, the door opened and Colonel
Venning came out.
A quick frown clouded the Colonel's brow as he
recognized who it was, but although it was gone in
an instant Peter had not failed to notice it.
"Afternoon, Colonel," he said cheerfully. "I didn't
"know you lived out here. I was just looking at your
little summer-house."
"Why, Bryan, what brings you so far away from
Seabridge?" Venning rejoined with a pleasant smile,
closing the door behind him. "I thought you spent
every afternoon among the poets."
"Thought I'd give 'em a rest for a change and try
and correct that pull I've developed with my brassie,"
Peter said easily. "The course is so dashed crowded
these days there's no chance of practice without

making yourself an infernal nuisance to everybody. Jolly good sands these—Atkinson was telling me about them yesterday."

"Atkinson?—that's the fellow with the racing-car. He's about the only soul who ever comes this way bar a few trippers. You must come up and have some tea with me now you're here, Bryan—I live in a farm- house about half a mile away."

The invitation seemed so spontaneous and was made in such a friendly fashion that, in spite of the recollection of the angry frown with which the Colonel had first greeted him, Peter's vague suspicions began to disappear. What more natural than that a man living near such a stretch of sand should practice golf on it every afternoon? And why should he not use an old tea-hut as a golf-house if he so desired?

Probably he only kept his clubs there. Peter felt he ought to beg the man's pardon for ever having harbored such distrustful thoughts of him.

"I shall be delighted. I didn't know you lived in these parts till yesterday—" he began—and just then a bell trilled inside the hut.

This time there was no doubt whatever about the Colonel's vexation.

"How tiresome," he exclaimed. "Excuse me a moment."

He unlocked the door, and disappeared inside, the door swinging to after him.

Peter turned away conscious of a certain feeling of excitement. Were his misgivings going to be justified after all? A telephone in a shore-hut!—and a telephone with an underground cable at that!—for there was no overhead wire—the circumstance was, to say the least of it, unusual.

"I'm afraid we shall have to postpone our tea-party," said the Colonel, when he had once more locked up the hut and rejoined Peter. "I've got a private wire between here and the farm-house, and a rather important business message has just come through. How did you get here—ferry?"

"Biked," said Peter.

"Right—you don't want a lift then. I shall see you to-morrow morning at ten as usual. Going to put in a bit more brassie-practice?"

As he said this his deep-set eyes looked so searchingly into his companion's that Peter had the unpleasant feeling that his thoughts were being read. Light-heartedly enough he announced his intention of staying there for another hour or so, but there was little of light-heartedness in the mood in which the Colonel's departure left him.

He was both perturbed and puzzled over what he had seen. Was Venning really other than he professed to be, or was he, Peter, degenerating into a meddlesome busybody with a propensity for imagining suspicious circumstances where none existed? This was the immediate problem before him, and lighting a pipe he sat down on top of one of the dunes near the hut, in the hope that steady reflection would reveal some aspect of the case which he had hitherto over- looked.

About half an hour had passed in this way without having brought any illumination, when a droning in the sky made him look up, and he saw an aeroplane flying at a considerable height. Taking off his spectacles he shaded his eyes and followed its progress. It was a seaplane, and apparently moving

111

in his direction.

Suddenly the engines were switched off and it commenced to glide down towards the shore. What was the notion, Peter wondered?—there was no water nearer than the sea, two miles away. Down the machine swept until Peter could hear the wind whistling in the wires; then, when it was a couple of hundred feet above the level of the mud, the engines started with a rising roar, the 'plane swooped round in a graceful curve and proceeded to thunder along the edge of the sands, keeping just sufficiently clear for safety. The whole length of the sands was traversed in this manner until it was but a speck in the distance; then it turned and commenced to fly back again, still keeping over the sands, but much nearer to the dunes. Peter saw it would pass almost over his head.

With a roar that seemed to fill all heaven the sea-plane flew by, not a hundred feet from the place where Peter sat, and as it passed he had a clear view of pilot and passenger, who were looking in his direction. And to his unutterable amazement he recognized the passenger. It was Sir Mortimer Drude.

Peter sat very still, his heart beating with uncomfortable rapidity, while the seaplane continued its course over the sands towards Whale Head. Were they looking for him? The thought made a cold perspiration break out down his spine. For if they were, and had come to try and kill him, he stood about as much chance of escaping alive as a beetle of crossing the Brighton Road on a Sunday. There was not an atom of cover anywhere to be seen;

save for a few sparse tufts of grass growing here and there the sand-dunes were as bare as bunkers. If they were armed with rifles it was simply a case of potting him at their leisure.

Yet had Sir Mortimer recognized him? He had no means of telling, but even if he had, there was nothing to be done—except perhaps dodge behind the hut, and that was a game which could not last forever.

The aeroplane was once more turning, and Peter had to fight hard to resist the desire to run for the momentary shelter of the hut as the machine again began its journey down the length of the sands. But he had sense to realize that in the event of Sir Mortimer having failed to recognize him, a sudden rush for shelter would only serve to draw their attention. He dug his nails into the palms of his hands with the effort to keep motionless as the 'plane for the second time zoomed overhead, but the occupants made no sign of recognition. And then, in a happy moment for Peter, it began to ascend and circle towards the mud-flats, until in a moment, still rising, it was making for the open sea. Peter took out his handkerchief and mopped his brow. He realized that his hands were trembling.

What was the meaning of this mysterious survey from the skies? Had Sir Mortimer been searching for him or not ?—and if not, what in the name common-sense did he mean by flying along the sands in that amazing fashion? And where in all this did Colonel Venning come in?

These were questions Peter tried to answer in vain as he cycled thoughtfully back to Seabridge. On the outskirts of the town he perceived Colonel Venning coming towards him in his two-seater. He was driving at a much faster rate than was usual with him, and he did not see Peter; and as they passed, Peter noticed a new expression on his face. If a formidable frown and a mouth set like iron were any indication, Colonel Venning was in a stormy temper.

CHAPTER VII
THE THREE RAYS

Peter went at once to the post-office, where he sent off a couple of telegrams—quite ordinary telegrams they would have appeared to a casual reader, though perhaps a trifle on the lengthy side. Their statements that the writer had seen Leonard in Seabridge, accompanied by his little son Percy, together with an intimation that unfortunately the writer had had no opportunity of making himself known, afforded Peter considerable amusement: he felt he was playing the part of the secret agent of fiction to the life. When he got back to the hotel he confirmed the telegrams by letter.

At dinner that evening he found he had a table-companion—a tall young clergyman with glasses and a long neck, and an unmistakable appearance of belonging to nonconformity. With his eye for irrelevant detail Peter watched with surreptitious amazement the exceptionally large Adam's-apple which the clergyman possessed, wholly fascinated by the undulations it caused in his lean throat whenever he swallowed. He occupied himself in the intervals between eating by solving a cross-word puzzle, and presently he leaned courteously across the table.

"Pardon me," he said in a pleasant voice. "Could you give me a synonym for trifling? Seven letters— the first 't' and ending in L?"

"Trivial," said Peter promptly.

Wilfrid Usher

"Dear me—how very stupid of me! Trivial, of course," said the clergyman, thoughtfully popping a piece of dry bread into his mouth as he filled the letters in. "No doubt, sir, you will think I am engaged in a very trivial occupation, but I work under such high pressure as a rule that I am compelled to relax my mind whenever I can, and I find the solving of cross-word puzzles an agreeable and instructive way of doing so. Er—no wine, thank you, waiter. A little plain water, if you please. Are you making a long stay here, sir?"

With his mind full of his recent discovery Peter was inclined to be suspicious of anyone making any attempt to enter into conversation with him, but this young dissenting clergyman, with his be-spectacled eyes and his rather pompous but quite agreeable manner, was so obviously harmless that Peter was soon listening sympathetically to the trials and difficulties of a minister whose work lay among the working-class population of Birmingham. So interested, indeed, had he become, that the clergyman, waxing enthusiastic, took from his pocket the projected plans of a mission it was proposed to erect in a particularly rough neighborhood, and insisted on Peter examining them. It was refreshing to see such keenness in so young a man; it was refreshing to see the enthusiasm with which he leant across the narrow table the better to point out the details of the projected mission-house, absent-mindedly fingering Peter's half-empty bottle of Bass with his free hand as he did so. But it was something more than refreshing to see him, in the midst of an eloquent dissertation on the urgent necessity of maintaining

some form of religious instruction among the
children of the poor, drop a small pellet into the
open neck of the beer-bottle with a movement so
subtle that it was only by a miracle Peter chanced to
observe it.

"And it is only by methods such as these—by
counteracting the deadly poison-gas of materialism
that is advancing over the life of this country—by
planting our outposts here and there—that we can
hope to arouse in the people that hunger for
righteousness which is the only thing that will save
their souls. The tide must be stemmed," said the
clergyman, leaning back and eyeing Peter
enthusiastically through his spectacles, "and only
the clergy can stem it. I could tell you things. . . ."

Peter was not listening so attentively now; he
was searching his mind for some way of getting rid
of the beer left in the bottle without rousing the
other's suspicions. For without doubt it was either
poisoned or drugged; he had plainly seen the tiny
pellet dropped in; and while the clergyman
continued to orate over the mission. Peter marveled
anew at the perfection of his disguise. For obviously
here was one of those attempts of which Tremayne
had warned him, and he wondered what would
happen if he suddenly accused the man of trying to
poison him. Astonished incredulity, perhaps, or
outraged indignation?—"My dear young man, I
greatly fear that beer has upset you more
than you realize." It was ten to one the man had
some excuse ready, and Peter could not very well
demand an analysis of the beer upon a mere
suspicion.

No, there was nothing to be gained by denunciation;

the game to play was to pretend to drink the beer
and await developments. He emptied his glass.
"There's no doubt a very great deal in what you
say," he remarked, re-filling his glass and taking it
in his hand. "Next time I visit Birmingham I must
come and see how the mission is getting on." His jaw
dropped suddenly and his eyes, goggling, stared over
the clergyman's shoulder. "Who in the name of
heaven is this!" he cried.

The clergyman spun round, and immediately Peter
tipped his glass on to the carpet beside him. He was
sitting next to the wall, and his action was invisible
to anyone else in the room. By the time the
clergyman had twisted himself back into his original
position Peter was apparently draining his glass, still
gazing over his companion's shoulder.

"Jove, that gave me a turn!" he gasped, as he set
down the glass. "Thought I saw a man who was
killed in the War. Is there anything, I wonder, more
startling in the world than thinking you see a man
who you thought was dead?"

"It is extraordinarily upsetting," agreed the clergyman, his eyes lingering for a moment on Peter's
empty glass with an expression of satisfaction. "I
remember once in my student days thinking I saw
the ghost of my uncle—a singularly stout man and
addicted to port, unfortunately—an hallucination
which, if I remember aright, I attributed to salmon."
He rose and bowed courteously. "You will excuse me,
I'm sure," he said, and Peter watched his lean back
disappear through the door with a faint feeling of
admiration.

He beckoned to the waiter.

"That clergyman I've been talking to—I know him

quite well but can't recollect his name. Can you find
out for me?"

"No. 47, sir—I'll inquire, sir." He came back
presently with the information that it was a Mr.
Septimus Tringle of Birmingham, and Peter stored
the name in his memory for future reference.

The drug, or whatever it was with which the clergyman had tried to dope him, would not be one that
was quick-acting, he decided, for it would never suit
Mr. Tringle's book for Peter to be taken ill at table.
What was more probable was that its strength had
been nicely adjusted to exert its maximum effect at
night, so that its victim would know nothing more
than that he was overpoweringly sleepy.

He shuddered a little as he wondered what would
have happened if he had not chanced to see that
little movement of Mr. Tringle's hand.

He retired a little earlier than usual, for he wanted
to make a thorough examination of his room. Almost
at once he received a shock, for his air-pistol, which
he kept locked in his suitcase during the daytime,
was gone. He looked carefully at the lock—it was one
that any bunch of keys would probably open, and he
blamed himself severely for leaving the pistol in a
place so easy to burgle. Was Venning the culprit, he
wondered, or Tringle, or both? Somehow he didn't
associate Venning with that kind of work.

Presently he undressed and got into bed, putting a
couple of heavy-headed golf-clubs near to his hand.
He had examined all the cupboards and drawers,
looked behind the wardrobe and washing-stand,
seen that the door was locked and bolted, and finally
he had inspected the window. It was on the second
floor and had no balcony, the wall falling sheer to a

garden rockery thirty feet below, as he had noticed
by day- light. He did not think Mr. Tringle would pay
him a visit from this direction. Nevertheless, he felt
confident that it was Mr. Tringle's intention to visit
him that night; indeed, he felt he would be
disappointed if that gentleman failed to materialize.
He had become greatly interested in the personality
of Mr. Tringle.

For a little while he lay staring at the electric-
light, pondering over the tangle of mysterious events
of which he seemed to have become the centre. He
had no fear that he would unexpectedly fall asleep,
for his brain was as active as a fox-terrier's. How
long his vigil would last he could only guess; he
imagined Mr. Tringle would come to complete the
good work begun by the drug about midnight.
Switching off the light he composed himself to wait.
Half an hour passed—an hour—finally midnight
struck somewhere in the town, and still there was no
sign of Mr. Tringle. It seemed to Peter that perhaps
he had seen through the somewhat clumsy
subterfuge he had adopted, and had left the hotel
never to return, fearing Peter might hand him over to
the police and have the remains of the bottle
analyzed. If that were so it looked as if he was going
to have a peaceful night after all. Yet he still thought
Mr. Tringle would come; that satisfied gleam in his
eyes when he had glanced at the empty glass had
been real, not simulated.

All at once he heard something fall softly on to the
carpet. As noises go it was a mere nothing, and in
ordinary circumstances it would probably never have
arrested his attention. But in the state of disquiet
induced by the discoveries of the evening his hearing

was acutely sensitive, and he lay quiet as a mouse, his heart beating a little faster than usual, waiting for the noise to be repeated. Profound darkness filled the room—darkness in which the vague outline of the window hung ghost-like. Sure enough presently plop near the window again, very faint, followed by a peculiar slithering noise, like human hands feeling the surface of a door. A man was crawling along the floor on his hands and knees, very quietly! Or was it some kind of animal?

Peter gripped his mashie and waited, sitting up with one hand on the electric-switch. For a time the noise had ceased—the intruder, whoever he was, was listening. A plan suddenly presented itself to Peter. To remain in bed was asking for trouble; therefore he gave a strangled snore such as a man might make in turning over; at the same time he silently threw back the sheets and slipped from the bed on the side furthest from that where he imagined the intruder to be hiding.

Then he stood listening. He was convinced that to anyone else in the room it must have seemed that he had merely settled himself into a more comfortable position and continued to slumber. And presently he heard again the sound which had disturbed him, suggestive of someone stealing barefooted over the carpet.

Quietly he moved backwards until his hand came in contact with the edge of the washing-stand, and as quietly removed the soap from the soap bowl. Next, his questing fingers came upon the tooth-brush jar, and this too he removed soundlessly and tucked under his left arm. Then he approached the side of the bed, and leaning over the pillow, sought the

electric-light switch that hung from the wall. Having
found it he listened again, but the intruder was
making no sound.

Peter curled his fingers round the cake of soap; it
was hard and dry—an excellent missile for his
purpose. The course he was taking entailed a certain
risk, for the intruder was certain to be armed, but he
banked on the fact that a badly-startled man is for a
few moments a man bereft of reason—and in those
few moments Peter did not propose to remain idle.

He threw the soap at the window with all his force.
The glass broke with a crack like a pistol-shot, and
immediately Peter switched on the light, the china
jar poised ready for instant discharge at the head of
the intruder. The room leapt into being—empty.

The closed door, the furniture, the window with its
gaping black hole, the bed—Peter ran his eye rapidly
over them, but there was nothing to be seen to account for the noise he had heard.

"Funny," he muttered, "I could have sworn—"

The next instant he drew in his breath sharply, the
words transfixed in his throat, as he saw the
loathsome object that sprawled along the floor half
under the wardrobe. It was a snake, four feet long,
thin almost as a whip, and bright green in colour,
and as he gazed at it, horror-stricken, it was joined
by another that writhed its way gently along the
carpet, making the soft slithering noise that had
attracted his attention. For perhaps two seconds he
stood as if paralyzed; then with a frantic bound, he
leaped on to the bed.

From this comparatively safe vantage-point he
counted no less than five of the creatures in different
parts of the room, one actually being in the attitude

of attempting to climb a leg of the bed. With its head poised motionless, its tiny eyes seemed to be watching Peter with an odd expression of wariness, until in a sudden fury of repulsion Peter picked up his mashie and slew it unscientifically but efficiently. The sight of its corpse encouraged him to pursue the next, which he did with the help of two chairs. Fortunately the snakes seemed only too anxious to avoid him making no effort to attack simultaneously, with the result that in a short time everyone had its back broken.

The slaughter, however, was attended by considerable noise, and Peter was not surprised when there came a knock at the door.

It was the night-porter, and when Peter let him in his face blanched. "Good Lord, sir," he gasped. "How did these get in?"

"Through the window unless I'm much mistaken," returned Peter. "By Jove, yes—look! there's a rope."

He pointed through the broken window, where a rope was plainly visible. "What numbers are above here?" he asked quickly.

The man considered. "Somewhere about 46 and 91," he replied thoughtfully.

"He's in 47," said Peter. "We'll have him out of it before he can escape. Come along."

He pushed past the astonished man into the corridor where the light was on, and several people in various stages of deshabille were standing at their doors.

"What is the meaning of this?" demanded a stout gentleman indignant. "Are you aware you have disturbed half the hotel, sir?"

"So would you disturb half the hotel, my friend, if you had half a dozen snakes crawling up your legs." Peter could not resist saying.

A muffled scream came from inside the stout gentleman's room.

"Snakes, sir!" echoed the stout gentleman, turning pale and retreating. "What do you mean, sir? Louisa, pray be calm. How dare you try to frighten my wife, sir. Snakes, indeed!" he went on, from the shelter of his doorway. "How dare you have the impertinence to talk to me about snakes, sir. Brrrh!"

There was quite a little crowd at Peter's heels as he reached the landing above and approached No. 47.

"What's the trouble about?" asked a young man with red hair and green pyjamas.

"Something about snakes, he said," volunteered a little man with a Yorkshire accent. "Say, lad, what's oop?"

Peter, however, did not reply, but rattled the door of No. 47. "Open the door, please," he said in a peremptory voice.

"What's this?" demanded a fussy little man with a bald head, coming forward. "What's all the row about? Man, you're waking up everyone in the hotel!"

Peter ignored him. "Tringle, open this door!" he called angrily.

"Wouldn't it perhaps be better if you left it till to-morrow, sir," urged the night-porter, remembering his responsibilities.

"Stand clear!" cried Peter, and taking a little run he planted the sole of his foot (he had fortunately remembered to put on his slippers) over the lock of the door. At the second attempt the door burst inwards, and Peter darted in, feeling for the electric light as he went.

The room was empty. Tied to the foot of the bed was a rope which led to the open window.

"Gone!" said Peter bitterly.

The following morning, when he had done interviewing managers and policemen, Peter went to the golf- club determined to try to come to some sort of understanding with Colonel Venning. He had come to the conclusion that the Colonel was on the same side of the game as himself, and after the attempt on his life he felt he wanted an ally. The difficulty was how to approach him. Then he remembered the sign, scratched on the wards of a key, which Bridgewater had used to make himself known at Tregenneth, and he decided to try its effect on Venning.

Rain began to fall soon after breakfast, and he was relieved to find Venning at the club-house, deep in the Daily Telegraph.

"It's hopeless to-day I'm afraid, Bryan," he re- marked with a glance out of the window at the leaden sky. "Enjoy your practice on the sands yesterday?"

"I think I've succeeded in straightening out that pull at last," replied Peter. "I stood a little more open, and they seemed to be keeping in a straight line for once."

"Good!" They talked golf jargon for a little while; then the Colonel said casually: "By the way, did you see that seaplane that came over soon after I had gone?"

Peter nodded. "Yes, it came down quite close to the sands. Rather a curious place to choose for a visit."

"Very. It didn't alight, I suppose?"

125

"There was no water anywhere near for it to alight on. It simply cruised backwards and forwards up and down the sands, almost as if—as if it was looking for someone."

"Really?—very curious thing to do in such an out-of-the-way place," was Venning's comment as he picked up the paper. Peter, watching his face slowly, could detect no other expression on it except perfunctory interest. He glanced quickly round the room.

For the moment it was empty. He drew a score card from his pocket.

"D'you mind checking this, Colonel—it's my round yesterday," he said. "I rather think I only took four at the dog-legged seventh—do you happen to re-member?"

Venning's eyes fixed themselves expressionlessly on the card, in the corner of which Peter had drawn Bridgewater's sign—not obtrusively, but conspicuous enough to catch the eye.

"I daresay you're right," he said thoughtfully.

"Good morning, Marsden," he broke off as the door opened and the secretary came in. "Not much chance of play to-day."

"Filthy weather!" said the cherubic secretary cheerfully. "Always is here with the wind in this quarter."

He sat down at a table and began to write a letter. Venning rose to his feet.

"Marsden's a pessimist," he declared. "I believe myself it's going to clear up after all. Come and have a look outside, Bryan."

Venning did not speak again until they were standing by the eighteenth green.

"Brown, the Rugger man, aren't you?" he asked,
his keen eyes searching Peter's face.
"Yes."
"I've had my suspicions of you for some time,"
Venning went on, "but why do you make yourself
known to me now?"
"For two reasons," said Peter. "Firstly, because
Sir Mortimer Drude was in that seaplane that came
over yesterday; secondly, because my life was at-
tempted last night at my hotel."
Venning's face did not alter by the least movement.
"Do you suppose Drude recognized you?" he
inquired.

"I don't think so at the time, but after what
happened last night I'm not so sure." Briefly Peter
related the episode of the noncontormist parson. "I
was warned my life might be attempted," he added,
"but I hardly expected that kind of attempt." He
gave a little laugh. "I can see that horrible snake
trying to climb the leg of the bed still; I shall
probably dream about it for days. I take it that
Tringle is one of Drude's gang, of course."
"There's no doubt about that, and he's not the only
one in the neighborhood. That telephone message
yesterday afternoon was a bogus one to get me out
of the way, and it was the first intimation I had that
my listening-post was discovered. You must leave
the hotel, Brown, and come and stay with me, for
unless my calculations are wrong matters are
coming to a head." He gave one of his rare laughs.
"Ours is a funny trade, Brown—though, as you're
new to it, you may not see the humor of it in quite
the same light as I do. You see, we never know our
colleagues except in an emergency, and sometimes

127

the most absurd mistakes arise. I don't mind
admitting that when I found you outside my
observation post yesterday I was silly enough to
think for a few moments you were on the other side."
Peter laughed. "I confess I very nearly entertained
similar suspicions about you," he admitted.

That afternoon he took up his quarters at the farm-
house where Venning lived. It was a place suited to
a man of the Colonel's solitary habits, for there was
not another house within half a mile. It was kept by
an elderly man and his wife who possessed the
reserve of people who had long lived apart from their
kind, and they greeted Peter with the courtesy of a
past century. Indeed, so old-fashioned was
everything in that house that it was with a sense of
incongruity that Peter came across an up-to-date
wireless set, though he suspected it was not only for
the entertainment of the old people that it had been
installed.

One of the first things Venning did when the couple
had retired to bed was to supply Peter with a small
but serviceable-looking revolver. "I needn't tell you
not to use it unless you're downright obliged," he
said.

"Personally, I always carry one at night—more for the
confidence it gives than anything else. And let me
give you a tip. In an emergency, carry it in your coat-
pocket. The essential thing in dealing with the people
we are up against is quickness, and unless you're an
expert at the draw—which I don't suppose you are—
you might as well carry your gun in your boots as on
your hip for all the use it will be to you in a crisis.
Do you feel like a stroll along the sands? Yes, I
should bring it along if I were you."

The Great Holdup Mystery

Imperceptibly the older man had taken command, nor did Peter resent it. Venning was the professional, while he was only an amateur, and as they walked towards the shore he was glad rather than otherwise to be under authority. Venning had obviously had so much more experience in matters of this kind that it was futile to think of any other arrangement. Darkness had fallen some time past as the two men descended the dunes on to the firm sand. There was no moon, and the night was so still that they could hear the faint honking of a motor on the main road two miles away. Out to sea the tide was swiftly making with a faint murmuring sound as it stole over the mud-flats, while in the distance a dot of red light appeared and vanished with mechanical regularity, like the beating of a tiny pulse.

Venning presently left the sands again for the uneven surface of the dunes, until a darker patch against the dark sky told Peter they had reached the hut. There was a rattle of keys and a sound as of a door being opened; then a faint light appeared framed by the doorway.

"Come in," said Venning's voice, and he entered. The Colonel immediately closed the door.

There was little but bare boards to meet the eye inside. A table, on which there were a few books, a small electric lamp, a tin of cigarettes, and a newspaper; and an upright chest and a deck-chair comprised the furniture. There was also a cupboard, minus its doors, containing a bottle of whiskey, a siphon, a tin of cocoa and some glasses, together with a spirit-stove.

"I'm afraid I'm not equipped for hospitality," Venning said almost apologetically as he pushed

over the cigarettes. "The glasses, however, are clean.
Whiskey?"

"Thanks."

They pledged each other in silence, Peter noticing
that his companion drank nothing but plain soda.
Then, with a word of excuse, Venning bent over the
floor and proceeded to prise up a couple of planks,
revealing a cavity from which he took a telephone.
"Hello, hello speaking. Right. Right. No. I can't say.
Very good,

Myers—right." He rang off, replaced the telephone
and stood up. "When you're ready, Brown," he said.

"Seeing if everything is O.K.?" Peter asked curiously.
"Do you anticipate trouble to-night?"

"I expect it every night, my dear fellow. What
exactly will happen I know very little more than you
do, but this much I can tell you. I have excellent
reason for believing that some night this week a
certain mutual acquaintance of ours will visit these
shores—here. Why he should choose this spot in all
England, except that it's a pretty lonely one, I can't
tell you. All I know is that I have received certain
information that he may do so. Though you can't see
them, I have a dozen men posted along these sand-
hills, ready at any moment to obey my signal."

"You expect him from the sea?"

Venning nodded slowly. "And I have some reason
to hope he won't come alone. It's a much bigger man
than Sir Mortimer Drude I hope to have my hands
on before the night's out. If my calculations are right
this place will be the rendezvous for two of the
biggest criminals in Europe—men beside whom
Drude, Kreller, Zorloff and the rest are mere
commonplace crooks.

130

And one of them is the most dangerous scoundrel
alive to-day—the old spider who is the centre of the
whole vast web of criminal intrigue that stretches
from Moscow to Lisbon. And we haven't the slightest
clue to his identity. . . . Silly, isn't it?"
"But you say they know you are here? That bogus
telephone message yesterday. ..."
"They know I'm here, but they don't know how—that
you, Myers?" he called. "Yes, many men I have under
me. If I know anything of the kind of people we're
dealing with, it won't be fear of one man that'll stop
'em coming. They'll come looking for trouble, I don't
doubt. Please God, it'll be a different kind of trouble
they'll find when they get here! Well, it's half-past
eleven, and high tide is in an hour. It's time we were
in our places."
He switched out the light and opened the door.
Peter followed him over the dunes with a feeling of
growing excitement.
Never had Peter known a darker night. As he lay
among the sand-hills half an hour later, his heart
beating a little faster than usual with anticipation,
the intense blackness closed upon him like
something tangible in every direction. A slight drizzle
of rain had begun to fall, so gently that any sound it
made was lost in the murmur of the tide, which had
now advanced beyond the level of the mud and was
creeping up the sands, as Peter could tell by the sh-
sh-sh at intervals of a breaking wave. Assuredly a fit
night for evildoers to be abroad.
Somewhere near, within hailing distance, was
Venning, armed and alert for any eventuality, as
were the dozen or so men picketed along the shore;
yet Peter could not rid himself of the feeling that he

was alone.

It was a creepy business, this waiting for someone to come out of the sea, and he wished it was over. The damp rain was beginning to chill his spirit. Unaccountably, too, he had developed a headache. He wondered how long he would have to wait if no one came. Presumably it would be until the tide had turned, and ebbed far enough to preclude the possibility of a boat landing.

Suddenly his heart pounded, for clear and plaintive came from somewhere behind him the call of a night-bird, instantly bringing back to his memory that night when he stood among the shelter of the trees by the creek of Tregenneth, waiting for Horstman and his men. It was the same cry—he remembered noting the peculiar sound of it at the time and wondering what kind of bird had uttered it—and the significance of it brought him to his feet with a rush. Venning must know at once what it portended.

A moment's reflection, however, showed the foolishness of such a course. It was almost certain that the night-bird's cry had reached the ears of the Colonel, who, whether he knew its true meaning or not, would need no warning from him as to the possible importance of such an unexpected sound. To go blundering across the dunes in the inky blackness might only inform their enemies that a watch was being kept, besides upsetting Venning's plans, and Peter resolved to keep to his original instructions, which were to remain where he was until ordered, or actually attacked.

He stood listening, revolver in hand, but as the minutes passed and the call was not repeated, he

began to wonder if he had not perhaps been
mistaken. After all, he knew nothing about night-
birds and their calls.
He felt his ears tingling as he thought what a fool he
would have looked if he had sought Venning with
such a story, and it turned out to be a false alarm.

His headache forced itself on his attention once
more—it was almost as if a band had been fastened
round his head and suddenly tightened—and for a
moment he felt giddy. It struck him that he must be
out of sorts, and he was on the point of resuming his
seat when it was borne upon him, with a renewed
quickening of excitement, that he could hear, over
and above the complaining of the sea, a peculiar
throbbing noise. Immediately afterwards he was sure
of it—somewhere over the waste of waters a motor
boat was moving.
The drizzling rain had ceased by now, and he stared
into the darkness in the direction of the sound until
his eyeballs ached with the strain, while the
throbbing grew steadily louder. A light appeared out
to sea—a pin-point in the screen of darkness. He
stared at it as if hypnotized; then the light seemed to
give a sickening dive, and he remembered no more.
The first thing he realized when he recovered
consciousness was that he was bound hand and
foot.
It was still dark, but lights were moving about near
him, and he was aware of the proximity of men. He
discovered that he was lying on his back on the
sands, but his head was free, and by twisting it
round he could make out similar forms beside him
that were also prone. Venning's men! The bitter
truth dawned on him instantly. They were

prisoners—prisoners in the hands of Sir Mortimer
Drude it was more than likely.

Clearly Venning had been outwitted—but how in the
name of sanity had it been accomplished? He
remembered his last conscious moments—the
intolerable headache, traces of which still remained.
Had his food been doped, he wondered? And then he
caught sight of one of the men moving about a short
distance away, and he guessed what had happened,
for the man wore a queer-shaped headgear that sent
Peter's mind back to the War—it was a gas-mask! He
had been gassed—presumably they had all been
gassed, and the night-bird's call had been the signal
that the deed was done. Even in the ignominy of
defeat he was conscious of a faint satisfaction that
he had not been deceived in this respect.

His interest became fixed on what was occurring
near him. There seemed to be a considerable number
of men present—a dozen at least—and it looked as if
they were engaged in erecting something on the
sands, for there were various goings to and fro to the
sea, where a group of lights suggested the presence
of a small boat. As the men became momentarily
visible against the light on the sands Peter could see
that they all wore gas-masks, and it struck him that
they were fitting up some kind of gun. He recollected
the five-mile stretch of sand that ran straight as a
Roman highway, and Sir Mortimer's survey of it from
a sea- plane, and all at once he thought he saw light.
Was Sir mMortimer about to give one of his
"demonstrations"?

Fantastic as the thing seemed, it certainly fitted the
facts so far as he knew them. If Sir Mortimer wished
to give a secret trial to some engine of destruction

which necessitated a level stretch of several miles long, there could be no better place than these sands— in England at any rate—though it was strange that he should make such an attempt knowing, as the gassing of Venning and his men proved that he did know, that his operations were suspected.

He became aware that two figures had detached themselves from the group and were walking in his direction. One of them struck a match, which burnt steadily in the still air, and then appeared to remove his mask.

"It's clear now," said a voice which Peter had no difficulty in recognizing as Sir Mortimer's.

The other evidently followed his companion's example, for he replied in a refined, drawling voice: "A useful gas, this of yours, Mortimer, but dangerous to handle, I should imagine. It has no smell at all, you say?"

"None," answered the scientist. "It gives no warning at all, so far as I have been able to ascertain. Its composition is no secret, for something very similar was used by the British forces during the War. Its chief merit lies in its variability for punitive purposes.

Administered in a certain form the merest whiff is death. To-night, however, it was sufficiently mild to induce temporary unconsciousness only. Taafe did his work well."

"You are wise," rejoined the other. "There is nothing to be gained by unnecessarily irritating the official forces of the law. Where's this man you spoke of?"

"Here," said Sir Mortimer, and an electric torch was flashed in Peter's face. "Ah, so you have come round, have you, Mr. Peter Brown?"

Peter blinked at the light. "Will you be good enough to tell me who you are, and why I am in this position?" he asked, after a pause.

"All in good time, Mr. Brown, all in good time. You do not recognize my voice, then?"

"I do now," said Peter grimly. "Staying at Seabridge, Sir Mortimer?"

"I have not that pleasure," was the silky reply. "Had I been, I am under the impression you would not be here to-night, Mr. Brown. It is the old story: if you want a thing done well, do it yourself. A certain friend of mine bungled rather badly last night. Now I should not have bungled."

"I thought at the time it was one of your playful experiments," murmured Peter. "Have you got any more in store for me?"

"Certainly, Mr. Brown, certainly—why not? Your friend Colonel Venning and his brave men—well, I have no particular quarrel with them, and I have just given them another sniff of gas which will keep them quiet for a little while. To-morrow they will awake in the same positions as they were gassed, and will all probably wonder how on earth they ever came to fall asleep at their posts. You, however, will not be among them."

"Really?" said Peter. "How do you know?"

"Because, my dear Mr. Brown, I intend to have you thrown—alive—into the mud of the River Yatt." The words were uttered in such a conversational tone that the meaning took several seconds to sink into Peter's brain. Sir Mortimer mistook his silence for fear, for he went on:

"That makes your cheek blanch, eh? I am told the

mud is twelve feet deep in places—and you won't
float, you know. No doubt the mud shifts in the
course of time, and perhaps in a few years to come
some fisherman may find a few old bones and rags
which may be identified or may not. In any case, it
will not trouble me. And I am sure it won't trouble
my niece."

"Your niece?' repeated Peter slowly.

"The lady upon whose good-nature you so cruelly
imposed," said Sir Mortimer quietly. "Let me assure
you that she has bitterly regretted her action in
helping you to escape. In fact, I have been compelled
to—er—to take certain measures with regard to her
for which I am sorry. You see, she defied me. And I
do not like being defied."

"You damnable villain!" cried Peter, roused at
last. "What have you done to her?"

"I have merely put her where she will be under no
temptation to thwart my plans," was the calm reply.
"If you wish to know, she is imprisoned on an
island."

"If you so much as hurt a hair of her head—" Peter
began furiously, and then stopped, conscious of the
emptiness of the threat. Sir Mortimer laughed.

"I hardly think you will be in a position to do me
any harm, Mr. Brown," he said blandly. "For, you
see, in a couple of hours' time you will be dead.
There is no doubt about it, I assure you. You are like
the brave man in Newbolfs poem—'untroubled of
hope'. In fact, so certain am I of your decease that I
am going to let you witness an experiment. You were
always interested in my discoveries, Mr. Brown,
weren't you?—well, to-night you shall see how one of
them operates.

Good-bye for the present."
He turned away, followed by the other man, who
had not opened his mouth during this colloquy.
Peter was left a prey to mingled feelings. On the face
of things his number was clearly up, with the
prospect of a horrible death in front of him, yet he
refused to despair. Once before he had been faced
with death at Sir Mortimer's hands and had
miraculously escaped, and his position was a no
worse one now—indeed, it was rather better, for
there was yet time for him to set his wits to work and
devise some means of avoiding the fate prepared for
him. And in the meantime he was at last going to
learn whether Sir Mortimer's vaunted knowledge was
capable of producing material results. His curiosity
to know what was about to happen was so great that
he almost forgot his fear.
He wondered who was the scientist's companion.
He spoke perfect English as if it was his own tongue,
yet Peter could not help wondering if it was the
mysterious individual whom Venning had described
as the biggest criminal in Europe. As he recalled the
lazy, drawling tones of his voice there came to him a
conviction, which had not been present previously,
that it was one with which he was vaguely familiar,
and he searched his memory for the occasion upon
which he had heard it before.
He did not dwell for long on the problem, however,
for his thoughts were switched into an entirely
different direction by the darkness being suddenly
pierced by a searchlight. It seemed to come from the
machine which he had supposed to be a gun. The
white beam wavered a little over the sea and came to
rest on the slopes of Whale Head, two miles away.

The Great Holdup Mystery

While Peter wondered what its appearance
portended, another beam, violet in colour, sprang
into existence from somewhere among the sand-hills;
this, too, hovered and settled on Whale Head. For a
few minutes the two search-lights, the white and the
violet, remained concentrated on the same place;
then, as Peter watched, yet a third ray, vivid green
this time, shot up into the sky from another point,
and commenced to sink slowly down towards the
headland.

As it descended it seemed to the wondering Peter
that a sudden hush fell on the group near him; he
was subconsciously aware of tenseness, as if
everyone was bracing himself to receive a shock. The
green ray reached the point of concentration, and
remained there. For two seconds there was a
strained silence; then the amazing thing happened.

A vast tongue of fire leapt to heaven from the hillside like a gigantic candle-flame, dissolving the
darkness on the instant into a kind of yellowish
daylight in which the sea, the headland, the shore,
and the men on it were visible as in a nightmarish
picture of yellow monochrome. It flamed silently and
magnificently for a space of time that a man might
count five; then, with a shattering roar and a
vibration that shook the earth even at that distance,
the disturbance reached the group on the sands. The
searchlights went out immediately; the flame
vanished into the sky; and in the darkness, above
the wind which had risen, was heard a curious
sound like shingle being drawn down the beach by
the backwash of a wave. And then came the sea.

It is strange to reflect that the group on the sands
had omitted to prepare for this perfectly natural out-

139

come of their experiment. Peter put it down to that absence of practical application which is popularly-supposed to be typical of the scientific mind. Whatever the cause of this lack of foresight, the huge wave, when it came, clearly caught the experimenters by surprise, and it was certainly due more to luck than management that no one was drowned.

As it was the wave rocked the motor-boat like a cockleshell, and went surging up the beach as far as the sand-dunes. The group were wet through to the skin, as were Peter and his fellow captives. Fortunately for them it was only the first wave that was such a great size; those that followed did not reach half-way up the sands.

In the darkness Peter could hear men running about, and presently lights flickered, converging on the edge of the sea. The experiment was over, and the experimenters were re-embarking. There was some trouble in starting the engine, but at length it fired with a splutter, and the men seemed to be crowding into the boat. Hope rose in Peter's heart. Perhaps he was being forgotten in the confusion caused by the miniature tidal-wave. But this hope was doomed to disappointment, for soon after the motor-boat had left the shore a car was started behind the sand-hills, and two men approached him. He was gagged with a hand- kerchief and carried to an open touring-car, into which he was unceremoniously thrown. The car started at once, and Peter perceived it was heading in the direction of the river.

In the car he made a supreme but ineffectual effort to free himself. He tried hard not to think of his

coming fate, but all the while he saw in imagination
the banks of the Yatt, thick with soft grey mud, and
steep as a railway cutting, with the dirty tidal river
running between at the bottom. With his hands and
feet tied he would be helpless and sink at once—but
he would not die at once. That was the worst
thought of all. There would be a few moments—a
whole minute, perhaps—when his face would have
sunk below the mud, and he would be conscious,
holding his breath, waiting for the dreadful moment
when the intolerable pressure on his lungs forced his
mouth open. . . .

The car stopped and he was lifted out and carried
over some level ground. He could smell the mud
now.

He made a final unavailing effort to break his bonds;
then his captors stopped and, one holding his feet
and one his shoulders, they began to swing him.
One—two—three—four—then a mighty heave; and
our Mr. Brown described a half-circle through the
air, to land with a sickening squelch into the mud of
the River Yatt

CHAPTER VIII
THE CLERGYMAN WHO DIED

In that awful moment, as he landed face downwards in the mud, Peter gave himself up for lost. So powerful was the instinct of self-preservation, however, that even as he felt the slap of the wet mud in his face he struggled, bound as he was, to turn on to his back, though the movement could at most result in adding only a few minutes to life. The effort ploughed him deep in the mud, but he succeeded, and lay gasping through the handkerchief, which had in one way proved useful, for it prevented the mud from choking up his mouth and nostrils. But mud was in his eyes and ears, mud pressed against his sides, clung to his legs and gripped his feet; and as he felt himself sinking deeper a frenzy of horror seized him, and he struggled like a maniac, until the impotence of it came over him, and he stopped, exhausted. The mud was over his neck.

And then a mood of fatalism swept over him, and he determined to struggle no more. It was the finish of the course, and he would try and meet it like a man. He prayed that the end would come quickly—and then once again there rose in him the desire to struggle frantically, and he fought it down, hard. The mind, at such moments, thinks of queer things, and his imagination conjured up a picture of a fly caught by a spider—the impotent struggles at intervals, gradually growing fewer and feebler as the spider increases its hold. He felt like that fly—only he would

142

not struggle.

He prayed again that he would not give way to panic—like the pitiful fly.

All at once his pulses raced with the tenth part of a hope. It struck him that for the moment he had ceased to sink. For the first time he forced open his eyes. He had to close them again immediately, but by blinking rapidly he succeeded in shaking some of the mud from his lids, and at length he was able to keep them open. The drizzle had come on again, and he could see nothing. With a terrible anxiety he waited. Had he stopped sinking or not? The suspense was agonizing; and then, as he found part of his head was still uncovered, hope flamed up again in his heart. Scarcely daring to breathe he thought things over: either he had come up against a layer of harder mud, which might soften with the warmth of his body, or else the mud was only of a slight depth, and he was resting on firm sand. His hands were bound behind his back, and with his fingers he tried to feel the consistency of the substance that was bearing his weight.

He discovered hardness; it might be caked mud or sand, but for the moment it was clear that he had ceased to sink.

The revulsion of feeling was so great that life seemed to spread itself out before him with unusual sweetness. He forced down the inclination to dwell upon the future, and tried to concentrate on the present. If he was lying on sand covered by a mere veneer of mud, as he was beginning to be convinced he was, then he would be safe until someone found him. He had no fear of the tide, for it had been approximately high-water when he was thrown in.

143

Wilfrid Usher

But would anyone find him, half-buried as he was, even in daylight? It was not at all certain, for the Yatt was a lonely river. He realized that he must try to extricate himself by his own exertions. It occurred to him that he might roll up the bank. It would be an unpleasant business and there was the danger of coming across a deeper patch of mud, but he considered it worth attempting. First of all, though, he must try sitting up. It was one of the hardest physical efforts Peter had ever made. The mud seemed loath to let its prisoner go. Strong as his abdominal muscles were, they ached with the strain. He could lift up his legs but could not move his trunk. Once, in the midst of his efforts, he desisted in a sudden fright, under the impression that he had sunk in deeper. At last he was forced to the conclusion that the feat was impossible. There remained rolling.

He began by trying to turn over on one side, but what had been easy when he lay on the surface of the mud he now found to be extraordinarily difficult. He could turn his head easily enough, but move his body laterally he could not. The mud held him fast. He lay back for a while, considering. The only satisfaction he had got out of his efforts was the confirmation of his suspicion that he was on firm sand, for he had sunk in no further. For a time he kept motionless, husbanding his strength for a new effort.

Slowly, almost imperceptibly, the darkness grew less. Presently he could make out the dark bank of mud, sloping like the roof of a house above him. The sky began to lighten and he could soon perceive the stark outline of Whale Head in front of him. This

gave him his bearings and at the same time made
his heart sink, for it told him he was in a part of the
river where no chance visitor was likely to come. In
half an hour's time the whole cheerless prospect lay
before him— high banks of brown-grey mud, steep
as a railway-cutting, with the slate-coloured Yatt
running swiftly seaward at the bottom. The sky was
heavily overcast, full of the promise of more rain.
Only one grain of comfort did the daylight reveal—he
was several feet above high-tide mark and not in
danger of drowning.

Twice during the next hour Peter struggled to move
his position with no result. Gulls, past-masters in
the art of acrobatic flying, swooped over him, and
once a particularly courageous one alighted on his
chest, only to jump off in a panic as Peter gave a
muffled shout. Its presence suggested a contingency
upon which he did not dare dwell. It was shortly
after this that he heard the first sign of human
activity. The course of the Yatt was so devious that
he could not see the ferry, which was half a mile
away, but he knew its whereabouts, and when he
heard a faint hail in the distance he guessed some
early riser was waiting to cross. There would be
much traffic on the ferry-boat that morning, he
surmised, for thousands of people must have heard
the noise of the explosion, and they would be sure to
visit the scene of it if they could.
It would be a nine days' wonder, for no one could
possibly guess the cause of it, and it would probably
be put down to some freak of the elements. Venning
and his men, if they were alive, might have their
suspicions, but they would not broadcast them;
indeed, they would probably say as little as possible

about the night's work, for their part in it had hardly
been a distinguished one. He wondered if they would
organize a search for him. The probability was that
they would assume he had been taken prisoner. The
prospect was not bright.

The morning wore on. The river dwindled to a
muddy trickle and commenced to fill again. No one
came near, and a kind of apathy gripped Peter. It
looked as if he had escaped suffocation only to die of
starvation and exposure. At intervals he tried to
move, but the mud was a safe gaoler. A mood of
despair came over him at last, and he made no
further efforts.

As Peter had surmised, the inhabitants of Seabridge, awakened at one o'clock in the morning by
an appalling explosion that shattered half the
window- panes in the town, thought of earthquakes.
Those who happened to have been lying awake when
it occurred, however, agreed that a terrific flash of
light had preceded it, and were inclined to put it
down to a gigantic thunderbolt. For an hour or more
the streets were dotted with people discussing the
phenomenon, but as it was not repeated, they
presently went back to bed. It was in the morning, at
breakfast, that excitement rose high again in
boarding-houses and apartments, for strange
rumors were flying about. It was said that a
foreign warship had attempted to bombard
Seabridge in the night; some averred that they had
heard the hum of aeroplanes, and talked darkly of
another war; while not a few saw in the occurrence
yet another instance of the Government's weakness
in not dealing more firmly with the Red menace. . . .

But at length rumor thickened in one particular direction, and it soon became generally known that a mysterious attempt had been made to blow up part of Whale Head. The chars-a-brancs and motor-boat proprietors did a thriving trade that morning, while the ferryman at the mouth of the Yatt found himself utterly unable to cope with the hundreds of people who demanded passages, and one fears that there was a certain amount of profiteering. It has been estimated that over nine thousand persons visited the scene of the explosion during the day and gazed wonderingly at the huge crater—the main part of St. Paul's could have dropped in it with ease—that had appeared on the hillside.

But while it was a great day for the transport-owners, there were others to whom it brought bitter humiliation. One would prefer to draw a kindly veil over the feelings of Colonel Venning and his men when they awoke in the grey dawn to find themselves trussed in a row like a lot of fowls. No mention of their plight fortunately get into the Press, for as it happened one of their number—it was a man named Myers, the same man Venning had rung up in Peter's presence the previous night—was not bound so securely as the rest and succeeded in releasing himself.

One gathers that there was not much said as the man Myers cut the ropes that bound the others. Venning, I have been told, looked a haggard old man when he realized what had happened to him. When he found that Peter was missing it was as if he had received a blow. He seemed utterly bewildered. The marks on the sands, which might have helped him to draw some conclusion as to what had taken place, had, of course, been washed out by the wave that followed the explosion. Only a few footprints and the faint mark of a boat's keel told him that his enemies had come and gone by the sea.

It was while he was dejectedly looking at the footprints that an exclamation from one of his men caused him to turn sharply. The man was staring at Whale Head.

"Look there, sir," he said in a startled voice. "That wasn't there yesterday."

They were the first people to reach the crater—the vanguard of that vast army of sightseers that trooped to Whale Head in the course of the next few days. By the time their speculations were exhausted—and, needless to say, not one theory bore the slightest relation to the true facts—Venning was himself again.

"We must find Brown," he said. "He may be lying helpless somewhere near."

But though they searched diligently enough not a trace of Peter Brown could they find.

It was one of the ferryman's assistants, hastily summoned from Yattbridge to meet the growing demands of the ferry, who discovered Peter. It was by this time well past noon, and he was floating downstream on the ebb with an oar over the stern of his boat by way of rudder. According to his own account it was by the merest accident that he noticed Peter at all, his attention being principally occupied in steering the boat. He quickly drew in to one side, and having got out and pulled his boat a little way up the mud, he climbed the steep bank. There was no danger in this, for in that part of the river the mud was nowhere more than a foot deep, though it was as deep as ten feet in other places.

His first thought was that it was a corpse which he had found. The middle part of the body was entirely below the surface of the mud, only the toes and the head being visible, and the eyes were shut. As he gazed on his discovery, however, the eyes opened and a low moaning sound came from behind the handkerchief.

"You could 'ave knocked me down with a feather," the ferryman's assistant used to say when relating the incident. "I tell yer it didn't 'arf give me a turn an' all. All tied round 'is face with a pocket-'ankerchief, 'e was. Gagged, ah! And when I come to pick 'im up blest if 'e wasn't bound 'ard an' fast, too! 'Lor lumme, mate,' I says. 'An' 'ow long 'ave you been 'ere, might I ask?'

"He couldn't answer for a bit—not even arter I got the 'ankerchief off of 'is face, 'e couldn't—but 'e kinder grinned like when I got out me knife and cut 'is ropes. 'Thank you,' 'e says, just like that, and tries to get on 'is 'ind legs—I'd got 'im up the bank by then —an' down 'e goes agin all of a blessed 'eap. I starts a-rubbin' of 'is legs to get the surkylation back, an' 'e says 'Don't—not yet,' like as if it 'urt 'im. Mud!

Lord, 'e was a sight; I never see so much mud on a chap in me life. "By and by 'e looks down at me boat and says: 'Did you walk up there?' 'Yes,' I says, wonderin', 'why?' 'Nothin',' 'e says, 'only I thought it was deeper, an' so did them as chucked me in.' 'Chucked you in?' I says. 'You ain't pullin' me leg, I suppose—not one of these 'ere movie men, are you?*

"'E gives a little laugh. 'No,' 'e says, 'I'm not a movie man.' Then 'e asked me the time, an' when I told 'im 'e seemed surprised—thought it was later-like. 'Look 'ere,' 'e says, 'kin you keep a secret?'

'O' course I can,' I says. 'Well, then,' 'e says, 'keep quiet about findin' me an' I'll make it worth your while.' An' blow me if 'e didn't give me a quid an' all! O' course you chaps won't say nothin' to no-body"

Thus Mr. Ted Morgan, greengrocer's assistant and sometimes ferryman, in the bar of the "Blue Boar" at Yattbridge, encouraged by the pints of kind friends.

Everyone was kind to Mr. Morgan, and signified affection in the usual manner, but there was one man whose kindness took a different form. Getting the garrulous Mr. Morgan into a corner he slipped half a crown into his hand.

"Look here, I'm a detective," he said in a low voice. "And I'm especially interested in this man you rescued.

Which way did he go when he left you?"

"Wish way?" repeated Mr. Morgan, blinking perplexedly. "Wish way did 'e go?"

"Yes," nodded the kind stranger. "Did he go back to Seabridge?"

"Did 'e go—back Seebree'?" said Mr. Morgan with a hiccough, "now you're arsked me summat. Lemme shee now!"

"You watched him go, of course?"

"Washt 'im go—corsh I washt 'im go! 'Don't tell nobody,' 'e saysh, an' gives me a quid. A whole— blessed quid! Nor I 'aven't—tol' nobody. Wan' me tell you?" he demanded with sudden sus-picion.

"No, no," said the stranger soothingly. "I only want

to know which direction he took."

"Oh, thash all ri'," returned Mr. Morgan, "thash en-
entirely diff' thing. Wish way did 'e go? Now lemme
she. 'E went—"

"Over towards the sands, eh?"

"Thash ri'. Over—over tor' sands. Nishe feller!"
Perceiving the unlikelihood of getting anything
further out of Mr. Ted Morgan in his present happy
state, the stranger left the "Blue Boar" and
proceeded slowly down the lane outside. Presently he
was joined by another man.

"Learnt anything?" inquired the new-comer.

"Very little," was the reply. "The filthy pig's as
drunk as an owl. It looks as if Brown went off
towards Venning's place."

"Better give up for the present, hadn't we?"
suggested the new-comer. "We shan't catch them
napping a second time.

"I will not give it up," returned the other, in whose
voice Peter, had he been listening, might have traced
a likeness to the Rev. Septimus Tringle. "D'you think
I'm going to let two hundred pounds go begging for
want of trying?"

"You've tried twice, anyhow" grumbled the new-
comer. "And he got away both times."

"The third time it'll be my turn to win. The fool
seems to have as many lives as a cat. Who would
have supposed the mud was only a foot deep just
there?"

"Horstman won't be pleased when he hears about it,
I might tell you. Failure isn't a popular word in his
vocabulary."

The man who had entertained Mr. Ted Morgan
cursed Horstman with great heartiness.

Wilfrid Usher

"There won't be any quesemphatically. "It's true he'll
probably tell a good many people about last night,
and as far as I'm concerned I thought it a fool trick
on Drude's part to let him see the experiment.
There's no harm done, however."
"Unless he recognized—"
He stopped significantly. The other shook his head.
"He couldn't possibly," he replied sharply, "it was
dark as pitch."
"I was referring more to his voice."
"When I've finished with Master Peter Brown he'll
be past worrying about voices," was the grim answer.

Peter was so exhausted and numbed from his
immersion in the mud that when he had parted from
his garrulous rescuer he could scarcely put one foot
before the other. His way lay across several large and
marshy fields, and as he plodded doggedly on he
could see, in the distance, a concourse of chars-a
bancs and motor-cars at the foot of Whale Head, and
people like ants climbing the lower slopes of the hill.
Gradually the exercise restored his circulation and
at the same time raised his spirit. He began to see
glimmerings of humor in the situation. There was
certainly irony in the fact that he was still alive, for
it was unlikely that Sir Mortimer would have allowed
him to witness what was evidently a demonstration
of the potentialities of one of his discoveries, unless
he was confident of his immediate decease.
No one met him as he crossed the field towards the
house where Venning lived, and he thought it just as
well, for his dreadful appearance would only have
aroused curiosity, and it was obvious that the fewer
people who knew about his misadventure the better.

It chanced that Venning was standing in the lane
talking to a police-inspector as he approached, and it
amused Peter to notice that he was quite
unrecognized.

"Well, my man, what can I do for you?" demanded
the Inspector, surveying the mud-covered apparition
which had stopped before him. "Been having a mud-
bath, haven't you?"

"Don't you know me, Venning?" said Peter with a
grin.

"Good God—Brown!" gasped the Colonel. "But—
where in the name of Heaven have you been?"

"In the mud," said Peter. "Chucked there last night
by some mutual friends of ours."

"In the mud?" cried Venning incredulously.

"Bless you, yes—stayed there all night. Nice place,
the Yatt, for a night's lodging. Especially when you're
bound and gagged like I was!"

He smiled cheerfully at the astonished policeman.

"This is Mr. Brown—Inspector Tolley," said Venning,
recovering himself. "We've been hunting for you all
morning. But come along inside, man, you
must be famished!"

"I'd rather have a bath first if you don't mind—I
feel rather—clammy," said Peter.

Half an hour later, clad once more in respectable
garments, he was telling his story to the two men in
between the intervals of making a hearty meal.

Venning made only one interruption, and that was
when Peter, repeating the conversation he had had
with Sir Mortimer on the sands, mentioned that the
scientist had imprisoned his niece on an island.

"An island," he said thoughtfully. "That's interesting.
Please go on."

153

When Peter had finished, the Colonel rose and stood with his back to the fireplace, filling his pipe.

"There's almost a kind of fate in the way you escape from Sir Mortimer's hands," he said. "If I were a fatalist I should say it looked as if it was ordained that you should be spared to put a spoke in his game."

"To tell you the truth, I'm rather sorry for Sir Mortimer," Peter observed; "the poor devil has so obviously got bats in the belfry. It's his chief of staff, Horstman, and one or two others, I'm reserving my dislike for."

"It's a lucky thing they chose that spot for you," said the Inspector. "There's a dozen feet of mud up by the mouth. Could you describe the two men or their car?"

"The car was an open four-seater. As for the men, they never spoke, and it was too dark to see their faces."

"How many men came in the motor-boat?" asked Venning.

"About a dozen, I should say."

"Was Horstman among them?"

"I didn't see him."

"Now about this man who was with Sir Mortimer. You say you formed the impression that you had heard his voice before. Can't you try and think where it was or under what circumstance?"

"I tried as I lay in that confounded mud, and it was no use," returned Peter with a slight laugh. "My idea is that I've heard him speaking—making a speech—somewhere—but it's only the vaguest of notions. Per-haps I shall come across it by accident—these fugitive memories often crop up when you're not

154

looking for them—perhaps not."

"I hope you will, for there's no doubt he is the man I told you of—the master criminal of the gang Sir Mortimer is dealing with. I rather think Sir Mortimer's remaining tenure of life will be a short one."

"You mean—"

"I mean that now Sir Mortimer has convinced him that his discoveries are of such extraordinary power, he's not likely to pay through the nose for what he can just as easily get by simpler methods. The only thing that will prolong Sir Mortimer's life is the ability to convince the gang that he has further secrets up his sleeve. Before that time comes, let's hope the whole lot will be laid by the heels, and the discoveries put in the hands of reputable scientists."

"It will have to be done by cunning. Those rays . . . an army would wither before them like saplings in a tornado."

"Undoubtedly," Venning agreed, "but you must bear in mind that poisons have their antidotes. The more powerful the gun the thicker the armour, and I have no doubt there is a defense against all artificial destruction. Perhaps defense is the more difficult problem at the present time, but it always levels up. And there is another thing. I gather that the zone of danger is only at the point of concentration of the three rays. I take it that there are certain peculiar properties in these rays that are harmful only when they combine. Obviously there are difficulties in the way of handling such a weapon in its present state."

"Difficulties which may be overcome."

"Perhaps. But, remember, Sir Mortimer isn't the inventor of the weapon; remember the strange

Wilfrid Usher

circumstances—fantastical, if you like—under which
it has come into his possession. The thing has come
to him ready made, so to speak; he is merely copying
instructions out of a book. Or, if you like, making
and assembling the parts according to the blue-
print. Is it likely that he, with his limited knowledge
of scientific possibility, will be able to improve on the
work of beings as far superior to him in knowledge
as we are to the Phoenicians?"

The Inspector smothered a yawn and looked out of
the window. Obviously the conversation had drifted
beyond his level of interest. Colonel Venning re-lit
his pipe, which had gone out.

"Well, Inspector, I think that's all that can be done
for the present," he said. "If you discover anything
else, come round and let me know, will you?"

"One moment, Inspector!" said Peter. "Has anything further been heard of the clergyman who was
so kind as to put snakes in my bedroom at the
'Royal' the night before last?"

"God bless my soul!" said the Inspector. "Was that
you, too? You seem to have been in the wars lately,
and no mistake. No, they haven't heard anything
more of him so far as I know. Cleared out of here by
now, I should think."

"I don't know," said Peter slowly. "I have a shrewd
suspicion that he was one of the men who threw me
into the mud. You know the queer feeling one gets
that a certain person is near—well, although I
couldn't see him and he was mum as a mute, I had
that feeling then. I confess I should like to meet the
Rev. Septimus Tringle again."

When the Inspector had gone Peter turned to
Venning.

"What did you mean by that interjection of yours
when I mentioned that about the island?" he
asked.
"It was only a passing thought," said the Colonel.
"Sir Mortimer owned a house on Sark some years
ago. I remember reading about it in his dossier. So
far as I remember he never lived in it himself. He
sold it soon after the War, though, so it couldn't be
the same.

"Colonel, have you ever had the feeling that you are
being watched?" asked Peter, as they sat at supper
that night.
"Oh, yes—nerves mostly. Why, d'you feel like
that now?"
"I do. I've had the feeling ever since I sat down
to supper. It may be nerves—I don't say it isn't—but
it's there, nevertheless."
He glanced uneasily out of the window, where the
setting sun was tinting the western sky to gold.
Colonel Venning smiled.

"A good night's rest will put you right," he said.
"You're still suffering from the efforts of your
involuntary mud-bath."
"I dare say," Peter replied absently.
"It's nearly half-past nine," said Venning presently.
"Let's hear the news. It'll be interesting to hear what
they have to say about this affair."
He rose and switched on the loud-speaker. After a
pause a pleasant voice began to speak.
"This is London station calling the British Isles,"
it announced. "We have been requested by Scotland
Yard to broadcast the following. The police are
anxious to trace the whereabouts of the relatives of

Mrs. John Matchup, who died in Helminster
Infirmary in August last year. Any friends or
relatives of the deceased are requested to
communicate at once with the nearest police station,
or with New Scotland Yard, S.W.I. Now here is the
weather fore-cast—"

But Peter was not listening to the weather forecast,
for he had caught sight of Venning's face, and it had
whitened perceptibly. Immediately the Colonel rose
and switched off the loud-speaker.

"I must go at once," he said hurriedly. "That message
was for me."

"Not—bad news, I hope?"

Venning shook his head. "No, no—not family news.
I can't tell you what it is—indeed, I don't know. But
it means I must go at once."

"Can I help?"

"Not this time; I must go alone. Stay on here for a
few days if you like."

"If you go, I go," said Peter. "There's no point in
my stopping on here."

It did not take Colonel Venning long to make his
arrangements, for in ten minutes his two-seater was
at the front door.

"Good-bye, Brown," he said, as they shook hands.
"Take care of yourself. I expect we shall meet again
very shortly."

Left to himself, Peter experienced a sense of
depression. After the adventures of the last few days
he felt that anything else would be in the nature of
an anti-climax. For some minutes he sat listening to
the wireless programme, but the music seemed flat
and uninteresting. Presently that curious sense of
being watched, which he put down to nerves,

158

returned to him, and he determined to go to bed.
Tired as he was, however, he felt so restless that he
was convinced he would never sleep, and it occurred
to him that a short walk might induce that state of
immediate physical fatigue in which sleep comes
easiest. He looked to his revolver—he was taking no
chances—and decided that a stroll as far as the
main road and back would meet the case.
At the garden gate he stopped to fill his pipe. As
he felt for his matches something like a great beetle
sung past his head and hit the brickwork of the
cottage with a crack. The instant he heard it he
ducked and ran, doubled up, along the lane till he
was past the farm; then he plunged into an orchard
on the same side of the road as that from which the
bullet had come. There he drew his revolver and
pressed back the safety catch.

It was almost dark by now; there was just sufficient
light for him to avoid the tree trunks as he stole
rapidly and silently to the back of the orchard. Upon
reaching it he dropped prone and continued to
wriggle his way forward until he arrived at the stone
wall which divided the orchard from the farmyard.
With his cap well over his eyes and his coat collar
up, he raised himself until he could see over. But
though the roofs of the buildings were outlined
against the sky, the lower parts were in deep
shadow, in which all detail was lost. There was no
sign of the man who had fired the shot.
Across the road the light from the room he had just
left gleamed dully through the yellow curtain. It was
evident that the old people were within listening to
the music—indeed, from where he was he could
faintly hear the strains of a fox-trot.

159

For a Quarter of an hour or more Peter waited as
still as a mouse, but his enemy gave no sign. As on
the preceding night when he had awaited bigger
game, it was very quiet, the light wind which blew
across the flats making little sound. This silence was
all at once broken by a little click and a noise like
the twanging of a bow-string, and Peter smiled, for
the twanging noise died away in the opposite
direction. What it was his enemy was firing at he
could not conceive, but it was certainly not him.
Peter climbed the wall and tiptoed as quietly as he
knew how in the direction of the sound. He was
beginning to enjoy the hunt, and hoped his enemy
would continue to advertise his position by firing at
imaginary targets. Behind the angle of a barn he
crept and then stopped still as stone, for across the
yellow patch of the window, but on the same side of
the road as himself, the figure of a man passed,
doubled-up conspirator wise—a long lanky man with
a lean neck—and Peter could have hooted with joy. It
was the Rev. Septimus Tringle.
From the shadow of the barn Peter watched him
take up a position by a wall, and presently there was
another faint click, and again a large flying beetle
seemed to soar away into the distance. It was a piece
of luck Peter had not counted on, and he hastened to
take advantage of it. With the utmost caution,
testing every footstep before resting his weight on it,
he moved towards the dimly visible figure against the
wall, ready at any instant to fire if the other should
discover his presence. When less than a dozen yards
separated them he spoke.
"Don't move or turn round, please, Mr. Tringle:

I'll shoot if you do," he said suavely.

The figure did not move. Peter took a couple of
steps forward.

"Drop the pistol and put up your hands," he went
on in a pleasant voice, then adding, with a sudden
change of tone, "And quick, too, or, by God, I'll drill
you where you stand!"

There was no reluctance on Mr. Tringle's part to
obey both orders. Peter picked up the fallen pistol—
a long-barreled affair with a thick chamber.

"Now march," he said. "And if you play any tricks
with me I'll kill you. Understand?"

"I understand—blast you!" muttered the other
between set teeth.

"Tut-tut, Mr. Tringle—a clergyman, too!"

"You can cut that out," snarled the captive. "What
are you going to do with me?"

"Can't you guess?" asked Peter quietly, after a
pause.

From his captive's silence it was evident that he
could.

"You tried to kill me with those snakes—and failed,"
Peter went on, a note of gravity creeping into his
voice.

"You tried to drown me in the mud—and failed. And
just now you tried to kill me again—and once more
you failed. Is there any reason why I shouldn't try
to kill you?"

The other was silent, and Peter thought he heard
his teeth give an involuntary chatter.

"I'm sorry to have to kill you—I'm really a soft-
hearted person and hate killing anything—but I'm
afraid there's no alternative. And you must admit I'm
only meting out a fate you intended for me. It was a

pity you didn't know the mud was only a few inches deep in that particular spot, because I shall know what spot to avoid. Please move along—and remember I have both pistols."

"You're going to murder me?"

"Of course I am. What else do you suppose?" asked Peter simply.

It was a fit setting for an act of violence, as they crossed the marshy fields towards the river. Far away the lights of Seabridge twinkled under a darkling sky in which traces of the past day still lingered, though it was long after sunset. For miles in front and on either hand there was no human habitation in sight, and the sense of desolation was deepened by the plaintive murmur of the sea.

Suddenly the man in front stopped, and there was just sufficient light for Peter to see that his face was working.

"You—you can't kill me like this," he faltered. "I know when I'm beaten—I've failed and I'm ready to pay the penalty. Hand me over to the police—shoot me if you like—I can bear even that—but not—" he gulped—"not in the mud."

"Did you think of that when you threw me in?" asked Peter coldly.

"I didn't—I admit I didn't. But you can't throw me in there—you can't—it's too horrible. I'll plead with you on my knees if you like—"

Peter raised one pistol. "Get on !" he said in a harsh voice. The journey was resumed.

At length the river bank was reached. It was wider here than the place where Peter had nearly met his end, though the mud-banks were if anything steeper.

Peter threw his captive's pistol into the mud. It sank from sight immediately.

"Deep here, eh?" said Peter.

The other looked down at the slow-moving river at the bottom and shuddered. "You're not going to throw me in there?" he cried hoarsely.

"I'm going to give you what you would never dream of giving me—a fighting chance," was the reply. "You and I are going to have a man-to-man, good old-fashioned scrap with our bare hands—and the loser is going in the mud. Can you think of anything fairer than that?"

"Fairer?" Hope had brought a little manliness back into the other's voice. "And you armed?"

"On the contrary, we fight on equal terms. And to prove it I will lay my pistol on the ground. All I ask is your word of honour not to touch it."

"Very well. I give it."

Peter placed the revolver on the ground and stepped back two paces. Instantly, with a wild laugh, the other stooped and picked it up.

"You fool! You utter idiot!" he cried. "Did you think for a moment you were going to get the best of me! My God, I'll give you something for the fright you've given me! It's you that's going into the mud—but this time I'll make certain you're dead before you go in."

Peter did not reply. He stood still, his attitude the image of dejection.

"Nothing to say, eh?" snarled the other, taking a few steps back, as if fearing Peter was on the point of making a despairing attack. "You were talkative enough when you had the upper hand. Do you know that I'm going to kill you—you swine!—now?"

"Yes." Peter's voice was sad. "I was afraid you'd try that. That's the reason I took the cartridges out first."

Quickly the other raised the pistol and fired. There was a succession of clicks. Peter laughed shortly.

"I rather think it's you for the mud after all," he said, and the next instant he had closed with his enemy. For a short time the man fought desperately, kicking and scratching like a wild-cat; but Peter had twice his strength, and in less than two minutes had his adversary under his knee.

He rose to his feet, breathing quickly. "Get up," he said.

It had become considerably darker in the last five minutes. Peter saw that the other was lying still in a peculiar attitude, close to the bank of the river.

"Are you hurt?" he asked.

A groan was the reply. It seemed to Peter that the man was trying to do something to his leg. He took a step forward, and was about to bend over him, when the man leaped to his feet with great rapidity, holding something in his hand, and without pausing aimed a sweeping blow at Peter's head.

Peter ducked just in time to avoid the blow, and then, a flame of anger rising in him at this second act of treachery, he swiftly dropped on one knee and collared the man's legs, at the same time giving a tremendous heave that threw him clean over his shoulder. He heard the man give a kind of sob, and then scrambled to his feet, only to realize that he was standing on the very brink of the steep bank of the river. He looked round for his adversary—and from below him there came a scream.

"Help!—I'm sinking—oh, quick!" The voice rose

to a shriek again.

"Hold on!—I'm coming," cried Peter. "Spread your coat out—"

He plunged down the slope, but in a moment he had sunk to his knees. Ten feet away a black mass was writhing and struggling. Peter tried to take another step forward, tearing off his coat as he did so, but the mud gripped his legs like glue.

"Try and catch my coat," he yelled, making frantic casts down the slope, but to no purpose—the coat fell short by a yard. Scream after scream rent the air; a man was dying the most horrible of deaths not four yards from him, and he was powerless to save him. And then, suddenly, silence fell—a silence broken only by the gentle rippling of the river at the foot of the slope, and the sighing of the light summer wind as it passed over the desolate flats.

CHAPTER IX
ON THE ISLAND

The steamer from Guernsey had just moored between the two stone piers that enclose the harbor at Sark.

Most of the passengers had crossed the gangway and were already bargaining with the drivers of horse-drawn vehicles anxious to take them for a trip round the island, when a man who had been standing in the stern, apparently lost in meditation upon the scene before him, came abruptly to the realization of his position and made for the gangway with some haste. He was a long, lean, untidy-looking man, with a bent back and a habit of carrying his head out-thrust like an inquisitive hen, which, combined with his large glasses, gave him the appearance of being short- sighted. Obviously a man of intellect, there was that about him that made one think immediately of libraries and the silence of reading-rooms. In years he might have been anything between forty and sixty, and it was evident that like a good many literary men he was inclined to be fussy over trifles, for he could not at first find his ticket, and showed signs of weak petulance at having to search his pocket for it. A young American who stood on the quay smiled a little at the scene. He had had a conversation with the old boy—as he mentally called the man with the glasses—on the journey across, and had been rather amused by his company. The old fellow's name was Juckes, he had discovered, and he was engaged on writing a history of the Channel Islands. The American had set him down as a "character," and had looked forward to seeing more of him, since it appeared they were staying at the same hotel. It is possible that he would have betrayed even greater interest had he known that a few weeks previously Mr. Juckes had been a prosaic garage-proprietor on the Brighton Road, and that there was at the present moment a small automatic pistol reposing in a canvas holster strapped under one armpit.

Arrived on the quay, Mr. Juckes was looking round for a conveyance to take him to his hotel when he became aware of the American standing beside him.

"Pretty little spot," said the American.

"Yes, indeed—most delightful," rejoined Mr. Juckes, surveying the scene through his spectacles. "One of those rare backwaters of the world which Progress and the rush of modern life seem happily to have passed completely by."

The American smiled appreciatively.

"Stopping long here, Mr. Juckes?" he asked.

"Possibly—it depends upon how long it will take me to complete my work," was the vague reply.

"Why, sure," said the American. "I'm stopping a week if I can stick it. Maybe we'll be seeing some-thing of each other."

"Quite—quite," said Mr. Juckes absent-mindedly. "Oh, certainly."

His tone was not particularly enthusiastic, for though he liked the look of the American, the last thing he wanted was company. The other, however, was far from thin-skinned, and continued to babble cheerfully, and for very courtesy's sake Mr. Juckes had to appear to show some interest in his remarks. It was natural that he should incline to look upon the American with suspicion—indeed, since his experience of the Rev. Mr. Tringle there were few people whom he had not so regarded—yet he could have sworn that here, for once, was someone who was not involved in the web of mystery in which he had been caught. The American —his name was Lamont—was a slim young man with an open, sun burnt countenance and clear grey eyes that were seldom without a glint of amusement, and it occurred to Mr. Juckes that under certain circumstances he might prove a useful ally. He looked the kind of man who could be trusted to give a good account of himself in an emergency.

An hour later, having partaken of a lobster lunch with rather more appetite than one would have expected of a man of his years, Mr. Juckes sallied forth to explore. His plans were of the vaguest. He had, however, ascertained before leaving England that the house which Sir Mortimer Drude had once owned was called "St. Cloud," the present occupiers being a family named Reddieson. It appeared that Dr. Reddieson was a Scotsman who had lived a good deal abroad, and was said to have at one time practiced in Paris; moreover, he was a widower who lived with an unmarried daughter. All of which was satisfactory enough so far as it-went; the omissions in the dossier Mr. Juckes proposed to supply himself. In his character of earnest student of the habits and customs of the islands, he thought, the task would not prove a difficult one.

It was a simple matter to find the house. It stood alone in a hollow about a furlong from the cliffs, a substantial building faced with stone, beset on all sides except one by a grove of short trees, and it had a considerable front garden running down to the lane by which it was approached. Guide-book in hand, Mr. Juckes scrutinized the place from the lane. There appeared to be no one about. He was considering various pretexts for gaining an entrance, when a sentence in the guide-book caught his eye— "There is only one dolmen on Sark—" and it gave him an idea.

Pushing open the gate he approached the house and rang the front-door bell. He was prepared for surprises; he was prepared to be faced by Sir Mortimer Drude himself; yet it needed all his self-control to preserve his countenance when the door opened and revealed none other than the ex-pugilist, Copping by name, whom he had last seen in Sir Mortimer's laboratory at Okewood Hall. And the nervousness in his voice, when he spoke, was not all simulated. "I am so sorry to trouble you," he began apologetically, "but I wonder if you would be good enough to tell me whereabouts in this neighborhood the dolmen is?"

The bruiser shook a puzzled head. "Don't know any place of that name here, sir."

"It isn't a place, it's—ah—a stone, a kind of cromlech," explained Mr. Juckes, who had only the vaguest notions about the subject himself. "Perhaps Dr. Reddieson ... if it isn't too much trouble. . . ."

The pug eyed his interlocutor suspiciously. Strangers were not encouraged at "St. Cloud;" yet this stranger looked harmless enough. And despite the company he kept there were germs of kindness beneath Copping's rough exterior.

Wilfrid Usher

"I'll just inquire if you'll wait 'arf a minute," he
said. And presently, for the third time in his life,
Mr. Juckes was face to face with Sir Mortimer
Drude.
"You wish to see me?" inquired the scientist, his
pale eyes searching Mr. Juckes'. And Mr. Juckes,
conscious of an uncomfortable feeling that few secret
were hidden from that keen gaze, began to wonder if
he had been wise in calling.
"I really shouldn't have troubled you, Dr. Reddieson
—it is Dr. Reddieson, is it not?—the matter is only
trifling ... I made sure your servant would know
... I didn't dream—"
The other cut short his apologies. "What is it you
want to know?" he demanded.
Mr. Juckes managed to force a smile. "Well, you
see, Doctor, I am writing a history of these islands,
and as I am naturally interested in megalithic
remains I am anxious to examine any dolmens on
the island. I understand—"
"The only dolmen on Sark is nearly half a mile
away," the other interrupted. "Anyone will tell you
where it is; why do you bother me? I really cannot
allow my work to be interrupted by such trifles, and
I wish you good afternoon, sir."
The front door was open, Dr. Reddieson's marble
eyes were fixed on his with the old inscrutable
expression, and there was nothing to be gained by
staying longer. He had found out one of the things
he had come to Sark to discover; the rest could wait.
For the present it was enough to know that Dr.
Reddieson and Sir Mortimer Drude were one and the
same person.
"Thank you so much—I am so sorry to be a

nuisance!" he said effusively. "Good afternoon."
He raised his hat with a clumsy gesture, and Dr.
Reddieson bowed coldly in reply. As soon as the door
closed, however, the doctor's expression altered.
With a grim frown he summoned Copping.
"Send Arthur to me at once," he ordered.'
Almost immediately a little man with a white face
appeared.
"Follow that man who has just been here," said Dr.
Reddieson. "Find out where he's staying, when he
arrived, and everything you can about him."
An hour later Mr. Juckes entered the little post-
office in the centre of the island. Was it possible to'
send a telegram? he inquired. Certainly he could; the
post-office was open until seven. That was most
satisfactory, but would a wire dispatched that afternoon reach England before night-time? The postmaster was on the point of replying when the
eccentric visitor suddenly changed his mind,
apparently for no reason at all, and announced that
he would send a picture postcard instead.

The postmaster saw no connection between this
trivial circumstance and the fact that a little man
entered the post-office at that moment and
purchased some stamps. But Mr. Juckes had noted
the man before he crossed the threshold, and
behold! It was the little fellow he had held up at the
point of the revolver that night at Okewood Hall, and
compelled to lead him to the laboratory door. And
something in his manner—a certain indifference to
his own presence which was just the least bit too
studied to be natural—suggested it was not mere
coincidence that was responsible for his being there
at that particular moment.

171

Wilfrid Usher

So Dr. Reddieson was curious to know his
movements, was he? Perhaps it was his pleasant
habit to have every visitor who stayed on the island
shadowed, until he was satisfied of their harmless ;
perhaps not. In any case it showed that the doctor
was fully aware of the danger of his own position.
Well, if the little man had been sent to spy on him
Mr. Juckes did not worry; he had perfect confidence
in the efficiency of his disguise. The telegram could
wait. Meanwhile, the views of Sark displayed in the
post-office were exceptionally interesting, and he was
in no hurry.
Nor, so it appeared, was the little man, for he, too,
appeared to be absorbed in the views. In fact, it is
doubtful if those picture post-cards had ever before
attracted so much interest. Minutes passed, and still
the scrutiny went on; and there is no knowing how
long it would have continued had not a most
awkward incident occurred—a most unfortunate
business altogether.

How it happened was not quite clear, but it seemed
that just as the short-sighted Mr. Juckes—always a
singularly clumsy individual—was leaning sideways
in an endeavor to peer at a picture-postcard he could
not properly see, his foot slipped and he
overbalanced.
That, in order to save himself, he should clutch
frantically at the little man, who chanced to be
standing a few feet away, was natural but
disastrous, for not only did he fail to regain his
balance but he brought down the little man with
him—and unfortunately the little man was
underneath.
Nothing could have exceeded Mr. Juckes' confusion

172

as he helped the little man to his feet, neighing his apologies with the utmost concern; and nothing could have exceeded the little man's indignation. Clearly he thought it had been done on purpose. "Why don't you look what yer doing, you great big clumsy owl?" he cried. "Ain't the 'ole world big enough without comin' and throwin' yer great 'ulkin' weight about in 'ere?"

"I assure you, really, I—I—really, I'm most upset," stammered Mr. Juckes. "I can't think how it happened—most distressing for you, I'm sure. I do hope you're not hurt.

"Hurt!" repeated the other angrily. "If I'd broken me leg it would 'ave been your fault! Ruddy old fool!"

"Tut, tut," said Mr. Juckes frowning. "An accident is an accident. I have apologized, and between gentlemen that usually closes the matter. There is no occasion for bad language."

"Oh, ain't there, Mr. Particular! Well, then—"

Mr. Juckes turned his back.
For a moment it looked as if the little man was about to commit a violent assault on his person. Then,
apparently thinking better of it, he shouted one more objurgation, and left the shop muttering. Over his shoulder Mr. Juckes watched him go with a distasteful expression.

"A vulgar fellow, that," he remarked. "Who is he?"

"One of the servants from 'St. Goud,' I believe," the postmaster replied.

"A singularly unpleasant character, I should imagine," said Mr. Juckes. "Now what was I about to do when he came in? Ah, yes, a telegram—I was on the point of sending a telegram, was I not? You are quite sure it will reach England to-night if I send it now?"

As he left the post-office Peter chuckled grimly to himself. By purposely irritating the man whom he was convinced Sir Mortimer had sent to spy upon him, he had made him momentarily forget his purpose and had then been enabled to dispatch his wire in secret.
True, there was nothing in the telegram to arouse suspicions in the most vigilant breast—it merely requested the recipient to forward on certain articles of clothing, his camera, and one or two books on geology—but he preferred Sir Mortimer to remain in ignorance of the fact that he had sent a wire at all. Of course, the little man would report to his master the whole scene in the post-office, but whether he thought him merely an eccentric old fool or something deeper did not greatly matter. His disguise, which was the work of a certain specialist in make-up to whom Venning had sent him, he defied anyone to pierce. Sir Mortimer might suspect what he liked, but he could prove nothing, if he searched every article of clothing he possessed.
While he had tea at a cottage near the Colinette he considered his next step. He believed that he had discovered the headquarters of the gang for whom the police of three continents were searching. At first sight it looked as if all that remained to be done was to summon efficient help from Guernsey and, with the assistance of the Sark authorities, put the whole house- hold under arrest. There was, however, a serious objection to this plan. Sir Mortimer, it was

clear, was fully on his guard, and probably had agents at Guernsey and Jersey who would immediately inform him of any display of official force that threatened his safety. For such an emergency he was bound to be amply prepared. No man would play with fire as he had done without having taken measures to ensure his own safety in case of discovery. Calling in the police to arrest him as if he were an ordinary criminal would be a proceeding foredoomed to failure, Peter was convinced. At the merest hint of danger the bird would fly—fly in the literal sense, perhaps.

Sir Mortimer Drude had chosen his hiding-place well.

Situated within an hour's flying distance of France and England it was ideally situated for sudden departure. Peter remembered Mr. Bridgewater telling him how the scientist had often disappeared for months at a time; here was the explanation. He had probably been leading a double life for years. And who, in such an out-of-the-way place, would ever think of identifying the retired Scotch doctor with the famous Sir Mortimer Drude? There was always the chance of recognition, of course, but it was so remote that it safely could be ignored.

How far his niece was implicated in the deception could only be guessed. Sir Mortimer had spoken of her being imprisoned on an island, presumably because of the part she had played in saving Peter's life. It was hardly likely he would go so far as to confine her to one of the lesser islands, few of which were habit- able; everything pointed to her being at "St. Cloud". If this was so he vowed that he would find means to see that she was free before the net finally closed around her uncle and his accomplices. It would be a poor way of showing his gratitude to allow her to be involved in the round-up he had every intention of engineering.

Later in the day he found the opportunity to ask the manager of his hotel if he knew anything of the Reddiesons. It appeared that the doctor moved abroad little, rumor having it that he was devoted to scientific research, an occupation which allowed small time for leisure.

"To tell you the truth I haven't seen him for months," the manager confessed, "nor Miss Reddieson either, poor thing. They are not a sociable family." "Why 'poor thing'?" demanded Peter. "Is she an invalid?"

The manager nodded and touched his forehead.

"Mental," he said. "At least, that's what I'm told. She never leaves the house now. Such a nice girl she was, too."

"To tell you the truth, I rather formed the impression that Dr. Reddieson himself was somewhat—er—peculiar," Peter remarked. "He was certainly strangely abrupt in his manner."

"He would be if you were a stranger to him. I happen to know he detests strangers. There was rather
an unpleasant incident a few weeks ago. A number of young fellows staying on the island started some horse-play and rang the bell at 'St. Cloud' and pretended they were pierrots. It seems the butler has been something of a boxer in his time, and he laid out three of them on the lawn. The Seigneur was very angry, I can tell you. By the way, do you believe in ghosts, Mr. Juckes?"

"When I see a ghost I will believe in it," replied
that gentleman.
"I wondered, because we have a pet ghost on the
island. Talking of 'St. Cloud' reminded me of it,
for it was near there it was last seen. I think you'll
admit it takes an original form. How would you like
to see a ghostly motor-boat?"
"A motor-boat? Dear me! I should most certainly
like to see it."
"Perhaps you will," said the manager, laughing.
"It's been seen three times up to date, and always at
night. One of the fishermen, Tom Damon, was the
last. He declared it headed straight for the cliffs at
full speed and vanished into the solid rock."
"Very extraordinary," said Mr. Jukes thoughtfully.
"And where do you say this—er—manifestation
occurred?"
"Just under the cliffs by 'St. Cloud'—according to
Tom Damon. The remarkable part about it is that
he's a steady old fellow, a most reliable man as a
rule, and a good Wesleyan."
"You interest me profoundly," said Mr. Juckes
(which was no more than the truth). "In a humble
way I have myself been something of an inquirer into
the mysteries of the unseen world, and the more I
learn the more I am amazed at the vastness of our
ignorance.
But I confess that hitherto I have never yet met with
a phantom motor-boat."
"You don't believe in the nonsense?" the manager
asked incredulously.
"The man Damon may be the victim of an
hallucination, of course," admitted Mr. Juckes with
suitable gravity, "yet do you know, I incline to the

177

view that it was one of those cases of a photoplasmic materialization of the electra, corresponding to what is known in the poltergeist world as pre-actuality of experience.

I confess I should like to view the scene of the manifestation."

"If you're interested in such things I've no doubt one of the fishermen would take you round," said the manager, obviously rather impressed. "I should like to know how you get on."

Peter promised that he would let him know. Secretly he was delighted with the story to which he had just listened; for not only did it suggest possibilities of discovery in connection with Sir Mortimer Drude's method of leaving and arriving at the island, but it also gave him an excellent excuse for nocturnal rambling—a pastime in which he hoped to indulge to a considerable extent in the near future. If he was discovered prowling about the island in the small hours he could always say he was ghost-hunting—of course in suitably impressive language. It occurred to him it might be useful to swot up some book on spiritualism, if the hotel library ran to such a subject, and a fortunate search revealing an old copy of "The Survival of Man", by Sir Oliver Lodge, he retired with it to his room.

Until that evening Peter had always been a hearty supporter of Daylight Saving, but as he sat in his bedroom waiting for darkness to fall he appreciated the fact that it had certain disadvantages, especially from the point of view of the burgling classes. Half-past ten went by and still the faint remnant of daylight lingered; it was not until a clock downstairs struck eleven that he decided it was dark enough to commence operations.

Quite by chance he had been put in a room that overlooked a kind of yard, occupied in the daytime by ducks and fowls, and underneath his window was a long, gently-sloping wooden roof that made his descent to the ground child's play. There was fortunately no dog, and he melted into the shadow beyond the low stone wall without causing a sound. A certain risk of being made to look rather foolish if he was discovered lay in this method of leaving the hotel; but the alternative, which was to spin some yarn of his being addicted to walking at night, and get the staff to let him have a latch key, he had dismissed. News travels quickly on an island, and if it came to the ears of Dr. Reddieson that one of the hotel guests was in the habit of walking abroad during the night hours, he would probably draw his own conclusions and be rendered doubly on his guard.

Through the low fringe of trees surrounding the hotel Peter slipped and gained the roadway. The moon was occasionally visible through the sailing clouds, and whenever it shone clear he stopped still until it was obscured again. His rubbered feet made no noise as he drew near to that part of the island where Dr. Reddieson lived. He was aware of a certain tenseness in his mind, a feeling rather akin to the nervousness he had experienced during the solitary occasion on which he had appeared for his county at cricket, when he was waiting with his pads on to go in and bat.

Peter was really no more than a good second-class cricketer, and his one venture in the ranks of the first class had not been crowned with success, but he well remembered the state of his feelings as he had watched the trundling of the fast bowler whom he was presently to face. And were not the circumstances now very similar ?—for here was he, an amateur burglar, about, in the vernacular, to crack his first crib, with the certain knowledge that a highly-skilled professional in the world of crime was only waiting for the opportunity to bowl out such as himself neck and crop.

There was a queer comfort in the weight of his automatic as he thought with what glee Dr. Reddieson would gloat over him if he was captured and his real identity discovered. For though, thanks to dye, electric treatment and the judicious use of a paraffin wax, he bore no resemblance facially to that importunate person, Mr. Peter Brown, late Major in the R.A.F., his artificial eye and the scar beneath it would infallibly give him away once his spectacles were removed.

Presently he reached the lane that led to "St. Cloud". Here he climbed a stone wall on the side opposite to the house, and picked his way through the scattered trees that grew there until he reached a position commanding the building. He had prospected the place by daylight, and it afforded an excellent view. The house was in darkness save for two windows, one on the ground floor and one on the next story, but in each case the blinds were drawn. For half an hour nothing happened. Once, indeed, a shadow passed across the blind of the lower room, but that was all. Then at last the light in the top window went out; there was the rattle of a Venetian blind being raised and the window was opened from the bottom.

Peter raised the field-glasses he had brought with him.

After a few minutes' waiting the moon slid from behind a cloud and shone full on the window; and with a thrill Peter focused a white figure that leaned out with arms resting on the sill. One of the women servants, perhaps, he thought. And then the figure made a little movement of the head, entirely characteristic and quite unmistakable, and Peter knew he was looking at the girl who had scarcely ever been out of his thoughts since that memorable night at Okewood Hall.

Had he dared he would have tried to attract her attention, but the risk was too great. Seeing an elderly man in the garden at that hour she might easily rouse the household before he could make himself known.

And what grounds had he for supposing that she would not immediately rouse the household even if she did know who he was? He had to admit there were none; like a faithful dog she might still be loyal to the hand that ill-used her.

But he determined now to run one risk and try to see who was in the lower room! and when, five minutes later, the girl gave an audible sigh and withdrew from the window, he crossed the lane and, pushing open the gate, sought cover in some bushes. Then, dodging silently from bush to bush, he approached the window.

It, too, had a Venetian blind, with the slats sloping upwards from the outside, and by peeping through the lowest he had a clear view of the upper three-quarters of the room.

At a table in the centre sat Sir Mortimer Drude,

his white head bent over a microscope. A pad on which he appeared to be making notes lay beside him, while the table was loaded with books and papers. There was another person in the room, a good-looking man who wore a monocle, and had the clean-shaven, incisive features of an English barrister. He was reading a newspaper, and, as he moved his head, with a shock of amazement Peter recognized him. There were indeed few private members of the House of Commons whose faces were so familiar to the world as Newsome Eversdale, the well known die-hard and leader of the group of reactionaries who had been dubbed "The Last Gaspers" by an irresponsible Labour member. Wondering what in the name of sanity a man like Eversdale could have in common with Sir Mortimer, the watcher was about to withdraw to the safety of the bushes until such time as the members of the household should retire, when the scientist leaned back in his chair and spoke.

"A harmless ass, my dear Newsome, that's all—I had inquiries made about him at his hotel. A fool, and what is more a writing fool, but dangerous, no. His inquiry was a coincidence, nothing more. One of those ineffable persons, Newsome, who go about the world collecting innumerable data about the trivial ... a counter of dead leaves—pah! I have no use for such twaddlers. Let us talk of something else. Tell me again what Zorloff said."

"What part?" the other replied, looking lazily over the top of his newspaper, and Peter received his second shock, for the voice of Mr. Newsome Eversdale was the voice he had heard at midnight on the sands near Seabridge.

"About the Plymouth arrangements. You know I dislike having them altered," said Sir Mortimer testily.

"I'm afraid there's no alternative, my dear fellow," drawled Eversdale. "I shouldn't worry, the other places can easily be brought into line."

He yawned, while Peter tried to readjust his ideas to this new discovery. Newsome Eversdale, M. P., the mysterious individual whom Colonel Venning had described as the most dangerous man alive—the thing was incredible. Yet it was undoubtedly his voice that he had heard on the night of the experiment on Whale Head. He remembered now that it had been vaguely familiar to him at the time, for he had once heard Eversdale address a meeting at Reading.

"What was the matter with the Queen Anne that she was delayed at Malta?" the scientist demanded presently.

"Don't ask me, my dear chap, I know nothing about a ship's technicalities," returned the M.P. with another yawn. "Something about the turbines, so I understood. What about bed, Mortimer? I'm as tired as a tramp."

"Wait a moment, I want to get this clear, Newsome. Are you certain there is no doubt about Toulon, Cherbourg, Portsmouth, Spezia and the rest falling into line? Remember that unless we act simultaneously we may as well not act at all."

Newsome Eversdale laid down his newspaper and allowed his monocle to fall.

"It won't pay them not to," he said dryly. "I don't allow my orders to be broken lightly, Mortimer. It's a nuisance having to alter all the dispositions in

order to suit Devonport as it is. Kreller I'm sure
about; he's in charge at Spezia and won't fail.
Pagleiro is safe enough at Toulon; so is Zorloff, who's
looking after Cherbourg. Lammiter can be relied on
to see after things at Chatham, and Marris won't
bungle Portsmouth so long as the little devil gets
sufficient reward, curse him. What day do you
expect Pagleiro and Kreller to arrive?"

"Horstman's fetching them to-morrow night from
the usual spot, weather permitting," was the reply,
as the scientist lit a cigarette. For a while he smoked
in silence; and then he added: "Newsome, this
business is telling on me. I shall be glad when it's
over and done with. I feel what you younger people
call 'being on edge'."

"Nerves, my dear Mortimer," returned the other,
leaning back and putting his hands behind his head.
"I feel the effects of it myself. I assure you that when
I was addressing that meeting up in Yorkshire last
night I was more than once conscious of an overwhelming desire to yell the truth at the fools. I tell
you I had to keep a firm grip of myself—especially
when old Wiggins with his red face and white
whiskers began referring to me as a pillar of the
Empire. I was afraid I'd be lulled into complacency,
and get caught off my guard. Curiously gullible
crowd, the English. I should never have had the pull
I have now if I'd toured the country on the red-flag
racket. As it is I dine with Duchesses and Cabinet
Ministers, and the working-man, who secretly loves
blue blood as much as any Yank, whatever his
political views may be, looks upon me as a hard-
hitting, plain-spoken, downright John Bull sort of
man he thinks he can understand. Heavens, if he

184

only knew!"

"Let's hope they'll never find out, for your sake."
Eversdale shrugged his shoulders. "Oh, I daresay
they will one of these days. Politics is the easiest
game in the world for a man to get into who wants
notoriety, and it's about the most difficult to stop in
if he's a humbug. I say the public are gullible, and so
they are; but they have a most unpleasant knack of
sorting the wheat from the chaff in the long run. Old
Lincoln was just about right—'you can't fool all the
people all the time'. That's why one of these days
you'll find Mr. Newsome Eversdale, M. P., applying
for the stewardship of the Chiltern Hundreds lest
worse befall.

As it is I'm already suspected in one or two places."
"Suspected?" The scientist raised his eyebrows. "By
the public?"

"By one or two people who count."

"Indeed! And by whom, pray?"

"That fellow Tremayne of the Foreign Office for
one; Cartwright, the secret-service man for another.
Oh, I'm not imagining things, my dear Mortimer;
I'm the least fanciful man alive. It's nothing more
than a suspicion in each case, but I've seen them
once or twice in unexpected places where there's no
sound reason for their being there, and it's set me
thinking."

"Coincidence," suggested Sir Mortimer.

"Possibly. I've no proof, of course. If I had I rather
think it would not be long before there would
be a couple of vacancies in the permanent staff of
the Foreign Office. Two regrettable accidents, say,
some- thing on the lines of that unfortunate
business of Geoffrey Hangerson. You remember—

185

that cricketer chap who stole those papers of yours."
"I'm not likely to forget. It was recovering those
papers that led indirectly to the trouble at Okewood
Hall," said Sir Mortimer grimly.
Eversdale nodded. "You mean that man Brown.
I'd forgotten he was mixed up with the Cornish
business, but curiously enough I was just going to
mention him. He's another of the men I'm afraid of."
"Because I was unwise enough to let him watch the
experiment with my rays?"
"Because he heard my voice that same night,"
corrected Eversdale. "If that fool Daniels hadn't
bungled it wouldn't have mattered, but as it is he's
the one man outside ourselves who knows me for
what I am, if he happened to recognize my voice. I
only pray and hope he's dead."
"A pious wish in which I won't join you, my friend,"
observed Sir Mortimer with the old singular smile.
"Not that I intend wasting my nervous force on anything so weak as thought of revenge; but death in
itself is such a slight thing I would hate to think of
Peter Brown passing the border-line without having
first settled his final account with me—a fairly large
account, you will admit."
"Mortimer, you are a sentimentalist," rejoined the
other with some contempt. "What the devil does it
matter who kills the man so long as he dies?"
"That," said the scientist, "is purely a matter of
opinion." And he once more bent his head over the
microscope.
Peter had heard enough. What devilry underlay
the reference to the great battle-cruiser Queen Anne,
and the naval bases of the three strongest Powers in
Europe, he could only dimly guess, but that it was

devilry he had no doubt for a moment. His original intention of entering the house and trying to get in touch with the girl held prisoner there he put aside at once. Desirable as he felt it was to give her the opportunity of escaping before the net closed round Sir Mortimer and his companions, the main issue had grown too important to be jeopardized by such an attempt.

To-morrow night!—that was the time arranged for what had every appearance of being a final meeting of the gang pending the mysterious operations which Eversdale and Sir Mortimer had just been discussing.

What an opportunity, if he could only make proper use of it! As he slipped away from the house and retraced his steps to the hotel he considered ways and means. The thing could be done easily enough; a wire would bring a score of men from England in a few hours. The difficulty lay in getting them to Sark without the gang's knowledge—seaplanes were such noisy things, and the sudden appearance of a squadron at the island would put Sir Mortimer on his guard at once. Then he had a brain-wave— Lamont, the American! He would come in useful after all.

Slipping into the hotel by the way he had left, he made his way to the American's room and tapped softly.

Five minutes later a tight-lipped young man was sitting on the edge of his bed, listening with rapt attention to an elderly spectacled gentleman of eccentric appearance, who spoke rapidly and earnestly in a low voice.

"Will you do it?" asked the eccentric-looking

gentleman anxiously, a little later.

"Sure thing," said Mr. Lamont with shining eyes. "Count me in every time. Why, if you hadn't put me wise about this I'd never have forgiven you. I've spent half my young life looking for a real hundred-per-cent crook scenario I could sell to Hollywood, and here's the thing kind of sitting up and begging for notice right in front of my face. I reckon Doug. Fairbanks'll have to open his eyes some when he sees me coming.

CHAPTER X
A NEW USE FOR A DOLMEN

The following morning Peter and Lamont rose early
and went down to the harbor. To avoid comment
they carried bathing towels and costumes, but they
did not bathe. Their business was with the
fishermen who were already pottering about their
boats, with whom they entered into earnest
conversation. The upshot was that presently the
American was conveyed Guernsey-wards in a motor-
boat, leaving Peter talking to an elderly seaman with
a grey beard. This man, whose name was Tom
Damon, had the slow manner and perfect courtesy of
the Sark native. He readily agreed to take Peter
round the island in a rowing-boat in order to explore
those caves which could only be reached by water;
moreover it appeared that the tide would be at the
right state that very morning, but it would be better
to start from Havre Gosselin, the anchorage on the
other side of the island.

Ten o'clock, accordingly, saw Peter descending the
ladder that leads down to the water's edge at Havre
Gosselin. He spent an interesting morning. The sea
was calm, and Mr. Damon rowed him into caves
which would have delighted the soul of a zoologist,
and even pleased Peter, whose ignorance of the
subject was vast, by the splendor and variety of
plant and animal life displayed on the walls.

And presently they made their way under the cliff near "St. Cloud", where, as Peter expected, Mr. Damon began to relate the story of the mysterious motor-boat. At first he spoke with some diffidence, probably for fear of ridicule; but as his passenger listened with a perfectly serious face he soon expanded with that wealth of detail beloved by fishermen the world over. The story he told was practically identical with the manager's, and encouraged by Peter he even went so far as to point out the exact spot in the rocks where the alleged boat had disappeared. When Peter suggested that they should go nearer, Mr. Damon was nothing loath.

"Pretty deep here," Peter remarked, as the fisher-man stopped rowing, and the boat rocked gently within a short distance of the high wall of the cliff.

"'Tis deep, sir," said Mr. Damon, with a shake of his grey head. "Deeper than anyone knows."

Peter glanced up at the cliffs. "Curious formation those rocks have. You might easily imagine some giant had been amusing himself by piling those great blocks on top of each other as a foundation for the whole cliff."

"Granite, sir—solid granite," said the fisherman. "Though I did once take a gentleman round who called them by another name. What was it now?"

"And it was here you say you saw the boat making for?" Peter asked.

"It was, sir. Making straight for't sure as I'm talking to you now. 'Twas a bigger motor-boat than any we have here, too. More like what they call a motor launch, I reckon. There was a bit o' moon

showing, and I caught sight of her once again when I
was in my boat with Peter Masson. Heading right
for shore, she were, with not a light showing aboard
of her. When I see the way she was going I shouted
loud as I could to stop her, but 'twas no use. Like a
dart she went, straight at the cliff—and vanished
clean away."

"What an extraordinary thing. Smashed to pieces,
I suppose, on the rocks?"

"No, sir she didn't smash up, for Peter and me rowed
there fast as we could, and there wasn't sign nor
sound of her, not of boat nor man. Swallowed up she
was, like a miracle."

"Do you think she went down?" asked Peter.

"What else was I to think, sir? She must have sunk
in a second, crew and all. And as I say, 'tis so deep
hereabouts no one would ever find her."

"It's curious there was nothing, though; no caps
or seat-cushions or anything like that?'

"'Tis curious, you're right, sir; so curious that half
the folk won't believe me and try to make out as I
seen a ghost. Not but what there's ghosts on Sark,
but who ever heard of a motor-boat being one?"

He gave a deep rumbling laugh, and added: "Besides,
there's John Duboy and Tom Pegane seen it before
me; ghosts don't appear to several like that—not in
Sark."

Peter returned to the hotel for lunch well pleased
with his morning's work, and with an appetite that
considerably astonished the waiter. Early in the
afternoon he received a telephone call from Guernsey
and spoke to Lamont, who informed him that he had
been in communication with England and all was
well.

Afterwards he sat in a deck-chair on the veranda
with a book on his lap, but he made only a pretence
of reading. He felt restless and unable to think
clearly of anything save the task before him.
Outwardly calm enough, his brain kept worrying
over details, wondering if there was any contingency
that he had omitted to provide for, any loophole of
escape he had over-looked.

The main part of his plan was simple enough. Time
did not permit of assistance arriving by boat, it must
come by air; but the arrival of two or three seaplanes
in the vicinity of Sark, or even at St. Peter's Port,
which could be seen from Sark, would indubitably
warn Sir Mortimer that something unusual was
happening and rouse his suspicions. It was
extremely unlikely that he had neglected to station
someone at St. Peter's Port, the capital of Guernsey,
with the idea of immediately informing him of any
special movements on the part of the police. Peter
had therefore instructed Lamont to direct the
occupants of the seaplane to land in some secluded
bay on the further side of Guernsey, and to make
their way as secretly as possible, and by whatever
means available, to Sark, where he had arranged a
meeting-place. The house would then be
surrounded, precautions taken to prevent the
occupants escaping by any other exit, and then
Peter was not quite certain what would happen
then. The obvious thing to do was to walk in and
arrest the whole gang, but somehow he did not think
it would be accomplished quite so easily as that.
There would, he calculated, be at least eight or nine
resolute men in the house, men utterly
unscrupulous in the taking of human life, hardened

by constant defiance of civilized law, and they would certainly not allow themselves to be captured without a fierce struggle.

Peter had asked for twenty men, and even with that number the task would be a dangerous one. He recalled how, years ago, a few armed, desperate men had defended a London house for hours against a small army. For all he knew Sir Mortimer might be in possession of machine-guns, or even deadlier weapons.

It was a situation demanding subtlety and cunning rather than daring and brute-force; yet for the life of him he could not at the moment see how it was to be brought to a successful conclusion without loss of valuable lives. And then there was the question of the girl. . . .

He rose and flung his book in the chair. Perhaps a sharp walk would clarify his thoughts; this sitting-still business was intolerable. His brain seemed absolutely barren of ideas. There must be some way of getting hold of the girl and saving her from the humiliation of being captured along with the rest. Duty and desire tugged fiercely at him from opposite directions. On the one hand, plain as fate, was his duty as a man to do his utmost to lay these outlaws of civilization by the heels; on the other was the cruel realization that this course must inevitably bring about the ruin of the woman who had saved his life. More- over, any attempt to get into touch with her and help her to escape before the final arrest might quite easily imperil the success of the whole operation.

He was savagely filling a pipe when he became aware

of a figure approaching from the hall-door of the
hotel, and he stiffened suddenly. It was Sir Mortimer
Drude.

Smiling urbanely, the scientist approached him
with outstretched arm.

"I hope you will forgive this intrusion, Mr. Juckes,"
he said pleasantly. "They told me I should find you
here. I have really come to ask your forgiveness for
what I fear was my unbearable rudeness yesterday."

"You are very kind, Dr. Reddieson," said Peter,
"but I assure you I was not aware of.."

"Ah, but my dear sir, I was, though I greatly
appreciate your generosity in pretending not to have
noticed it. I was most unbearably discourteous, Mr.
Juckes, and you must allow me to apologize. We old
men are rather apt to get a little irritable at times,
I'm afraid, and yesterday was one of my bad days. I
trust you succeeded in finding the dolmen of which
you were in search?"

"As a matter of fact I was reserving that pleasure
for to-morrow," Peter had to confess.

"That makes my errand all the easier," the scientist
said. "I was indeed hoping that such would be the
case, for it allows me to offer to make some amends.
May I suggest that you afford me the privilege of
acting as your cicerone to the island? I gather that
you yourself are not uninterested in the stone
monuments of primitive ages, Mr. Juckes?"

"Only so far as it bears on my present work," Peter
returned. "My interest is merely that of the man in
the street, Doctor."

"Excellent, Mr. Juckes, excellent. You will the more
readily be able to assimilate all I shall have to tell

you. In my youth the subject of alignments, menhirs
and cromlechs formed one of my earliest studies,
and though our one dolmen on Sark is hardly a Kit's
Coty House, I have no doubt I shall succeed in
interesting you in it, poor specimen as it is."
Peter's first inclination was to invent a strained
ankle, and beg to be excused. But he foresaw that if
Sir Mortimer had only visited him, as he surmised
was the case, in order to satisfy himself fully that
Mr. Juckes was no more than a harmless crank, a
refusal to accompany him might reawake his
suspicions.
After all the scientist would not be likely to attempt
any violence in broad daylight, whatever his
suspicions were, for Sark was very far from being a
desert island.
"I'll come with pleasure," he said. "I shall be glad
of the chance to stretch my legs. Excuse me one
moment."
Returning to his room he unbuckled the small
canvas pistol holster under his left armpit, and
transferred his automatic to his pocket. He was
running no risks where Sir Mortimer was concerned.
The scientist was in an amiable and discursive
mood. As they walked together—Peter always with
an eye to unexpected contingencies—he talked in a
way which in happier circumstances would have
delighted his companion. But Peter was weighed
down by his knowledge of impending events. The
face of Una Drude kept coming before his mind.
Some picture which he had seen somewhere or other
kept recurring to him: the gloomy picture of a court-
scene, with the judge and all the paraphernalia of
the law, and in the foreground a girl standing in the

witness-box, white-faced and scornful—and the girl
had the features of that girl he had once met in a
Devonshire lane, who had called herself "Jane
Smith". There was contempt as well as scorn in her
eyes, contempt for him, the man whose life she had
saved, and who had repaid the obligation by bringing
her to this ignominy.

It was conceivable that she herself would escape
prison, but even so, what could she think of his conduct, save that it was hateful and despicable? What
would be the use of pointing out that he had only
done his duty, in face of the overwhelming fact that
he had brought about the downfall of her uncle?
The strange bond of attachment between her and
Sir Mortimer probably still persisted, in spite of his
treatment of her; women were made that way, he
supposed. Whatever happened, so far as Peter could
see, the very thought of the man whom she had once
so pluckily rescued would be insupportable to her.
His thoughts travelled to the man beside him, now
holding forth learnedly about monoliths, and his
depression deepened. He had no ill-will at all against
Sir Mortimer; his main feeling was one of regret that
the destiny of a man of such tremendous intellectual
capacity should be so warped. What was the cause,
he wondered? Up to the end of the War he had been
a responsible and highly-respected citizen. The
shock of an air-raid, perhaps: such things were
known sometimes to subvert men's moral balance,
and if the cause was pathological, how could the
man be blamed? Perhaps all crime, all sin, was
pathological, and in the distant future a murderer,
instead of being hanged, would undergo an
operation.

He came out of his reverie and forced himself to
pay attention to the other's conversation, for they
had left the roadway and were approaching a group
of stones which had some appearance of having
been put in their present formation by human
hands. They stood in a field by themselves, a
lonely monument of a past age, with a few bushes
growing round the two flat slabs that lay flat on the
ground.
"Curious how little we know about the people who
erected them," observed the scientist. "We don't
even know for certain what they were for, though the
fact that the smooth surface of the stones is
invariably turned inwards suggests they were
intended to be used as vaults rather than altars."
"Stonehenge and Avebury were temples, I understand," remarked Peter, who felt he must make some
intelligent comment.
"Precisely," Sir Mortimer agreed, "and both
Stonehenge and Avebury were probably erected by a
race considerably further along the path of human
advancement than the builders of these relics.
Nevertheless, these are not without their interest to
the archaeologist. Look at the marks on this stone
here."
He pointed with his stick.
"Marks?" said Peter, interested in spite of himself.
"I don't see any."
"Here," said Sir Mortimer, tapping the stone.
"They're not very plain, but they're quite decipher-
able, if you look."
Peter bent down, and then, arrested by some
singular quality in his companion's voice, he turned

his head. But he was too late, for like a madman
Sir Mortimer struck at him with his stick.
Half-stunned, Peter tried to reach his pistol, but
before he could do so the scientist had rushed at
him and thrown his arms round his middle. Peter
felt his breath hot on his cheek; the next moment a
blow on the head from behind brought oblivion.
Horstman lowered his weapon, a short piece of
weighted rubber-tubing, and bending his huge body
over the prostrate man, pulled off the spectacles,
and catching sight of the grey hair, twitched away
the wig.
"It's him right enough, blast him," he squeaked.
Sir Mortimer bent over and examined the white
face.
"It is," he agreed. "The young fool! A clever
disguise, though, Horstman, eh? A lucky chance
you had that chat with Tom Damon—I thought such
excessive interest in those rocks seemed peculiar.
Pah!—it's too easy. Get him under quickly and take
him along."
A minute later the field was empty, save for Sir
Mortimer Drude, walking thoughtfully towards the
road.

"So it amounts to this, my adventurous young
friend—you are at last absolutely in my power;
absolutely, you understand, without the remotest
chance of escape or of being rescued. Make no
mistake about it, Mr. Brown, this time you are going
to decease; I am not going to delegate such an
important business to other people again. I am going
to kill you, and in my own way; and from what I
understand it will be neither sudden nor pleasant."

The Great Holdup Mystery

Peter, lying on the floor of an inner room, his hands
and feet tightly bound, did not answer. His voice
might not be so steady as he wished, and he refused
to give this man the satisfaction of knowing that he
was afraid. And he was afraid—there was no denying
it. But mingled with his fear was another emotion—
disgust with himself for allowing himself to fall into
such a simple trap as the one Sir Mortimer had set.
At such times a man's self-criticism is apt to err on
the side of severity, and when the other seated
himself on the edge of the table and spoke again,
Peter had to admit that his strictures were just.
"You are a fool, you know, Brown," he said candidly.
"You have no brains. It really gives me very little
satisfaction to beat a man of your mental caliber—
you fall so easily. I am perfectly willing to admit that
up to the present the extraordinary vendetta which
you have thought fit to engage in against me and my
interests has met with a certain amount of success.
But if you will take the trouble to analyze that
success I think you will find that it has been
principally due to the element of luck, coupled
perhaps with a little of that recklessness which is
the result of an incapacity to measure risks at their
true value. You are a failure my friend, and I hope
you realize it. I know your sort well. You are one of
those ineffable young men who have taken the place
of the strong, silent hero in modern sensational
fiction: stupid, muscular, brainless creatures who
think that all that matters in life is to be a
sportsman and a good fellow; whose main ambition
is to roll little balls over the grass into silly tin holes
in a smaller number of strokes than anyone else;
whose creed is good form and whose only

commandment is 'Thou shalt not do what is not done'; who accept ready-made conventions and opinions but scorn ready-made clothes; who affect to despise intellectuality, and all it stands for—the things I stand for . . . Why, I do not suppose you have ever really tried to think about a thing in your whole life! And yet just because your ideas are not my ideas and your conventions are not my conventions, you presume not only to judge my actions, but actually to step in and say this and this shall not be done!

Who are you, pray, to be the arbiter of my behavior? What special qualification do you possess which entitles you to question my judgment on affairs or decide the legality or otherwise of my actions?"

Sir Mortimer's voice, which had begun quietly enough, had grown shriller as he proceeded, until his final words were almost a scream. His eyeballs protruded and a fleck of foam appeared on his lips. Leaving the table he approached the bound man.

"Well, you young puppy, can't you speak?" he snarled. "What do you mean by playing the spy and following me about? Isn't it enough to have half the secret-police of Europe to deal with without having to suffer the impertinence of your damnable intrusion!

Answer me!—or, by God, I'll find means to make you!"

He stood over his prisoner shaking like a man in some kind of fit. Painful as the exhibition was, its effect on Peter was to harden into a certainty the long held suspicion that he had to do with a madman.

And with the conviction came a gleam of hope. Had

he not heard that it was sometimes possible to deceive the most cunning madman by a simple ruse through which normal people would see at once? "Your threats are very fine, Sir Mortimer," he said quietly. "I'm just wondering if they'll sound as fine in a couple of hours' time."

The scientist composed himself with an effort. "A couple of hours' time! What do you mean?" he demanded.

"Simply this. That unless you release me at once I'm afraid things are going to be rather unpleasant for you in two or three hours' time."

"Oh, this is very interesting. And pray what is likely to happen to me in two or three hours' time if I don't release you at once?" asked Sir Mortimer with a sneer.

"You called me a fool just now," said Peter. "Don't you think the word might be more fittingly applied to you for supposing for an instant that I should be so rash as to venture out in your company without taking ample precautions against trickery? I took good care to inform the hotel people I was going out with you and should probably spend the evening at 'St. Cloud'. They will certainly want to know where I am if I'm not back by a certain hour."

"Oh, no, no, no, no, Mr. Brown, that doesn't follow at all," declared the other, shaking his head. "I assure you, you are quite mistaken. I might, for instance, 'phone the hotel and inform them that you have changed your mind and decided to stay the night.

But I have other plans in view. I think, in fact I am sure, that we parted soon after examining the dolmen, and I last saw you walking in the direction of the Coupee. A dangerous place, the Coupee, Mr. Brown, especially if anyone should take it into his head to climb down. What is to prevent your mangled body from being found at the foot of the cliffs to-morrow morning? I know of nothing to stop it, in fact it seems to be the obvious solution to the difficulty of disposing of your body—always supposing that your body hasn't been mutilated previously, of course. . . ."

He stopped, while a look of unholy anticipation stole into his face. But if Peter felt a renewed chill of fear at the innuendo he gave no sign.

"Not very original and not very convincing, I'm afraid, Sir Mortimer," he replied steadily. "You see, the hotel people aren't the only ones who happen to be interested in my safety. I can assure you that if anything happens to me, it's as certain as anything on earth that you'll hang for my murder. The situation is a very different one to when you had me at your mercy at Okewood Hall. Then not a soul except the members of your household knew where I was. In a few days' time the whole world will know the truth about Dr. Reddieson"

"And I can assure you I am prepared for every emergency," said the other blandly. "Even if what you say is true your friends would arrive here only to find me gone. There are peculiarities about this house, Mr. Brown, that would make a search a difficult and dangerous undertaking. I agree, however, with what you say about the unwisdom of allowing your body to be found at the foot of the Coupee. Possibly the air-shaft of the old silver-mine would suffice instead... or even . . . However, that may be decided later.

Time is getting on, and we must get to business."
He rang the bell and Copping appeared. "Tell
Horstman I'm ready now. Then go and tell Mrs.
Black to ask Miss Una to be good enough to come
down."

A few minutes later Horstman limped heavily into
the room. "Come round, has he?—good!" he
exclaimed in a voice of satisfaction as his eyes fell on
Peter, and he began to laugh shrilly, rubbing his
great hands together.

And then Una Drude came in, followed by a lean,
forbidding-looking woman of sixty. One glance Peter
gave at the girl: noted the great change in her
appearance, the white, thinned face and the dark
eyes, which seemed to him to be unnaturally large;
and thereafter he kept his own gaze fixed on the
ceiling.

"You wanted me," she began, and stopped as she
saw Peter.

With a look Sir Mortimer dismissed the elderly
woman; then he turned to his niece with a malicious
smile.

"I think, Una, you have met Mr. Brown before,"
he said in his silkiest tones. "In a Devonshire lane,
was it not? When he was dressed as a clergyman,
unless I am mistaken—ah! you remember now, do
you! Mr. Brown has been kind enough to honour me
with a further visit, attired this time, as you see,
in the garb of an elderly gentleman. Strange, this
fancy for disguises, is it not? Mr. Brown—my niece,
Miss Una Drude."

Narrowly watching the girl as he effected this
ironical introduction, during which Peter was made
to feel the menace underlying the suave sentences,

the scientist saw a flush of colour steal into her cheeks, and the sight seemed to goad him into a kind of wild fury.

"Yes, you may well blush, you—!" he said in a voice that shook, and the unspeakable word set Peter struggling impotently at his bonds. "Perhaps it escapes your memory that if it was not for your ridiculous infatuation for this man we should still—"

"Stop it!" cried Peter, beside himself with anger. "Leave her alone, damn you I Leave her alone, I say!" He made another frantic effort to free himself and Horstman tittered gleefully. "If I had only half an arm free"

"Delightful!—most excellent!" crooned the scientist, clapping his hands gently together. "Quite in accordance with the best traditions of melodrama."

"Have you brought me down here simply to insult me?" the girl asked scornfully.

"On the contrary, my dear Una, I have brought you down especially to show you a little exhibition. Doubtless you cherish the view that your Mr. Brown is a gallant hero, brave in adversity and uncomplaining in misfortune. Well, I am going to show you what he is really like. You shall see him whining piteously for mercy, like the skulking cur he is. I trust the spectacle will be edifying."

"You'll have to wait a long time for that," said Peter contemptuously. "I wouldn't beg a favor of a hound like you if I was at my last gasp!"

"We shall see," replied Sir Mortimer complacently. "Tie his eyes up Horstman, and put him on his feet." He was lifted into an upright position, and a hand-kerchief tied round his head. The next moment a painful blow on the mouth sent him headlong, and

he heard the high voice of Horstman tittering with
laughter.

Actuated by an overwhelming impulse Una started
forward, but Sir Mortimer caught her by the wrist
and held her, grinning wickedly.

"You coward! Oh, you vile coward!" she cried,
struggling fiercely but in vain to release herself. "Let
me go, you fiend! You devil!"

"That'll do, Una, that'll do," warned Sir Mortimer
in a dangerous voice. "Or I may find cause to mete
out something of the same to you. D'you hear that?"
He scowled at her, and then, suddenly swinging her
round, he flung her into a chair. Then he once more
ordered Horstman to stand Peter on his feet. But
no sooner was Peter in an upright position than
another blow on the face sent him down again, with
such a rage in his heart as he had never known
before.

"By God, Horstman, if ever I get my hands on you
—" he began in a strangled voice, for the last fall had
jerked the handkerchief from his eyes and he could
see who his assailant was.

Horstman kicked him violently in the ribs.

"But you won't—see? You won't get the chance!"
squeaked the giant. "Who pushed me in the river
when I wasn't lookin'? You did, didn't yer?—well,
now I'm payin' yer back. Payin' yer back in yer own
coin! If I 'ad my way I'd twist the head off yer ruddy
shoulders, blast you!"

There was a kick between each sentence that made
Peter gasp with the pain of it, but at this point Sir
Mortimer interposed.

"That'll do for now, Horstman," he said
authoritatively. "I don't want him dead yet. I haven't

finished with you yet, my friend," he added,
addressing Peter.

"That was merely a little preliminary chastisement
to get you used to it. Beginning to wish you'd never
had anything to do with the business, eh?"

Peter did not answer. At the moment he could not
have spoken if his life had depended on it. It was the
first time he had ever been bullied without having a
chance of retaliating on the bully, and the knowledge
stuck in his throat and almost choked him.

Sir Mortimer's eyes switched round to his niece.

"I'm wondering if a little chastisement wouldn't be
good for you, too, my lady," he said reflectively.

"What do you say, Horstman?"

"All the same to me, guv'nor," piped Horstman.

It was at this moment that a sudden wild hope
sprang up in Peter's heart. He had moved his arms
and discovered that the rope which bound him had
become slack.

"Bring her over here," said Sir Mortimer
peremptorily.

"Don't you dare lay your filthy hands on me!"
cried Una, springing to her feet as Horstman moved
in her direction. "Uncle, if you allow him to touch

"If you speak like that to me, Una," interrupted
Sir Mortimer, "I'll tie your mouth up!" "Speak!—You
dare to tell me not to speak, after..."

With a sudden movement Sir Mortimer placed one
hand roughly over her mouth before she realized his
intention, and gripping the back of her head with the
other hand, shook it vigorously; then he let her go.
And once again Horstman chuckled.

Una looked at her uncle with flashing eyes. "This
is the end of everything," she said vehemently. "I

hate you! I hate you more than I thought I could
hate any man. For years I trusted you, gave you my
affection . . . even when you kept me here a prisoner
I tried to think well of you . . . now that's over.
Do what you like with me, I'm past caring."
She turned her back contemptuously, and Peter
stealthily enlarged the slack of the rope. Indeed, he
felt that he could now withdraw both arms without
difficulty. Only a little longer and he would be able
to rise to his feet. . . .
"Bring her over here," said Sir Mortimer again.
With an evil smile Horstman caught hold of the
girl's wrist and swung her round so that she faced
the room. At the same time Sir Mortimer walked
sharply towards them both. For the moment the
backs of both men were turned towards Peter. It was
his opportunity at last.
Something in the girl's expression made the scientist
glance over his shoulder, and what he saw made him
cry out in alarm. For Brown on his feet, his face
white and tense, his whole body crouched as if for a
spring. Even as Sir Mortimer beheld him he gave two
tremendous hops towards Horstman, who released
the girl with an oath and tried to get into a position
of defense. But Horstman was no boxer. Peter made
a quick feint for the mark; down went the giant's
guard; and then, with every ounce of his thirteen
stone behind his arm, Peter hit him a terrible blow
on the jaw.
Owing to his feet being tied together the blow was
not timed as perfectly as he could have wished, but
it did not fail in its intention. Horstman went over
like a falling tower and lay still, while Sir Mortimer
shouted for help at the top of his voice.

Peter, hampered by the rope round his legs, realized
that escape was impossible, and unmindful of the
bursting in of the door and the inrush of men into
the room, he went up to the girl and put one arm
round her shoulder. In that hectic moment it seemed
to be the most natural thing in the world to do.
"He didn't hurt you, I hope?" he said, smiling down
at her.
She smiled back at him and said something which
in the uproar he could not hear. And the next
instant, urged on by Sir Mortimer, who was yelling to
them to take him alive, the men were upon him. His
right hand was still tingling from contact with
Horstman's jaw, but he nevertheless tried to defend
himself. One he felled at a blow, and another
staggered out of the fray gasping for breath, but the
odds were farcical. He had a vision of the thin face of
Sir Mortimer in the background, baring his teeth like
a wild animal, his pale eyes shining with excitement.
And then, even as he had knocked out Horstman, a
fist caught him on the chin and knocked him
senseless; and they all crowded round and looked
down at him.

"Everyone out of the room except Copping and
Bates," cried Sir Mortimer. Then, when the room
had cleared, he stood gazing at his fallen enemy.
"What are you going to do with him now?" asked
Mr. Newsome Eversdale, who had entered the room
while the fight was in progress.
"Do!" said the scientist, lighting a cigarette with
shaking fingers. "God in Heaven, but if he were to
die now I think I should go out of my mind. He shall
die with agonizing slowness, Eversdale, with every
nerve flinching; he shall see his death approaching,

inch by inch, until he screams for mercy. Oh, I'll
make no mistake about Mr. Peter Brown this time."
His voice trembled with the intensity of his hatred.
"He shall go in the cave, Eversdale."
"Not to the—?" The other did not complete his
sentence, but gazed at the scientist with a startled
expression. "You don't seem to love him exactly,
Mortimer," he added with a short laugh.
"Love him? Dear God!" Sir Mortimer raised his
clenched fists to Heaven, and his lips moved silently.
Eversdale glanced at him again curiously, and then
shrugged his shoulders. After all, it was no concern
of his. And it was just then that he noticed, behind
Copping and the man Bates, who were bending over
Horstman, the figure of Una Drude. She was very
pale, and her eyes were fixed intently on her uncle's
face.
"Hello, Miss Una," he said with a forced smile,
"I'm sorry you've had to witness a scene like this."
Her gaze met his across the room. "Not at all.
Mr. Eversdale, thank you," she answered
composedly.
"I assure you it has been most illuminating." She
seemed on the point of saying something further,
and then, appearing to change her mind, she gave
one glance at Peter's prostrate form, and quietly left
the room. Sir Mortimer immediately followed her.

CHAPTER XI
CEPHALOPEDA

For the second time within a few hours our Mr.
Brown recovered consciousness, to find himself lying
on his back in complete darkness. His head ached
intolerably and he was conscious of a feeling of acute
nausea, but there was present none of that confused
groping towards mental clarity which characterizes
the return to consciousness of most men who have
been knocked insensible by a blow on the jaw. On
the contrary, the events preceding his lapse into
insensibility were singularly vivid in his recollection,
and when he put out one hand to feel the surface of
the floor on which he lay, and discovered it to be
bare rock, he realized at once that he was in some
kind of underground cave or cellar, and in all
probability still a prisoner. A peculiar fetid smell and
a certain heaviness in the atmosphere suggested
that the chamber was a small one, possessing little
communication with the outer air, while an
occasional muffled thud and the subdued murmur of
moving water told him that the sea was not far
distant.

He shifted his legs, and discovered with some
surprise that he was unbound. Painfully rising into a
sitting position, he felt under his left armpit, where
he had strapped the pistol-holster. The holster was
still there, but the pistol was gone. He went through
his pockets hurriedly. Nothing else seemed to have
been removed. On the contrary his possessions had
been augmented by a cylindrical object which had
certainly not been in his pocket when he left the

hotel.

It was an electric-torch, and he switched it on.

He was lying in a natural cave, close to a glistening wall on which several unpleasant-looking insects were scurrying for shelter in the sudden light of his torch.

Remembering Sir Mortimer's predilection for animal life, Peter scrambled hastily to his feet, only to call himself a fool the next moment, for these were obviously nothing but the natural denizens of the cave. He gave a short laugh of self-contempt. There was no doubt his nerves were in a shocking condition. He leant against the wall, breathing quickly, shining the torch round the cavern. And what he saw both scared and puzzled him.

The chamber was some forty feet wide and roughly rectangular in shape. The place where he stood appeared to be a ledge which ran round three sides of the cave, the edge falling sheer into unknown depths.

Creeping to the brim he could see the reflection of water fifteen feet below. He shuddered as he thought of his fate if, in the darkness, he had staggered into the pool, for the sides were like the walls of a house. Doubt-less that had been Sir Mortimer's intention— but why in the name of common sense provide him with a torch, when a torch was, in the circumstances, the one thing likely to save his life? He wondered if Una had somehow managed to slip it unobserved into his pocket; or perhaps it was Copping, who wasn't a bad sort of fellow. . . .

He dismissed the conundrum as unanswerable, and proceeded to explore his prison. Almost at once he came upon the door to this singular cave; it was set in the wall opposite the blank end, and looked as if nothing in the world would open it but the key. Several times he threw himself against it desperately, but it easily withstood his efforts. It was clear there was no escape that way. He continued to explore. Five minutes later he was back in his original position, feeling his chances of ever getting out of the cave to be hopeless. Short of finding some subterranean tunnel communicating with the sea, it looked as if he would be left there till he starved.

The idea of there being some under-water communication with the sea gave him the tenth part of a hope, and he went to the edge again and peered down.

There was certainly an opening somewhere, for he could clearly see the marks of high tide seven or eight feet above the level of the water. Yet the surface was quite undisturbed, which seemed to prove that communication with the sea was at a considerable depth.

As he flashed his torch about he noticed a peculiar feature of the ledge by the door, which, unlike those on either side, fell back like a shelf. He could see now that it was artificial, and apparently made of concrete. It was, in fact, a platform, and Peter wondered for what purpose it had been constructed. Like the natural ledges on either side of the cave, it was about ten feet wide, and was not unlike a large diving-board.

Absorbed in his conjectures as to its purpose he was startled by a sudden rippling of the water below him and instantly shone his torch in the direction of the sound.

Emerging from the water was the most frightful-looking object he had ever be held. As his horrified gaze took in the two enormous eyes, the loathsome ragged head, and the curious umbrella-like formation of the body, he thought at first it must be some strange nightmare of a fish of a species unknown to him.

And then an incredibly long tapering arm rose from the pool and wavered uncertainly in the air, and he knew why he had been left unbound in the cave. It was a gigantic octopus.

Panic gripped him—that cruel, hopeless panic which crushes reason and leaves its victim temporarily paralyzed. Like a man hypnotized into immobility, with dilated eyes he watched the creature propel itself leisurely to the end of the pool; saw it clamp itself to the rock, and stretch three of its tentacles slowly towards him, and still he did not move. He felt the sweat start from his forehead. In a strange, almost subconscious way he noticed that one of the tentacles had been cut or broken off, and idly wondered what could have caused it. Higher they came, so that in the glare of the torch he could see the fine whip-like ends with their twin rows of suckers. And then the spell broke. With a yell he sprang backward to the wall and stood trembling, waiting for the tentacles to rise above the level of the ledge. Would they be long enough to reach the walls? This was the question that burned itself in his brain, for if the monster could reach him where he stood, there was not the shadow of a hope. The rocky ledges were higher than the concrete platform by several feet, and to attempt to escape by running to the other ledge would only precipitate matters. Besides which, the ledge he was now on was if anything the higher of the two.

He tried to remember whether an octopus worked by sight or smell; but, before he could decide, one of the tentacles appeared over the ledge and moved towards him, grotesquely reminding him of the out- stretched arm of a man playing blind-man's buff. And the next moment, with renewed terror, he saw another tentacle appear further down the ledge. This, too, explored the surface with horrible deliberation, and then stopped motionless, lying right across the path. Meanwhile the first tentacle had stopped also, about four feet away, its end, which was slightly flattened like a ribbon, waving aimlessly in the air.

Peter remembered the tide-marks in the pool; the water had still five or six feet to rise. He became aware of a strong inclination to take a running jump into the pool, and end the business. Anything was better than this waiting for death. And such a death! Sir Mortimer was getting his revenge all right.

And then, from the direction of the platform, there came with startling suddenness the sound of loud, high-pitched laughter. Immediately following there was a faint click, and the cavern was lit by electric light in the roof which Peter had failed to notice. With an effort he moved his eyes from the threatening tentacle a few feet away and glanced towards the door. A trap had opened in one of the upper panels, and Horstman, with a bandaged face, was grinning at him. So they had come to view the kill, had they?

Well, at least they shouldn't have the satisfaction of knowing that he was afraid.

"Hee-hee!" tittered Horstman. "Quite a nice little
picture. All accordin' to Cocker, as they say. Didn't
expect to see me again so soon, did yer?"
Peter did not answer. It seemed to him—it might
have been imagination—that the tentacles had
moved a few inches nearer, and he was conscious of
a wild longing to throw himself on Horstman's
mercy, to plead with him to shoot the monster—
anything to end his torture. Fiercely he choked the
weakness down. Whatever happened he would not
give this brute the satisfaction of speech.
"Lost the use of yer tongue, eh?" Horstman thrust
his great head through the trap and peered down
into the pool. "Ah well, you'll lose more than that
before the next half-hour's up. Plucky, ain't yer—
knockin' folks down when they ain't lookin'?"
Peter continued to ignore him. By not so much as
the flicker of an eyelid did he show that he was
aware of the giant's presence, and Horstman, who in
his limited way had probably expected that Peter
would make some sort of appeal to him, began to get
annoyed. There was, after all, not much fun in
taunting an unresponsive man.
"A ruddy little coward!" he cried through the trap.
"A blasted, ruddy little quitter, that's what you
are." He paused expectantly; and then, as Peter still
remained silent, his temper increased. "And you
needn't pretend as you can't hear me, either!" he
added shrilly. "Just you wait!—just you wait till the
tide's a bit higher, that's all. You'll ruddy well soon
find your tongue then, I reckon!"
Peter's reply was to yawn slowly and elaborately,
as if in the last extremity of boredom, and it was this
yawn which did that for which he had scarcely dared

215

to hope. It seems possible to believe that Horstman's original intention was only to jeer at his victim through the trap, but that his ungovernable temper, fired by Peter's assumed indifference, overcame his caution.

At any rate, there was the sound of a key being turned, the door opened, and he stood on the threshold of the cave, his face red with passion. He held a revolver in one hand.

"I'll teach you to yawn in my face," he shouted angrily in his high-pitched voice. "What's to stop me shootin' you now, I'd like to know?" His eyes fell on the tentacles of the octopus: the nearest was fully twenty feet away, so he came out upon the platform. "I'll plug you through the 'ead, blast you, if you can't speak civil and answer. D'ye hear?"

Peter thought rapidly. If he rushed Horstman suddenly, and succeeded in avoiding the tentacle stretched across the path, the giant might either retreat through the door or attempt to shoot him as he rushed, most probably the latter. Remembering what Bridgewater had told him at Tregenneth about Horstman's poor marksmanship with a pistol he determined to risk the attempt. Unarmed as he was with nothing but a heavy torch, it was a desperate course to take, yet what other was there? Better surely to be shot down by Horstman than fall a victim to the creature in the pool.

And just as he was collecting himself for the effort he saw something that sent his pulses racing with a wild hope. The two tentacles on the ledge were still motionless, but under the platform, unseen by Horstman, another was creeping silently upwards, like some enormous serpent. If only he could hold

Horstman's attention a little longer! He decided to abandon his air of indifference, and as his lips began to move a grin of satisfaction spread over Horstman's face.

"Shoot away!" Peter remarked carelessly. "It would be about your form to take pot-shots at an unarmed man. I can't stop you, you know that. Incidentally, what's this place used for, Horstman? I'm rather curious to know." He took a deep breath; the strain of acting naturally while that undulating arm crept steadily nearer the platform was almost unbearable. The tentacle was now within a couple of feet of the top, and still Horstman hadn't seen it. "What are these electric-lights in the roof for? Peter added, and his voice cracked.

Horstman evidently mistook this for a sign of fear for his grin widened as he cast his eyes to the roof. "Experiments, if you want to know," he squeaked, and glanced down as something touched his foot. At the same moment Peter, utterly unable to restrain himself even though the action cost him his life, gave a yell of warning. But it was too late.

With extraordinary rapidity the thin, whip-like tentacle had twisted round the man's ankle, and was pulling him towards the edge of the platform. Horstman screamed and fired his revolver madly at the body of the octopus, while Peter, regardless now of anything but the fact that a fellow-creature was being dragged to a dreadful death, dashed to his help. But the platform, when he reached it, was empty. One glance only he gave into the pool; then, utterly sickened by what he saw, he managed to stagger through the door and close it behind him. Then he fainted.

A little later, coming to himself, he found he was in
a natural rock-tunnel, on which was laid an artificial
concrete path, leading to the door of the cave. Not for
anything would he have gone through that door
again.
In front the path ascended steeply, and he followed
it for a long distance until it branched into another.
At the junction he hesitated before deciding which
way to take, finally resolving to continue uphill. Soon
he came upon a flight of steps, at the top of which
was a door. Switching out his light he cautiously
tried the handle. It opened easily.

Alphonse, the chef at "St. Cloud," was in an
uncommonly bad temper. What had upset him none
knew, but so unpleasant had his manner and
language been all day that Fred, his assistant in the
kitchen, as he took the dirty dishes out of the
service-lift which communicated with the dining-
room upstairs, was strongly minded to throw them
at Alphonse's head.

The knowledge that Alphonse, when roused, was
inclined to take violent physical exercise—usually at
another's expense—restrained him; and he therefore
relieved his feelings in the time-honored manner by
grousing at the world in general.
"'Arf-past eleven an' only just finished," he grumbled. "I tell you I'm fair sick o' this job."
Alphonse, instead of commenting on this
observation, pointed to the dirty dishes.
"To-night," he said gruffly, "you will wash up."
"What?" demanded the other indignantly. "Wash
up now? At this time o' night?"
Alphonse lowered his weight carefully into a chair

and placidly lit a cigarette. "Take this tray," he
ordered, pointing again. "Then come back for the
other." And he closed his eyes with an air of finality.
His assistant glared at him as if he would have liked
to kill him. Then, with an angry gesture, he picked
up the tray and walked resentfully into the back-
kitchen. The door shut with a bang.
Alphonse opened his eyes and frowned at the closed
door. Then he looked at the second tray of dishes.
Several minutes passed and his scowl deepened.
This was downright insubordination. Did Fred dare
to think he could disobey him, Alphonse? Jumping
up with more alacrity than one would have supposed
possible in a person of his bulk, he marched to the
door with the light of battle in his eyes.
Throwing wide the door he opened his mouth to
pour forth the torrent of invective which the
situation demanded, when an arm was twisted
round his neck and the next instant he was
sprawling face-downward on the floor in the grip of
an exceedingly unpleasant arm-lock.
"Don't make a sound," said a quiet voice. "If you
do I shall have to break your arm, and I know you'd
hate that. Your other arm, please. That's better."
He felt his wrists being tied together. "I'm sorry to
be so rough with you, but it can't be helped, and you
aren't the only one. No, your friend isn't visible, he's
tied up in that cupboard, where I'm going to put you
in a minute when you've answered my questions.
And I needn't add that if you attempt to call for help
I shall most certainly kill you. Just wait till I've tied
your feet up."
His boots having been lashed together with their
own laces Alphonse was rolled over. When he saw

who his assailant was his cheeks paled.

"Yes, it's me," nodded Peter. "Didn't expect to
see me again so soon, did you? I seem to have a
recollection of seeing your fairy face among the
crowd before I was bowled out. Tell me, have Pagleiro
and Kreller arrived?"

The man was silent.

Peter sighed. "I'm not a cruel man, but I must
admit there are merits in the methods of the Middle
Ages," he said regretfully. "It would be so easy to
tie a shoelace round your forehead and twist it with
a pencil until you answered—and it might save me a
deal of trouble."

Forthwith he proceeded to gag his victim with a
handkerchief, and then, dragging him to the
cupboard, bundled him in beside his companion and
turned the key. This done, he closed the door and
went into the kitchen, where he stood listening.
Apparently his encounter with the two men had not
attracted attention.

As he listened he became aware of the murmur of
conversation, which puzzled him for a moment, since
it seemed to come from the direction of the wall
facing him, which, as he knew, gave on to a passage.
And then he could have kicked himself for his
stupidity— the service lift, of course! Here was a
piece of sheer gratuitous luck. He thrust his head in
the lift and listened again. Conversation was
certainly going on amongst a number of people in
the room above, but to his disappointment he could
distinguish no words.

And more than anything else in the world just then
he wanted to overhear what was being said in that
room. Had he not heard Sir Mortimer say that

Pagleiro, Kreller, and probably others were coming
that night to a conference? It looked as if he would
have to try to listen outside the door, a very
hazardous undertaking.
And then a wild notion entered his head. The lift
was sufficiently large to enable a man to squeeze in
with an effort, and it worked on the endless-rope
system. It took food up and down—why shouldn't
it take him? That he would run a tremendous risk
he fully realized. The pulley at the top might squeak,
the rope break, the doors at the top might be open.
With Peter, however, to think of a plan of this nature
was to act, and tucking himself into the lift he began
to haul himself slowly up the shaft.
Fortune was with him. The door of the lift-opening
was shut, and he could hear every word said.

Mr. Newsome Eversdale forced a cigarette into a
thin amber holder and, having lit it, allowed his keen
gaze to travel slowly round the table.
"Well, gentlemen, I shall not detain you for long
to-night. You all have your instructions, and I am
perfectly confident in your ability to carry them out
without any further advice from me. There are,
however, one or two points to be considered, and as
this is probably the last opportunity we shall have
form discussion before our operations begin, it may
be as well to mention them now.
He paused to readjust his monocle and glanced at a
slip of paper in his hand. For all the emotion in his
level, slightly drawling voice, he might have been
taking the chair at the committee-meeting of some
suburban tennis-club. It was only when one
considered his audience that it could be seen that

here was a set of men of very different calibre. With
the exception of Sir Mortimer Drude they one and all
bore on their countenances those unmistakable
marks which indicate the man who lives on the
weaknesses of humanity; hard-bitten and
unscrupulous, utterly devoid of those considerations
of kindness and conscience which link society
together, but formidable, full of character and
the ability to pursue their own interests with
resolution and decision.
It was Pagleiro, the swarthy little fat man, who
answered. "We are all attention," he said agreeably.
"But first of all, these walls—" He waved an arm with
the expansive gesture of the Southerner and looked
quickly round the room. "Are they . . . '
"They are," replied Eversdale with some shortness;
and then, after once more referring to the paper, he
went on; "First of all there is the matter of the
Queen Anne. The fact of her being delayed in the
Mediterranean necessitates a slight readjustment of
our plans. Obviously, all our operations must take
place on the same day, and in order to allow the
Queen Anne time to reach Devonport I am therefore
postponing the date by ten days. There will be no
difficulty about that, I suppose?"
"It can be done, of course," Pagleiro observed. "But
it will be a pity."
Kreller, who sat on Eversdale's right, next to a
silent man with a black beard, gave a harsh laugh.
"A pity!" he cried. "It would be madness. Insanity!
Rather than that the dispositions should be
changed at this hour I would advocate leaving out
Devonport altogether. There are still Portsmouth,
Chatham and Portland. And will there not be other

warships at Devonport besides the Queen Anne?
Pah!

What is the Queen Anne that she should upset all
our arrangements!"

"She happens, my dear Kreller, to be the most
powerful battle-cruiser afloat to-day, and easily the
biggest vessel in the British Navy," returned Eversdale mildly. "If you can suggest any other warship
whose destruction would shake England to an equal
extent, I shall be most happy to consider it."

Kreller eyed him fiercely. "And does that warrant
running the risk of endangering the whole plan
through delay?" he demanded. "I am a believer in
timetables and sticking to them. The Queen Anne is
only one ship, and we are going to destroy six in
England alone.

It isn't as if we are one nation going to make war on
another. Our aim is intimidation. We have got to
prove to England, France and Italy that we possess
a weapon against which there is no defense, and are
determined to make use of it until they meet our
demands. Whether we prove it by blowing up battleships or the Houses of Parliament cannot matter a
tinker's curse, so long as we only impress them with
our power. Therefore I say, let the arrangements
stand. One battle-cruiser more or less can make no
difference whatever."

Eversdale shook his head. "You don't understand
the psychology of the British people," he said. "On
the surface you might not suppose they cared a jot
whether they had a navy or not, so little interest do
they seem to take in it. But in their heart of hearts
it's the most sacred pride of their lives. They've stuck
Nelson on top of a great column in a London square,

and it typifies the position the navy holds in their
vanity. And the Queen Anne is at present the flower
of the flock. It's as important in their eyes as the
old Dreadnought was in Fisher's day; it's their
proudest possession, and they are as keen on it as a
child with a new toy. Its destruction would rank as a
national disaster; far more than half a dozen other
battleships put together. Coupled with the blowing-
up of the other five, the moral effect on the nation is
bound to be incalculable."
"Very well, very well," grumbled Kreller impatiently.

"It is for you to decide. I have made my protest.
It is enough for me to look after the fools I have
under me in Italy."
Pagleiro laughed. "You are not very well to-night,
are you, Franz, my friend. Mon Dieu! Nor do I
wonder! You should buy a bigger motor-boat, Sir
Mortimer, and your guests would arrive in a better
temper."
"We may regard that as settled then. The date will
be August the tenth instead of the first." Eversdale
carefully readjusted his monocle. "The next question
is the ultimatums. I suggest that as soon as these
have been delivered to the heads of the governments
concerned, copies be sent to the leading organs of
the Press in time for insertion in the morning
editions.
It does not follow that they will print them, of course;
they may choose to regard the matter as a hoax. But
the very fact of their being received will contribute
to that mental attitude of uncertainty we wish to
bring about." He smiled grimly. "And you may be
in no doubt as to whether they will print them when
they find that the very threat which they contain has

been carried out."
"How long do you suppose it will take before we
bring them to their senses?" asked the man with the
black beard.
"That is a question I can't answer," replied Eversdale with a laugh. "If I could it would simplify
matters considerably. You may be sure we shall have
to give more than two or three demonstrations of
what we are capable before we convince them we
mean business.
No notice will be taken the first time, obviously.
They will simply look upon our threat as the work of
a lunatic. It will be a different matter when the next
batch of warships is blown up a week later, but even
then I hardly anticipate any weakening. There will,
perhaps, be a few signs of panic—not much,
especially in Italy, where belief in authority is
strong—but perceptible to a keen observer.
Remember, an unknown danger is always more to be
dreaded than a known. As each nation's morale
becomes affected there will be a corresponding
reaction in the world of finance. There will be a
tension in the air, a knife-edge of expectancy.
There may even be some mobilization of armies. And
then, at the right moment, when the fever of disquiet
is at its height, I shall launch the next ultimatum.
You will, of course, receive the instructions
through the usual channels. And this time, as you
know, instead of warships we shall threaten to
destroy things of more permanent value . . .
Westminster and Whitehall . . . Windsor Castle . . .
The Louvre . . . ."
For ten minutes he went on speaking, while a man,
crouched behind the door of the service-lift, listened

with an ever-growing amazement as the full extent
of the diabolical plot was unfolded. He felt he must
be dreaming, and that he should wake up and find
him- self in his bed at the hotel. That such a
scheme, involving the possible loss of human life,
should be calmly discussed by half a dozen men in a
common-place modern dining-room, seemed outside
the possibilities of ordinary existence. He had the
sudden illusion that they were playing some
monstrous kind of charades, and would presently
stop and converse like ordinary mortals.

Pagleiro was speaking now, his foreign accent
strongly marked.
"The sum of money to be paid—what have you
fixed upon? You had not decided last month."
Eversdale's voice replied, suave and cultured.
"One per cent of the national income in each case.
In England, for example, that will work out at about
eight million pounds. A mere trifle, of course—only
a little more than the cost of the Queen Anne. Less
than a quarter of what Great Britain pays annually
to the United States. Anything else?"
"There is!" Kreller brought his clenched fist down
on the table. "I say again, Eversdale, it's nothing
less than lunacy to change our original date. Every
moment that we put off time increases the danger of
our position. I am not such a fool as to suppose that
because the policy are silent they are inactive. We
know they have some inkling of our plans, and they
know of the rays. Do you imagine they aren't moving
heaven and earth to get on our tracks? For the
present not a soul knows our meeting-place here,
but at any moment discovery may come. I am not an
alarmist but the world is a small place, and our

enemies are too many for my liking."

"No," said Eversdale thoughtfully. "As you say not a soul knows our whereabouts—except one; and by now—"

"Except one? What one?" demanded Kreller fiercely.

Eversdale replied in the drawling voice Peter had heard the previous night. "What do you say his name is, Mortimer? I could never work up the same interest in the man as you. Brown, isn'- it?"

"Brown! That swine again!" Kreller swore vigorously. "What in hell has he been doing now? I thought he was put away weeks ago."

"On the contrary, he's very much alive—or he was a few hours ago," said Eversdale with a chuckle.

For the first time Sir Mortimer Drude spoke. "He is probably dead by now," he observed grimly.

"I should think so," cried Kreller. "He should have been killed before. Where is he now?"

In a few words Sir Mortimer explained the circumstances of the ruse by the cromlech and the subsequent uproar in the study.

"A man of spirit and enterprise," said Pagleiro when he had finished. "So that explains why Horstman didn't fetch us in the boat. What have you done with him?"

"Horstman? We left him on his bed to recover."

"The man Brown, I mean."

Sir Mortimer gave a sardonic laugh and glanced at his watch. "High-tide is in about half an hour's time. By now I should think it extremely likely he is gone where he will cease to trouble us further. An extraordinary specimen of Cephalopeda, my dear Pagleiro, of the sub-order Decapoda, and I think Ommatos-

227

trephidae."

"Talk English," growled Kreller.

"In other words an octopus of a singularly large size that happens to live in a cave under the island. It is, indeed, too big to get out, but fortunately there is a small hole communicating with the sea through which crabs and other stupid fish persist in coming, so it continues to survive. I myself used it to experiment upon with my rays in the early stages."

"Well?" Kreller demanded.

"Is it necessary to tell you the rest?" asked Sir Mortimer. "I give you credit for imagination, Franz."

Kreller gazed at the scientist with distasteful eyes. "You're a cold-blooded devil, Drude," he muttered. "But listen, tell me this. How do you know he was here alone? How do you know he hasn't friends on this island who know where he is, and are at this moment getting in touch with the police?"

"If he has any friends they haven't helped him much," said Eversdale with a short laugh. "He arrived alone, you said, didn't you, Mortimer?"

The scientist nodded. "Yes. He came alone, and so far as I have been able to discover he remained alone.

As for his friends in England, what can they prove, whatever they may think? Let them come and search the island and see what they can find."

"You say there is some doubt about his being dead yet," Pagleiro remarked, puffing a cloud of smoke from his thick lips. "Well, if he is still alive, have him in here and ask him. I will soon find out whether he is working alone or not."

There was silence for a space, and Peter in the service-lift shivered involuntarily. He began to think it was time to be making a move.

"Years ago in what you call Algeria," Pagleiro went on, "there was once a trader from the Epiros— a Greek, and rich, but obstinate. There was also a man from the mountains, a Cheg, who you would probably call a brigand, and he wanted certain information from the Greek. I repeat, the Greek was an obstinate man, but he told. Shall I tell you why? Because the other knew how to make him. Because I was that other man. There is much that may be done with a cigar, or even a cigarette. But then, per- haps, as you say, he is already dead."

Sir Mortimer rose and pressed a bell, and Copping entered.

But before Sir Mortimer had given his orders, Peter, whose fingers were nearly paralyzed with cramp through gripping the ropes, was silently slipping down the lift-shaft. His one thought was to get out of the house as quickly as possible. Such a course meant leaving Una, but greater considerations even than her safety were involved, and he did not think for a moment that Sir Mortimer would offer her physical violence. How to rescue her could be decided later; at the moment the imperative need was to convey his news to the outside world. This was easier thought of than done, for the kitchens were underground, and offered no immediate means of escape. It seemed pretty certain that he would have to make his way out on the level of the ground floor, and in the meantime, judging from the course the conversation in the dining-room had taken, someone would soon be coming down on a visit to the caves.

Taking off his shoes, he darted out into a dark
passage and hid in an alcove while a man, whom he
presumed from his heavy tread to be Copping, came
down the passage and passed through into the
kitchens.

Peter did not wait to learn if the man discovered
the absence of the chef and his assistant, but flew
up the stairs. There was a door at the top which he
opened cautiously, and finding that it led into the
hall and that the hall appeared to be empty, he ran
straight to the front door. It was an old-fashioned,
heavily bolted affair, with the bolts shot, and as he
worked them back from their slots a slight noise
from behind made him turn his head. There, with
his eyes wide open with astonishment, stood the
little man he had met in the post-office the preceding
afternoon.

It was a desperate moment, for Peter was unarmed.
So also, it appeared, was the little man, for as Peter
turned and made a frantic, hurried attempt to open
the door, he let out a yell for assistance. Abandoning
the door as hopeless, Peter made a rush for the man,
who scuttled back like a hare into the room he had
just left, and the next instant Peter had sprung up
the stairs, three at a time, and disappeared in the
darkness of the landing. As he reached the top he
heard the dining-room door open.

There was no time for thought. Switching on his
light, he flung himself at the first door he came to,
but it was locked, and he hastened to the next,
hurried on by the uproar which suddenly broke out
down-stairs. As he reached it the door opened and a
girl stood on the threshold. In an instant she took in
the situation.

"Quick! In here," she said, and a moment afterwards she had closed and locked her door. Peter
was about to speak when she held up a warning
finger. Voices sounded from the landing, and there
came a loud knock at the door.

"Una!" called Sir Mortimer's voice imperatively.
She caught him by the arm and hurried him to a
tiny dressing-room, where she pointed to a trap-door
in the ceiling.

"They'll never think of looking up there," she
whispered. "I can keep them a couple of minutes at
least."

"Una! Una!" The knocking on the door grew
thunderous.

She darted back into the room and answered in a
sleepy voice, as if she had just been awakened:
"Yes, what is it?"

"Open the door at once," demanded her uncle.

"Can't I be left alone even at night?" she answered
wearily from the bed. "Oh, what's the matter?

"I tell you to let me in!"

"Oh, all right," was the resigned reply. "Wait a
minute."

She ran back noiselessly to the dressing-room,
where Peter's legs were in the act of disappearing
through the trap-door. His face appeared anxiously
at the entrance.

"If they interfere with you I shall come down,"
he whispered.

She waved impatiently for him to be gone; then,
having removed from the dressing-table the chair by
which he had ascended to the trap-door, she went
back to the room and unlocked the door.

"What is the matter?" she asked, as her uncle strode furiously through.

"Where is he?" he demanded. "What have you done with him?"
"My dear uncle, do try to talk rationally. Where is who?"
"You know perfectly well who I mean. He came in here, I know he came in here. Every other door in this corridor is locked." He glared at her for a moment and then began to search the room. Una seated herself on the bed with a weary sigh.
"I suppose you'll explain what you mean sooner or later. You must think I'm fond of men if you think I'm likely to hide one here. I assure you the men I meet in this house have cured me of any desire for male society for ever. I suppose you think I'm hiding that poor Mr. Brown?"
"I don't think; I know," snapped the scientist, and called to the man who waited at the door. "Arthur, tell Mrs. Black to come here at once." Then he disappeared into the dressing-room. Una laughed. "He's escaped then, has he?" she called after him. "Well, I'm glad, and I hope he gets away." He came back angrily from the dressing-room, and she smiled up at him, insolently swinging her legs. "And if I did know where he was I shouldn't tell you—now." The significance of that "now" was not lost on Sir Mortimer, and he made an effort to control his temper.
"Don't you realize this man is trying to ruin us?" he asked, with a belated attempt at reasonableness. "Don't you understand he's a spy, in the pay of my worst enemies—and you go and befriend him."
Her eyes glinted viciously. "I certainly would if I

could. Men who knock people about like you let
Horstman knock Mr. Brown about seem to me not
far removed from savages, and their victims need
befriending. I don't care whether he's a spy or not;
he's a man, at any rate, which is more than can be
said for anyone else in this house. And now perhaps
you'll leave me, please; I'm tired."

As she spoke Copping appeared in the doorway
with an excited face. "Guv'nor, he's got away again,"
he cried. "I just found Alphonse and Fred—tied up
in a cupboard they were—I heard 'em kickin' the
door. . . ."

Una clapped her hands softly. "Oh, splendid," she
murmured. "One man against all of you and he
escapes every time!"

"How he got away this time I can't pretend to
understand, but I shall soon find out," replied Sir
Mortimer slowly. "But there is one thing you may
depend upon, Una, and that is that he will never
leave this house."

"Perhaps he's left it already," she suggested.

Sir Mortimer made no reply, and before anything
more was said Mrs. Black entered the room. Bidding
her stay there for the remainder of the night, the
scientist then addressed a final word to his niece.

"As for you, Una, I shall have something further
to say to you in the morning. Whether you really
know where he is or not I haven't yet made up my
mind. But if I find you have been helping him again
it will be him I shall punish, not you. Just think
that over."

"I will; but, you see, you've got to find him first,"
she retorted as the door closed.

CHAPTER XII
THE LOCKED ROOM

Peter listened to the conversation between Una and
her uncle with a quaking heart, determined to go to
the girl's help at all costs if they attempted to molest
her, but praying that the need would not arise. His
relief when he heard her more than holding her own
was great, although he realized that his troubles
were by no means over. The presence of Mrs. Black
in the bedroom made escape impossible in that
direction for the moment, and he accordingly set
about exploring his hiding-place.
The light from his torch showed that he was
standing immediately under the roof, in the space
left between the tiles and the ceiling of the room
below. Although built only two stories high, the
house was a large one, and he could see that the
joists extended a considerable distance; further,
indeed, than the torch revealed. He was still in his
stocking-feet, and he began to make his way like a
cat over the joists, hopeful of finding another trap-
door or some similar outlet. He soon ascertained that
the area over which he could roam was considerable,
apparently covering more than half the house, but
nowhere could he perceive any means of descent.
Once or twice he thought he heard voices in one
of the rooms below, and this presently gave him an
idea. He had a small penknife in his pocket and,

choosing a place where the lath-and-plaster was not
so thick as elsewhere, he lay down on his stomach
and commenced, with infinite caution, to make a
hole. It was a long job, for he dared not make any
noise, and though the plaster crumbled easily
enough there was always the risk that a stray piece
might fall into the room beneath. In addition to this
there was the necessity of working for the most part
in darkness, partly lest a chink of light should betray
him, and partly for fear that the torch itself should
begin to fail. At length the point of his knife met
with no resistance, and he applied his eye to the
hole.

Nothing could be seen; the room—if room it was—
was in darkness. Putting one ear to the opening, he
held his breath and listened, but could hear no
sound.

Very carefully he enlarged the hole with his fingers
and listened again; then, almost reassured that
there was no one below, he switched on the torch
and shone it through.

It showed an empty bed with the clothes thrown
back, as if someone had been lately sleeping there;
a table by the bedside on which was a book and a
candlestick; a chair over which the clothing was
carelessly thrown—women's clothing. For a few
puzzled moments he thought he must be looking
into the bedroom of one of the servants. Then he
remembered he had seen no women servants at St.
Cloud; this must be the room of Mrs. Black. He
grinned to him- self as he realized his luck, and
straightway began to enlarge the hole. He worked
quicker now, for the opening was immediately over
the bed, and when pieces of plaster fell they made no

sound. Finally, when he thought there was room for him to squeeze through, he clicked on the torch and dropped it neatly on the bed; then he lowered himself until his hands were gripping the top of one of the joists and let go.

It was a six-foot drop, and he landed with less noise than he expected, and immediately hurried to the door. Apparently the household was not yet abed, for there were lights in the hall below. Peter looked at his watch; it was three o'clock . . .

it would be several hours before Venning and his men could arrive. He waited a little to make sure his descent had roused no one, and then went to the window. The beginnings of dawn were visible in the sky, and by the uncertain light he made out that the window overlooked a yard, with a flight of steps, such as might lead into a coal-hole, immediately below him. To attempt to jump from that height, with the certainty of alighting on the steps, was not to be thought of, and there was no rain-pipe handy. He went back to the door and peered forth again. The odds, he knew, were that someone would be left on guard; on the other hand, there was just a chance they had come to the conclusion that he had got clean away. Creeping to the banisters he peered over.

Quite a considerable portion of the hall was visible, but there was no sign of anyone on guard. Should he risk it or attempt to slip away through another of the bedrooms? Neither course had much to commend it; for entry into a bedroom might arouse some sleeper, while there was the distinct likelihood that the hall, with its inviting emptiness, was nothing less than a trap to entice him out.

He began to descend the stairs, until most of the
hall was to be seen, and still there appeared to be
no one about. The impulse to make a sudden dash
for the front door was strong, but it was clear from
the lights that some of the household were still
awake, and he had no wish to repeat the experience
of a few hours previously. If there was an invisible
sentinel patiently waiting for him to emerge, the
front door was the very place he would watch,
besides which there was always the risk of the bolts
proving noisy.

Much wiser to try to slip away through the window
of one of the rooms.

As he neared the bottom of the stairs he noticed
a kind of alcove full of coats and hats which offered
temporary concealment, and he was about to make
use of it when he saw that a door at the rear of the
hall was standing half-ajar, the room into which it
led being in darkness. Here lay his way of escape, he
decided immediately. It was only a matter of half
a dozen yards to the door, and he had just reached
it when something sang past his head and hit the
woodwork with a vicious thud. For a fraction of a
second he gazed in astonishment at the knife that
stood quivering in the panel; then he swung round
and perceived, standing near the alcove he had
noticed, the grinning figure of a man, his arm still
extended with the effort of his throw. At the same
instant he recognized him as the dago with the scar
who had tried to kill him on the quay at Tregenneth.
What the other's instructions had been it is
impossible to say. Probably he had been ordered to
do no more than raise the alarm if the necessity
arose, but had been unable to resist the temptation

of such an easy target. How he came to miss his aim at such a short distance and why he did not at once call for help are questions that will very likely never be answered; what is clear is that when he did shout it was too late. True, he pulled out another knife and attempted to use it, but it was about as much use as a meat skewer against Peter's furious rush. There was only one blow in that fight—just one tremendous drive with all the pent-up feeling of the last twelve hours behind it—and it did not fail to reach its mark.

But the man's call had been heard. Even as Peter recovered his balance the dining-room door was flung open, and Sir Mortimer appeared, a revolver in his hand. Instantly he fired, but the bullet went wide, while Peter ran desperately for the only cover he could see, the room with the open door. Another bullet zipped past him as he dived through and flung the door behind him. A glance showed that it had neither key nor bolt, and he hurriedly swung his torch round the room, revealing two further doors in the opposite wall. Throwing open the first, he saw a long passage with a further door at the end, and he dashed down it as the chase broke noisily into the room he had just left. But when he opened the further door hope nearly left him, for at his feet were steps descending, presumably, to a cellar. There was nothing for it, however, but to go on, and he plunged down with the vague idea of finding a weapon and making a good fight of it before he was overcome.

At the bottom he found another door which opened to his joy, into a passage that he recognized as the one up which he had passed earlier in the evening; and he followed it unhesitatingly, remembering the

other track that ran past the tunnel leading to the
cave of the octopus. Where it would take him to he
had not a notion, but the pursuit was so perilously
close that he could see over his shoulder the
reflection of their light, and he was determined to go
on until it was impossible to go further. Presently he
passed the entrance that branched off to the octopus
cave, after which the walls fell away, and he seemed
to be descending through a series of caves. He
thanked his stars that the pathway was smooth, for
a pursuit over rocks would have played havoc with
the soles of his feet.

The slope grew steeper and more winding, and he
was compelled to proceed with greater caution. It
struck him that the air, which had been stuffy, was
becoming fresher, and he thought he could smell the
sea. He stopped a moment to listen. Down the tunnel
there still came the muffled echo of hurrying
footsteps, but also, in the background, was the
unmistakable murmur of moving water, and he
thrilled to the sound. Somewhere at the end of the
track there must be an outlet, and it could not be far
away. He put out his torch. Ahead, sure enough, the
pale gleam of daylight showed, and he hastened
eagerly towards it.

All at once the track ceased at the brink of a
precipitous fall in the rock and, peering over, he
looked down into a huge cavern, faintly illuminated
from above, in the depths of which water sobbed and
gurgled. The top of an iron ladder revealed a means
of descent, and he instantly availed himself of it.

To descend hurriedly an iron ladder of some
hundred rungs, however, is not an easy task for an
unpracticed hand, and he soon realized that before

he reached the bottom his pursuers would arrive at the top. Fortunately, the ladder leaned slightly inward near the ground, and he was thus enabled to rest a few moments in temporary security while he decided on his next move. He could hear Sir Mortimer's voice raised in excited argument overhead; from which he gathered, in the first place, that they were by no means in agreement as to whether he was still in front, and in the second that there was a certain reluctance to be the first to descend the ladder. This was all to the good, and he glanced rapidly round the cave for a possible hiding-place. And then he saw that in the middle of the cave, gently moving to the rise and fall of the water, was a motor-boat.

He stared at it in amazement. It was a large boat, capable of holding a score of people—yet how had it possibly got there? The walls of the cave were solid rock, and there was no visible opening; yet obviously an opening there must be. He noticed that below the surface of the water there was a hole in the rock which plainly led to the open sea, for the light filtered through greenly; but it was fully a fathom under water, and it seemed impossible that the tide could ever fall sufficiently low to allow a boat to enter.

The submerged hole, however, suggested an idea, and as he could hear sounds overhead which indicated that someone had commenced to descend the ladder, he divested himself of his coat and waistcoat. It was then that an extraordinary thing occurred.

Apparently from the solid face of the rock facing him there came a sound—the sound of a very loud and powerful sneeze.

Peter gaped at the wall of rock like a man struck dumb. There was only one man he knew sneezed in that hearty fashion: the man he had last seen lying unconscious in a Tregenneth cottage. But where in the name of sanity was he?

And then he heard a well-remembered voice say: "Well, Tommy, it ain't any use stopping here any longer. Let's go back."

Incredulity, a sense of enormous relief, and an unbelievable joy chased themselves across Peter's mind as he heard those familiar accents. He forgot that an armed man was hurrying down the ladder with the deliberate intention of killing him; he forgot everything save the fact that he was once more in touch with friends, and that whatever happened to him now there were others who would exact a just retribution from the gang. The sudden reaction made him careless of his own safety; he felt that nothing his enemies were capable of doing could hurt him now, and emerging from the shelter of the rock he waved his hand gaily to the man descending the ladder. Bullets spattered harmlessly about him as he ran to the edge of the water.

"Hello, there—Bridgewater!" he yelled. "Look out for me that side!"

The next moment he plunged into the water in the direction of the opening in the rock. As he swam through, he noticed that the wall of rock above the hole was of an almost incredible thinness, the significance of which struck him at once, and he realized the explanation of Tom Damon's phantom motorboat.

Rising to the surface, he found day had dawned, and

that, as he expected, he was in the identical spot
which he had visited with Damon on the previous
morning.

A few yards from the cliff-face lay a motorboat full
of men, every one of whom was staring at him with
a face of almost comical astonishment.

"God bless my soul, it's old Brown!" declared Mr.
Bridgewater, as Peter swam to the boat and was
pulled on board by eager hands. "Where in thunder
have you sprung from, and what was that firing?"
Peter held up a warning finger. "Shove her out a
bit," he said in a low voice. "I've got tremendous
news, and they'll hear if we stop where we are."

As old Tom Damon, who was handling a pair of
sculls in the bow, tugged the boat slowly away from
the cliff, Peter grinned at the company. Three besides
Bridgewater he knew—Lamont, Major Tremayne,
and Claggs; the other three had the appearance of
plain-clothes policemen, well-set-up fellows who
looked, capable of holding their own in a rough-and-
tumble anywhere.

"That's far enough," Peter said at length. "Half
the gang are in that cave—the one I've just left—
and as they must have heard your voice they'll know
the game is up. We must gather them in at once;
there's enough evidence to shop the lot a dozen
times over. They're mad, all of them—stark, staring
mad.

I listened last night to such a plan as I wouldn't have
believed it possible for grown men to discuss
seriously."

In a few terse sentences he told of the conversation
he had overheard in the service-lift. "It sounds like
the plot of a shilling-shocker, but the tragedy of it

is they are all in deadly earnest," he added. "They really believe they'd be able to hold up three countries and force them to disgorge cash. It's so infantile as to be past crediting. But though they'd never succeed they'd stir up the devil's own brew before we could lay 'em by the heels. How many men have you on the island?"

"Fourteen," said Bridgewater. "Including Venning and Cartwright. We'd better go back to the harbor straight away."

"Wait a minute; there's a motor-boat under the cave, and that wall of rock is a fake and either pulls up or lets down. It's the back door to 'St. Cloud,' and they'd slip away like a shot if we went off. They're probably watching us now through some spy-hole or other. Oh, the whole place is laid out like a fort. They've even got a pet octopus in a cave which Drude seems to have used to experiment on with his rays, and which very nearly experimented on me."

"Has he got any of his ray instruments with him?" asked Tremayne.

"I can't say; I haven't seen any," said Peter. "I imagine they've already been sent to the theatres of operation, but I can't be sure."

As he spoke there was the sound of a shot at close quarters, and something like a great beetle sang over their heads, while everyone ducked instinctively.

"Damn it, this won't do," said Bridgewater, producing a revolver and eyeing the cliff uneasily. "Start her up, Tommy, or we'll get potted. That was a rifle."

The engine fired at once, and the motor-boat had begun to move rapidly through the water when there came another shot, which again flew overhead.

"They're firing from the rock right enough," Bridge-water observed, "I saw the flash. It seems to me, Peter, you've had your share of luck in getting away from this crowd without being hurt."

"I know that," said Peter soberly. "But it isn't only luck that's been on my side. If it wasn't for that girl I shouldn't be here now, Bridgewater. It makes me sick to think I couldn't get her out of their clutches."

"She won't come to any harm," Tremayne assured him cheerfully. "A girl like that knows how to look after herself. Hello, another shot! Blaze away, my hearties! If you couldn't hit us before you certainly won't now."

"Pretty poor shooting, isn't it?" remarked Lamont.

"Shocking!" agreed Tremayne. "What's the program now, Jimmy me lad?"

Bridgewater pointed to a boat that had just come into sight round a bend, pulled lustily by a couple of fisherman in blue jerseys. "I'm going to send you round to the harbor in that. Peter and me and the others'll keep an eye on the cave entrance while you get in touch with Venning. Tell him to go ahead as soon as he likes; with a bit of luck we'll have every man jack of them in the bag before breakfast. If there's any shooting—well, he'll know what to do. And send a man back with half a dozen blasting cartridges; I'm going to have a look at Master Drude's back door."

The fishing boat was stopped, and its occupants, having been informed of as much as it was considered good for them to know, old Tom Damon, grumbling and protesting, was made to get in, and Tremayne followed.

"What about you, Lamont?" Bridgewater lifted
an inquiring eye to the American. "Going back with
them?"
Lamont laughed shortly. "I guess not. Not unless
you darn well make me."
"Right. Let her go, Tommy."
"There's one thing that puzzles me," said Peter as
the boat pulled away. "And that is how on earth you
happened to be hanging about outside that cave so
early in the morning."
"Better ask your friend Lamont here," was the reply. "It's his idea. Not that we expected to find you
swimming about in the water. To be quite candid,
I was in two minds as to whether I'd ever see you
alive again when I heard you didn't return to the
hotel last night. Lamont had a notion about there
being some kind of a passage up to the house
hereabouts."
"That's so," nodded Lamont. "I got thinking about
that mystery motor-boat you told me of, and got a
hunch there might be a hole of some kind which
you'd *****

Mr. Bridgewater produced a nasal spray and began
to apply it to his nostrils. "I hope they won't be long
with those cartridges," he observed.
In the semi-darkness of the cave three men looked
at each other with set faces.
"So long as I live," said Sir Mortimer slowly, "I
shall continue to regret that I didn't kill Peter Brown
when I had him in my power."
"Regret! What the hell's the good of regretting?"
cried Kreller angrily. "If it wasn't for your damned
ideas of revenge we shouldn't be in this mess now."
He flung the rifle he carried into the stern of the

motor- boat. "Muddle, muddle, muddle, all the time!
That blasted thing is about as much use as a piece
of wood!"
"It certainly won't be improved by your handling
it in that fashion," said Eversdale shortly. "We'd
better get back to the house and find out how many
there are against us. If they're only a handful we'll
fight them; if not, there's always the passage to the
dolmen.
But in any case, Mortimer, I think the career of Dr.
Reddieson has come to a close."
"What about having the motor-boat out and going
after 'em guv'nor?" said Copping hoarsely, joining
the group. "I'll have the wall up in a brace of shakes,
and they can't 'ave gone far."
Eversdale shook his head. "No good, Copping, I'm
afraid—waste too much time. Collect the rifles from
the boat—there should be half a dozen—and bring
them and any ammunition you may find along to the
house. And by the way, Mortimer," he added,
pausing as he was about to mount the ladder.
"Those tripods you used for the early experiments—I
suppose you could still use them if necessary?"
He disappeared up the ladder into the gloom, and
silently the others followed.

The accounts which have appeared in the Press of
the fight between law and disorder that took place in
the early morning of July 22nd are so fresh in the
minds of the public that to do other than
recapitulate them would be wearisome. Exaggeration
and invention, however, have played such a
conspicuous part in the accounts that a good deal of
misconception seems to have arisen as to the true

facts of the case. Peter Brown, for example, has been made out to be a sort of Galahad who overcame the gang single-handed; whereas actually the part he played in' their final downfall was a small one. The character of Sir Mortimer Drude, too, has been absurdly overdrawn. He has been described as a mixture of "Peter the Painter" and the Apache Bonnet, neither of whom he resembled in the least; the truth being that he was simply a brilliant physicist whose brain had become affected by a well-known disease notorious for its occasionally disastrous effect on the moral character of its victims.

The rumor that he was in the pay of a foreign government is all bunkum, and on a par with the sensational report that he was seen alive in Paris on the day following the round-up of the gang. Briefly, then, the facts are these:

Colonel Venning, it appears, had already posted his men in the neighborhood of "St. Cloud" before receiving Bridgewater's message, besides leaving two men at the Creux harbor. Upon being joined by Major Tremayne he gave immediate orders for the house to be surrounded, and himself marched boldly up to the front door, accompanied by three policemen.

No reply being forthcoming to his summons, and the door proving to be locked, a window at the side was forced, and an entrance made by the policemen, every precaution being taken against a trap. Their orders were to shoot at the least sign of armed resistance.

Finding the room empty, and seeing no one in the hall, they drew the bolts of the front-door and

admitted Venning, who was about to begin a search
of the lower rooms when a messenger came flying
with the news that men had been observed crossing
a field some distance away, and that upon being
challenged one of them had drawn a revolver and
wounded a sergeant.

The man who fired the shot, it was subsequently
learnt, was Pagleiro; which seems to prove that
Eversdale had quickly abandoned all idea of
defending the house —he probably had early
information of the extent of the forces against him—
and had escaped by the under-ground passage
leading to the dolmen.

Leaving a couple of men on guard at "St. Cloud,"
Venning immediately gave chase, and coming upon
some of the fugitives in a lane, a running fight of a
rather irregular nature ensued. Several of the gang
were armed with rifles, and more than one of the
attacking party were severely injured. Their intention
seems to have been to make for the landing-place at
Havre Gosselin, where they may have hoped to get
away in boats. Two of them actually succeeded in
reaching the landing-place and, stealing a boat,
rowed some distance in the direction of Guernsey;
but they were quickly overtaken and brought back
ignominiously to Sark, one of them—it was
Alphonse, the fat cook—with a bullet in his arm.
Another group was forced to surrender near the
Colinette after an exchange of firing in which one of
the gang was shot dead.

A little later word was brought that two men with
rifles had been driven towards Little Sark, and had
taken refuge at the far end of the Coupee with the
clear intention of shooting anyone who attempted to

cross. The Coupee, as everyone knows, is a natural causeway three hundred feet above sea-level, which stretches like a gigantic railway embankment across the hundred-yard gap between Sark and Little Sark. The road across this isthmus is in no place more than ten feet across, with a sheer drop on one side and a steep slope on the other, and a machine-gun company at one end could hold up a battalion. With these two men ensconced one on either side of the path it looked as if the task of dislodging them would prove a difficult one.

But they had reckoned without Venning, a former King's Prizeman. Having reconnoitered the position he took one of the captured rifles and disappeared among the gorse near the cliff-side. Presently there was the sound of a single shot, and the men peering towards Little Sark saw a figure attempt to rise and stumble forward, and then roll down on to the path of the Coupee, where it lay still. Immediately after wards the other man was observed to run, gun in hand and doubled up, over the slope leading into Little Sark.

The man on the path was quite dead. He was a tall, angular man with a goat-like beard, and his fierce face was twisted into an expression of anger that was somehow pathetically futile. . . .

"Kreller," said Venning briefly.

There was no sign of the other man when they reached the top of the rise. Venning moved cautiously down the narrow lane, his rifle ready for instant use.

Suddenly he flung the rifle to his shoulder, and then slowly lowered it; for, seated at the side of the road, placidly smoking a cigarette, was the man he was

seeking—a short swarthy man who smiled blandly at
his approach.

"Shoot, my friend, if you like," he said. "It will
make no difference. I am philosopher enough to
know when I am beaten. Only the weak and foolish
struggle in the net from which there is no escape—
and it is undignified to struggle." He held out his
wrists for the handcuffs with an amused expression.
"And I shall not trouble you for many minutes—
now."

Venning looked at him searchingly. "Where did
you leave the others—Drude and Eversdale?" he
demanded sternly.

Pagleiro continued to regard him with the same air
of quiet amusement, but his face had turned livid.
"No, no, my friend, you must not expect that. I
tell as much as I choose—no more. I have—what you
say ?—shot my bolt and failed, but I do not give
away my friends." He shrugged his shoulders
resignedly.

"Alas! We have all failed. As your Shakespeare
says—"

He broke off, and his face changed to a horrible
colour. And then with dreadful suddenness the end
came. . . .

Venning looked down at the still twitching body
with an inscrutable expression, and then, feeling a
touch on his arm, turned to find one of his men
gazing fixedly in the direction of the main part of the
island.

"Isn't that smoke over there, sir—like as if there
was a house on fire?" the man said, pointing to a
distant clump of trees beyond which a thick smudge,
visible against the clear morning sky, was rapidly

growing.

"It looks to me," remarked Venning thoughtfully, 'Very much like 'St. Cloud.'"

As the sound of firing reached the motor-boat, Bridgewater nodded for the man at the helm to start the engine.

"Time we were making a move," he observed.

"Pray Heaven they haven't left anyone on guard in the cave."

The motor-boat began to glide along under the cliffs towards the spot they had been watching. There was not a man among those on board who did not feel acutely uneasy as they drew near, half-expecting a rifle to blaze out from the face of the cliff at any moment; and the relief when the boat eventually reached its destination without any untoward incident was great.

But now a difficulty arose. As has been said, the cliffs descended sheer to the water, and the sea fortunately being calm they were enabled to approach close enough to fend off the boat with their hands. But though Bridgewater had ready his dynamite cartridges and firing apparatus, it was discovered there was neither nook nor cranny in which to fix them; nor had they any drills. The dilemma was settled, despite the protests of Bridgewater, who was not unnaturally anxious lest someone might still be lurking in the cave, by Peter once more diving for the hole under the rock. He was fully aware that he was running a considerable risk. But he reasoned that if the cave harbored an enemy he would have certainly fired at the boat through one of the invisible loopholes as they

approached; moreover, the proximity of danger
during the last twelve hours had so dulled the edge
of his apprehension that it is doubtful if he would
have hesitated in any case. The sound of distant
firing, which he supposed meant that the attack had
begun, had set him nearly frantic with anxiety.
Venning, he knew, would strain every effort possible
to save Una from hurt; nevertheless, his imagination
pictured horrible things happening to her. . . .
As before, he had no difficulty in negotiating the
hole, and as he rose to the surface in the dark
interior of the cave he perceived a man following him
through the opening, and recognized Lamont.
"Thought I'd better come along in case of trouble,"
gasped the American apologetically as he climbed
out beside Peter. "Anybody hanging around?"
Peter had brought with him a pocket lamp which
had luckily survived immersion, and he flashed it
round the cave. Except for the motor-boat it was
empty. The light, however, revealed a large wheel
attached to the rock, round the axle of which was
wound one end of a thin steel rope that disappeared
into the upper darkness of the cavern. Lamont at
once seized the handle and turned. For a few
seconds nothing happened: then the shape of the
hole under the rock began to alter, and gradually a
slab or panel in the wall of the cave rose dripping
from the water, leaving a passage several feet wide
open to the sea.
"Some craftsmanship," commented Lamont as he
made the handle fast. "Looks like concrete to me.
Rather awkward if some mineralogist had happened
along with a hammer, though."
Peter shouted for Bridgewater to enter, and the

two motor-boats were soon side by side. As a precautionary measure the piece of camouflaged rock was then lowered into its former position, and Peter led the way up the ladder. It was no easy task for Bridgewater, but at length all reached the top and began the steep climb up the concreted track. When they came to the passage leading to the octopus cave it occurred to Peter that some of the gang might be hiding down it, so accordingly two men were left behind with instructions to arrest anyone attempting to pass.

The rest pushed on until they reached the door through which Peter had escaped a few hours previously. Here the utmost caution became necessary.

Stealthily they crept up the stone steps and along the passage. No sound came through the door at the end, and Peter noiselessly turned the handle.

The room was empty, and when they reached the hall it was empty also, save for a large, stolid-looking man who sat on a chair with a pistol across his knee.

At sight of him Bridgewater uttered an exclamation. "Lambert! Why, man, what's this?" he demanded sharply. "What has happened?"

"They've got away, sir—cleared out entirely," said the man. "The whole house is empty; leastways, it was half an hour ago. How they done it I don't know, seeing as we had the house surrounded."

"I know," cried Peter suddenly. "The dolmen! Oh, what a fool not to have seen it before. There must be a secret passage between the dolmen and the house, and that explains how they got me here yesterday without being seen. Come on, Bridgewater, there's still a chance!"

"It's all right, sir, they've probably got the whole
shoot by now," returned the man, and then
proceeded, with provoking deliberation, to explain
the reason for Venning's absence.

"Why the devil couldn't you have told us that at
first, man!" said Bridgewater testily. "Which way
did Colonel Venning go?"

"I know the way to the dolmen," put in Lamont
quickly.

"Then for God's sake lead on," cried Bridgewater.
"I'll never forgive myself if I'm too late."

He hurried away with the American, followed by
Claggs and the remaining plain-clothes man. Peter
turned to the stolid-looking Lambert, whom he
wanted to ask several questions. He could easily
catch up Bridgewater and the others later.

"Have you been all over the house—in every room?"
he demanded.

Mr. Lambert stolidly resumed his seat in the hall.
"Pretty near," he said.

"What do you mean—'pretty near?'" asked Peter
irritably. "Is there any room you haven't been
in?"

"Well, there is one; but we'll have it open soon
enough when the others come back." He leaned
back and surveyed Peter in friendly fashion. "You
look a bit wet, mate," he said genially. "Been in
the sea?"

Peter wondered why the law did not permit such
men to be murdered out of hand.

"For God's sake answer my question," he cried.
"Which room is it?"

"It's up at the far end of the first landing," was the

calm reply. "You won't open it, though. I've tried, but it's made of steel, and locked, and there isn't no key. There's no hurry; we'll have it open soon enough when the rest come back."

And the stolid Mr. Lambert produced a crumpled cigarette from an inner pocket and proceeded to light it.

Peter waited for no further information, but flew up the stairs three at a time. Mr. Lambert, after making a move as if to follow him, thought better of it and resumed his cigarette. But the next instant he had sprung to his feet, cigarette forgotten, as the piercing scream of a woman rang through the house. Immediately he darted up the stairs in Peter's wake, but when he reached the landing it was empty. Peter had disappeared.

Lambert ran along the landing to the room with the steel door and, after listening a moment, shook the handle violently.

"Let me in—d'yer hear?" he shouted.

There was no reply, but he could hear a man's voice within, and he shouted again, kicking the door with his heavy boots. For all the effect it had he might have been kicking the door of a safe. There was again no response, and after a moment's thought he ran quickly downstairs.

Peter had taken the contents of the syringe full in the face the instant the door had opened. The liquid momentarily blinded him; then a curious dullness overcame his limbs, and he crashed to the floor, dimly conscious that the steel door had closed behind him. But the strange thing was that he did not lose consciousness. His body was completely paralyzed, yet when he was able to open his eyes his

faculties were working perfectly, and he could see,
hear, and understand all that was happening.
The room was fitted up as a small chemical
laboratory. Glass-stoppered bottles by the hundred
covered those parts of the walls not given up to
cupboards ,and there were several tables full of
apparatus tidily arranged. Three singular
instruments on steel tripods like theodolites
occupied different corners; they were cylindrical in
shape, and each was pointing to a chair in the fourth
corner on which Una Drude sat tightly bound with
ropes. And in the centre of the room, still holding the
syringe, stood the designer of this tableau,
benevolently regarding his captives.
"At last," he said gently, "at last I have the unique
honour, alone and unassisted, of offering you
welcome."
He smiled slightly as a voice became audible outside the door, but otherwise he ignored it.
"You have escaped me so often," he continued, "that
by the mere law of averages your luck was bound
to turn. I am ready to admit that, since you
have been instrumental in compelling my friends to
depart with rather more haste than they had
intended, you have some cause to congratulate
yourself; but I think you will admit also that now we
are alone it is possible that I may be in a position to
redress the balance."
He laid down the syringe and fixed his marble eyes
on Peter. "Luck for once has been with me. When I
saw your policemen blundering about near the
dolmen I realized that my chances of escape in that
direction were slight. To a first-class mind such as
mine, it was not very difficult to foresee what would

happen. The police would immediately try to cut us off from the boats, while you, as I imagined, thinking we were still in the house, would try to take us in the rear. I therefore returned to the house by the dolmen and succeeded in reaching this room, where I had already left Una, and where I hoped that sooner or later I should be privileged to offer you my hospitality.

This is where luck has been with me. Would you, when you heard of the locked room—as you were bound to do—investigate it at once, or would you follow your friends to join in the battle? That was the question I had to decide. And I decided rightly, Mr. Peter Brown. Your vulgar and insatiable curiosity has once more led you into trouble, and this time is the last. I think before I have finished with you, you will be sorry you ever escaped death at the hands of the Cephalopeda."

The suave, even sentences, uttered with cold passion, affected Peter far more than raving would have done.

That Sir Mortimer was abnormal he had long known, but hitherto, however strange had been his conduct, it had always halted at offering physical violence to Una. The fact that she was bound to the chair showed clearly that whatever restraint he had exercised on his hatred was at an end.

His eyes met hers, and he read in them terror.

Sir Mortimer moved towards one of the instruments, and standing behind it, with his eyes glued to the sights, adjusted a thumbscrew.

"People talk loosely about liberating atomic energy," he observed thoughtfully, "but few realize the power concentrated in light; in fact we are only at the beginning of understanding what light means to health.

I look forward to the time when we shall be able not only to concentrate the energy of the sun as we compress gas in a cylinder to-day, but also to store it and liberate it at so much per unit from a power-station. I do not mind telling you for your curiosity that the Drude rays are nothing more than light—bottled light, if you like. You would not understand it if I explained it to you. But you have already seen what happens when the three rays focus on a given point.

Well, I am now going to give you another demonstration, this time entirely for your own delectation.

In fact I am going to let you be your own demonstrator. Look at this, Mr. Peter Brown. It is a switch.

I have only to move it—so!—and the instrument becomes alive. The others are already alive; and I would point out that the focal point is—" He waved his hand vaguely in Una's direction. "Again, for the satisfaction of your curiosity, I have calculated that it will be roughly fifteen seconds from the time when the switch is moved until death puts an end to her—er—discomfort. And you, my dear Mr. Brown, shall yourself turn the switch."

Seizing the inanimate Peter he dragged him to a chair beside the instrument, where with some difficulty he proceeded to tie him up in the same way that Una was tied, except that he left his right arm free.

This done, he tied to the free wrist a length of twine, on the other end of which he made a small loop.

"That, I think, completes the preparations," he said.
"We will now bring you round."
From one of the tables he took a hypodermic syringe,
already charged, and injected his victim's arm. In a
few minutes the most excruciating agony began to
flow from the middle of Peter's body outwards to his
limbs. It was like cramp, only worse, but mercifully
its duration was short; and presently he could tell by
the way the thongs dug into his flesh that life and
feeling had returned. At the same time he recovered
his voice.
"What good do you suppose this will do you?" he
asked vehemently, and his voice shook despite himself. "It's murder; it's torture. I didn't think a man
of your intellectual attainments would descend to
torture, Sir Mortimer—on your own niece, too !"
"I have yet to discover that you are capable of
thinking at all," was the curt reply. "Believe me,
nothing you can say, no appeal you can make, no
money you can offer, can alter my determination in
the least, Mr. Brown. Your people may arrest me,
though I think it is extremely unlikely; but even with
the prospect of hanging in front of me I should go to
the scaffold joyfully if I knew I had revenged myself
on you."
Suddenly he seized Peter's free arm, and raising it
before the other realized what he was doing, he
slipped the loop of the twine over the switch on the
instrument.
"Now, Mr. Brown," he said. "You consider yourself
an athlete. Let us see how long you are capable of
holding out your arm unsupported." And with that
Sir Mortimer stepped backwards and stood watching
with a look of unholy expectation on his pale

countenance.

As the full devilish nature of the plan came home to
Peter the sweat broke on his forehead. He was a
strong man, and he knew he might be able to hold
out his arm for ten, fifteen, or even twenty minutes,
but his muscles had not yet recovered from the effect
of Sir Mortimer's paralyzing treatment, and he knew
there must come a moment when his arm would
drop from sheer weariness. Never had he conceived
such a refinement of cruelty. . Torture of a physical
kind he could perhaps stand; but this torture was of
the mind, the torture of knowing that the life of the
girl he loved depended on his own physical
endurance. He had no doubt that the madman had
told the truth; here was no mere play designed to
frighten. And already his extended arm was
beginning to tire. He set his teeth and prayed for
strength to hold out until help came—
that help which could not be far away now. And yet
he knew in his heart that when help did come the
chances were that it would be of no avail. Sir
Mortimer Drude would never allow them to leave the
room alive.

He glanced again at Una; her face was deathly in
its whiteness, and her eyes were closed.

"Are you still glad you chose to interfere with my
plans, Mr. Peter Brown?" said Sir Mortimer with
that deadly suavity which Peter always associated
with the scientist. And suddenly he grinned like a
maniac.

Peter did not reply, for just then, with a quick »
tightening of the throat, he perceived something
which Sir Mortimer had overlooked: the tiny flaw
that exists in most criminal schemes, and is so often

the means of wrecking them.

One leg of the tripod stood close to Peter's feet, and though his legs were bound immovably to the chair he knew he was capable of moving the front of his feet laterally, pivoting them, as it were, on his heels. A quick jerk would certainly disturb the delicate focus of the instrument, if it did not actually knock it over.

He kicked; the tripod-leg slipped some distance over the oilcloth; and instantly Peter snapped the string with a downward movement of his arm which completed the upsetting of the instrument. The next moment Sir Mortimer flung himself on him with a cry, trying to grasp his arm. And then Peter laughed softly. His opportunity had come.

Una, watching with dilated eyes, could at first see only that the scientist was beating fiercely on Peter's face with his fist, although his body seemed to be strangely contorted. And then she saw that Peter had seized hold of his wrist and was twisting it . . . twisting it slowly but inexorably with one powerful hand. Impotently Sir Mortimer was now plucking feebly at his hip-pocket with an arm that would not reach; and all at once there was a scream and a dull crack.

"I'm sorry for this," said Peter. "But it's your arm or our lives." Suddenly he released his hold of one wrist and grabbed the other. "Now," he said sternly, "just undo this rope."

Sir Mortimer's face was grey with pain. "Curse you, you brute!" he gasped. "You've broken my—"

"Do you want to force me to break the other, you fool?" cried Peter. "Undo the rope, I tell you!"

And, weeping and raving, the scientist obeyed. Sir

Mortimer was a man twice Peter's age and less than
half his strength, but no consideration of false
chivalry would have prevented Peter from carrying
out his threat if the other had refused.

The moment he was free Peter removed the pistol
from the scientist's hip-pocket and then, flinging him
aside, went to Una and cut the rope that bound her.
"There, there," he said soothingly, speaking to her
as he would have done to a frightened child as he
knelt beside her and took her hands in his. "You're
all right now, aren't you? Nothing more to worry
about now."

"I—I'm quite—all right, thanks," she said feebly,
with a kind of sob, and promptly proved the contrary
by fainting.

"Poor kiddie," murmured Peter, lifting her gently
in his arms and placing her in an arm-chair. "This is
all your doing, Sir Mortimer," he flung angrily over
his shoulder. "If there's any justice in the world you
should be flogged through the streets for this."

There was no answer, and he looked up; and what
he saw made him pull out his pistol and yell like a
man possessed. "Put it down!" he cried furiously, for
Sir Mortimer had righted the instrument and, one-
handed, was adjusting the sights. "Put it down, I
say, or by God I'll—"

A roar drowned his threat and a huge yellow flame
leapt to the ceiling from the chair on which Una had
sat. A fierce crackling sound followed, and
immediately the room filled with dense smoke.
Coughing desperately, Peter picked Una up in his
arms and staggered towards the door. Blinded by the
smoke he cannoned into one of the tripods, knocking
it over, at which the louder roar at once ceased; but

the fire had now a firm hold. He could feel the heat of it on his back as he fumbled at the door. He discovered a key in the lock and managed to turn it; and then, in a blessed moment, his fingers found the handle and, almost choked with the fumes, he tottered out into the corridor with his burden. The door, as if actuated by a spring, clanged to behind him.

Along the corridor he dashed, down the stairs and out into the garden, where he laid Una on the grass, and then proceeded, for the second time that day, to go off into a faint himself.
It was there, a few minutes later, that an alarmed Mr. Bridgewater found them and carried them safely out of reach of the burning house.

THE END

The Mystery Of Wilfrid Usher

When the world of fiction was altered nearly 200 years ago with the publication of the first mystery story, _Das Fräulein von Scuderi_ by E. T. A. Hoffmann (1819), it set off a rush of writing that has not slowed down to this day. This departure from the norm of fiction was used as an influence by Edgar Allen Poe as he began to write the most widely accepted mystery stories for an audience that soaked them up and clamored for more. Arthur Conan Doyle cemented the genre with the introduction of Sherlock Holmes and the introduction of the negative clue. ("I draw your attention to the curious incident of the dog in the night time. " "But the dog did nothing in the night time!" "That was the curious incident.")

Books and the rise of pulp magazines allowed many wonderful writers to enter the game of the mystery. Some were more successful than others. Agatha Christie, Wilkie Collins and the start of the Stratermeyer Syndicate for children, breathed life into the fast growing fiction market. The Hardy Boys and Nancy Drew took up where Grace Harlowe had started and wove mysteries for the young reader.

In the aftermath of WWI magazines encouraged amateur writers to try their hand at mysteries and some were quite good. One of these was a person named Wilfrid Usher. Although Usher was a better than passing writer and wrote charming and fast paced novels he never caught on with the wide public. He only published three novels as far as is known and there are no biographies on him or his work.

He created a world of heroes and spies, anticipating James Bond by nearly 40 years and his books are full of the British mystery touch stones. He creates suitably creepy villains (was there ever a more evil mad scientist than Sir Mortimer Drude) and gives them tools for great chase scenes and great solutions at the climax.

Usher published first in England with the Stanley Paul Publishers in London, a publisher known mostly for sports stories. In 1928 he published the first of his books *The Great Hold-Up Mystery*. In 1929 he issued *The Mystery Of the Seven*. One more

265

book also came out in 1930 and then, for no apparent reason, as the British sales were hardly worth noticing, his three books were picked up in the United States by the International Fiction Library of New York and Cleveland. Just as quickly all of the books vanished from view. This is a shame as the stories are taut, engaging and charming. A great rainy day read for those of us who love British manor house and the fight of the hero to get the girl.

So who is Wilfrid Usher? We don't know. Even in this age of Internet and mass depositories of information nothing comes to light about Wilfrid Usher. No reviews of his books, no author information, no history, no known magazine publication, and no way to trace him. Or is there?

Let us know who Wilfrid Usher is if you have information. Let the mystery reading world be introduced to a first rate story teller of the Bull Dog Drummond school.

And enjoy the magic of the mystery that starts one lonely, rainy night.....

www.ingramcontent.com/pod-product-compliance
Lightning Source LLC
Chambersburg PA
CBHW070327260626
47160CB00003B/973